KIND OF SORT OF FINE

KIND OF SORT OF
FINE

SPENCER HALL

Atheneum   New York   London   Toronto   Sydney   New Delhi

A
atheneum

An imprint of Simon & Schuster Children's Publishing Division
1230 Avenue of the Americas, New York, New York 10020

For information about special discounts for bulk purchases, please contact Simon & Schuster Special Sales at 1-866-506-1949 or business@simonandschuster.com.
The Simon & Schuster Speakers Bureau can bring authors to your live event. For more information or to book an event, contact the Simon & Schuster Speakers Bureau at 1-866-248-3049 or visit our website at www.simonspeakers.com.
Interior design by Rebecca Syracuse
The text for this book was set in Goudy.
The illustrations for this book were rendered digitally.
Manufactured in the United States of America
First Edition
2 4 6 8 10 9 7 5 3 1
Library of Congress Cataloging-in-Publication Data
Names: Hall, Spencer, author.
Title: Kind of sort of fine / Spencer Hall.
Description: First edition. | New York : Atheneum, [2021] | Audience: Ages 12 up. | Audience: Grades 10–12. | Summary: Told from two viewpoints, high school seniors Haley, who had a public breakdown, and shy Lewis, longtime member of the TV Production class, find that filming documentaries about their classmates' hidden talents reveals their own aspirations.
Identifiers: LCCN 2020035464 | ISBN 9781534482982 (hardcover) | ISBN 9781534483002 (ebook)
Subjects: CYAC: Interpersonal relations—Fiction. | High schools—Fiction. | Schools—Fiction. | Documentary films—Production and direction—Fiction. | Anxiety—Fiction.
Classification: LCC PZ7.1.H289 Kin 2021 | DDC [Fic]—dc23
LC record available at https://lccn.loc.gov/2020035464

ONE

HAYLEY

If you're going to have an emotional breakdown and stop your car in the middle of a busy intersection, let me suggest the main entrance of Groveland High School. It's wide, there's plenty of sunlight, and it's also Arby's-adjacent just in case you want to grab some curly fries after the police show up and pull you from your vehicle. You'll want to remember to dress appropriately, because several of your classmates will be filming the entire ordeal on their phones. Maybe wear something simple like jeans and a T-shirt but also have on a Batman Halloween mask, as if to say, "Sure, I'm crazy, but I'm the fun kind of crazy!" Or maybe wear a long flowing gown and wet your hair like Ophelia à la *Hamlet*, act four. That's Shakespearean crazy, arguably the classiest form of crazy. If you're hoping to use this moment to make some kind of statement, I suggest investing in a bullhorn or at least a poster board with large, legible writing. Because despite your other numerous accomplishments, this is what you'll be remembered for during your time in high school.

Sadly, it's too late for me to take my own advice. But even if I could go back in time and make these adjustments, I doubt it would keep me from ending up here—the school conference room with my parents and me on one side of the table and Principal Wexler and Mr. Keith on the other. Meetings like this are never good. Your school administration will never call you in two days before the start of your senior year to tell you how well you're doing and how thrilled they are to have you as a member of the student body. No, meetings like this start with "We're all here because we want what's best for Hayley, and we want to set her up for a successful school year." It sounds like they're doing me a favor, but the tension in the room and the forced smiles make it clear this is no happy occasion. People who are already doing well in life don't need a little committee to "figure out what we can do to get you to really thrive this year." In this case, "really thrive" means "please don't lose your mind again."

"You've certainly accomplished a lot during your three years here, Hayley," Principal Wexler says, looking down at what appears to be my transcript. Wexler is an intimidating figure. He has the broad chest of a retired football player, and he wears his green Groveland polo like a mob boss wears a finely tailored Italian suit. My ears start buzzing as he speaks, knowing already we're headed nowhere good. It's like our wasp mascot has escaped the stitching on his shirt and is now circling me, vigilantly watching for the best opportunity to sting. Wexler lifts his thick black reading glasses to his face to look over my file. "Your grades are impeccable. You're active in multiple clubs, and I understand you're quite the asset on our tennis team."

These are the words I always imagined coming from an admissions officer at a reputable college with a distinguished premed program. They should be paired with a handshake congratulating me on admission and a good scholarship offer and then followed by a trip to the campus bookstore where I triumphantly hand over too much money for an overpriced sweatshirt with UNC or Cornell or maybe Northwestern stitched across the chest. *Oh this? It's my Cornell sweatshirt. Yeah, I'm going to Cornell. No big deal. Bill Nye, Ruth Bader Ginsburg, and Toni Morrison went there too, but whatever. It's chill.*

This is not that conversation at all. The only thing that's about to follow these words now is a "but."

"However," Principal Wexler continues ("however" is just a fancier "but"), "we are concerned that you've inadvertently overpacked your schedule. We'd like you to scale things back a bit this year."

And there's the sting.

A nervousness tugs at my gut, pulling my stomach down like I'm at the front of a roller coaster peering over the edge of the first big drop, which makes sense because this conversation is only going straight down from here.

I didn't overpack my schedule. I selected my classes the same way I've been doing since my freshman year, carefully choosing the courses that will look best on my transcript and building an unblemished record that will land me a spot at a prestigious college, where I'll earn a diploma that can be matted and framed and hung with pride like Mom's and Dad's in the den. I'm on Groveland's Accelerated Track, which means I take advanced science and math courses every year, but these days being smart isn't enough to land a spot at a reputable college. Schools want well-rounded students; you can't just have a singular interest. So during the summer after ninth grade, I begged my parents to let me go to tennis camp because what admissions officer doesn't love a student athlete with a murderous backswing who also has a knack for writing killer term papers? I wore myself out learning the game. My best friend, Lucy, got tired of playing with me. Exhausted, she would just lie down on the court, and I would practice driving shots into the corner of the service boxes until the park's stadium lights would cut off at midnight.

I want to handle this conversation in a calm, mature way, but when I ask, "What exactly does 'scale things back' mean?" there's clearly an edge of annoyance in my voice. But how can I not be annoyed? I've been making all the best choices for three years, and now, just before what should be the culmination of my high school career, they're changing the rules of the game.

Mom shifts in her seat beside me, unbuttoning her blazer and releasing a small sigh. It's so humiliating that she and Dad are both getting a front-row view of what is gearing up to be one of the most unpleasant discussions of my life. I've been sandwiched between them for multiple parent-teacher conferences, conversations where all I had to do was sit there and smile as my teachers piled on the compliments. Mom would smile, and Dad would scratch the back of my neck in a way that was somehow embarrassing and wonderful at the same time. Now I don't know what's going to happen; we're in uncharted territory.

"Extracurriculars are important," Mr. Keith jumps in, "but these activities should be enjoyable. They should energize you. If they're draining or becoming a burden, you should step back and reevaluate." I bite hard into my lower lip to keep from lashing out as my irritation spreads, building like static over my skin.

Mr. Keith is my school-assigned guidance counselor, and he's basically what happens when a hippie decides they'd also like a 401(k). Keith is his first name, but he insists we call him Mr. Keith because it's just so cool and youthful, isn't it? He's always wearing sport coats over T-shirts emblazoned with cheesy graphics and only stops wearing his Birkenstock sandals when the temperature drops below twenty degrees. He'd probably make a great counselor at my little brother's middle school, or even here if I was interested in majoring in hacky-sackology or pan flute studies, but I'm not. I want a serious guidance counselor, not Bob Marley meets Bob Ross.

"We must learn that there's a difference between resting and quitting," he says. Mr. Keith loves to drop these sorts of phrases, corny positivity mantras that Instagram models like to use as captions for photos of themselves doing yoga on a mountain.

The weirdest part is that Mr. Keith and Wexler are basically best friends, and it doesn't make any sense. Wexler is a strict disciplinarian, and Mr. Keith has multiple rainsticks in his office. In high school, Wexler probably wore the prom king crown while Keith wore a flower crown, but it doesn't matter. Now they've united forces against me. Apparently, it takes both ends of the social spectrum to properly reorient my mental health.

"We want you to succeed here, Hayley, but we don't want you to burn out," Mr. Keith says, sliding a copy of my senior schedule across the table. I pick it up and my parents lean in. AP English. AP Calculus. AP Chemistry. AP European History. Looks great to me. "We'd like you to step away from the Accelerated Track program," Mr. Keith says.

It's like having a golden retriever tell you to give up on your dreams.

The charge of irritation I was feeling slides toward full-blown panic.

Ever since Mom told me about this meeting a week ago, I've been trying to imagine the worst-case scenario for how this might go—maybe weekly mandatory check-ins with Mr. Keith or not being allowed to drive to school—but I never imagined this. "No," I manage to say, my voice quiet, like I'm testing the waters. Wexler and Mr. Keith don't react. "No way," I say, more forcefully this time. "Dropping out of the AT program during my senior year will look terrible on my transcript." Mr. Keith gives me a pitying smile. It's the same look my mom gives my little brother, Tanner, when he talks about building his own tree house in the backyard, something that's never going to happen. I hate that look.

"Aren't you supposed to be encouraging me to keep working hard?" I ask, my voice too loud and too sharp for the small conference room. "It's like you're telling me to throw the car into neutral and just cruise to graduation." Wexler and Mr. Keith both flinch, and I realize, considering the circumstances, a car metaphor may not have been the best choice of words.

I catch my parents exchanging a glance over my head. Wexler and Mr. Keith might be a lost cause, but I can at least make sure I have Mom and Dad on my side. "I can handle the workload," I tell them. The words come out sounding more like a plea than an affirmation, but at least they're out there. I've spent years working toward an impeccable academic record, and I'm not going to let one moment of weakness bring that crashing down.

Mom puts her hand on my knee, and I realize I've been bouncing my leg so fast it's practically shaking the table. Not exactly the confidence-inspiring behavior of a self-assured individual. She gives me a weak smile. Dad puts a hand on my shoulder, and all I can think is it's not the back of my neck. I suddenly feel very small, like a toddler trying to elbow their way up to the adult table at Thanksgiving dinner. My parents—a woman who succeeded in becoming a partner at her law firm the same year she gave birth to my brother, and a man who successfully manages a team of corporate consultants and still found time to run three marathons last year—are having to sit here and comfort their daughter, who can't even handle high school.

Wexler takes off his glasses and rubs the bridge of his nose, like he's already growing tired of this conversation. "There is another option," he says, folding his large hands on the table in front of him. "If you want to stay in the AT program, you'll have to cut back on the extracurriculars. Resign from the tennis team and sign up for some, uh, less intense electives. Maybe TV Production."

"TV Production?" I scoff. "Like AV club?"

"TV Production is a class," Mr. Keith says. "They produce the announcements each morning. We actually have a pretty nice studio. Have you ever seen it?"

Of course not. I've never seen Groveland's art room either, but that's okay because Introduction to Pastels isn't exactly an impressive addition to your transcript when you're planning to apply for premed programs. Is this how they see me now, like some girl who's too fragile for real academic rigor? Is that who I am? I stare down at my schedule, running my finger along the edge of the page and testing how far I can push it without giving myself a paper cut. So I either drop out of the AT program or quit tennis and take some boring electives. They might as well be asking if I'd rather have them chop off my left leg or my right. Either way, my stride is wrecked. Dad must sense my apprehension because he says, "Are those really the only options?" His disappointed tone nearly cracks me open.

"At this point, we really believe one of these would be the best path forward," Mr. Keith says.

"Part of succeeding means knowing your limits," Wexler adds. Ironic considering his barrel chest is currently testing the limits of that poly-cotton blend. Ugh. Dr. Kim, my therapist, says I tend to get pretty judgmental when I'm feeling vulnerable, and I hate moments like these when I prove her right. Because really, who am I to judge anyone at this point?

Wexler leans back in his chair and crosses his arms like everything is settled, like he's made me an offer I can't refuse. Several moments of heavy silence pass, and it must become too much for Mr. Keith to bear because he digs into his blazer pocket and comes out with a handful of candy. "Would anyone like a Starburst?"

This is my life now.

I've reached an all-time low, but at least there's snacks.

I know I have the next line in this little play, but I can't form any words. Before my incident, I was all confidence because life made sense. It was a science: determine what you want, work hard, achieve your goal, repeat. But now that same equation doesn't seem to work. Because sometimes it leads to being pulled from your car at eight thirty on a Thursday morning. So as much as I might want to speak up for myself, I can't. Maybe I shouldn't. Maybe it's best for me to sit back and let people whose brains aren't malfunctioning make the decisions for a while.

"Okay," I say meekly. "I'll do the second one. I'll take TV Production."

We all get up to shake hands, and I thank them for their concern, but it's like someone else is speaking. It's like I've gone numb. Even when we conveniently run into the TV Production teacher, Mrs. Hansen, who just so happens to be free to give me a tour of the studio, I don't even care that this was clearly a trap. This had been the plan all along, and they only made it seem like I had a choice. People like me who make bad choices don't get to make real decisions.

My parents head off to the car while Mrs. Hansen guides me downstairs and through a large set of wooden doors with an unlit ON AIR sign hanging above them. I try my best to nod at the right times as she points out the editing bays and sound equipment, but it's difficult. Trading sunny afternoons on the tennis court with my team for this cinder-block room where I'll stare at a computer screen is not an even trade at all. My face must be telegraphing my disappointment because Mrs. Hansen says, "I know this elective wasn't exactly your first choice, but I think you'll really enjoy TV Production, Hayley. I tend to give the class a lot of freedom. You guys really get a chance to make this program what you want. Within reason, of course." She smiles at me, and I do my best to mirror her excitement, but I can feel my smile faltering.

"Check this out. Sit here." Mrs. Hansen pulls out one of the chairs at the anchor desk, and I take a seat. Then she goes over and switches on the monitor and points one of the stationary cameras at me. I appear on the TV, seated at the half-empty desk. Mrs. Hansen positions the camera so that my face is center in the frame. It's the same image I saw when I checked the mirror before leaving the house this morning—straight red hair, large brown glasses, freckles prominent from a summer spent in the sun. I bring my hand to the side of my temple, testing to see if I can feel it. Can I locate the part of my brain that's damaged? Is there a knot or a scar? Mrs. Hansen peeks out from behind the camera. "Pretty neat, huh?" she asks.

"Yeah. Pretty neat."

LEWIS

I'm lying on my back on the kitchen floor waiting for the room to stop spinning. My Mr. T T-shirt is soaked in sweat. I can feel the weight of it on my chest as I breathe in, out, and in again. There's a glass of ice water on the edge of the counter, and the thought of the cold liquid sliding down my throat seems so refreshing, but I can't find the strength to get up. I extend my arm, willing the glass to float down to my hand, but it doesn't move.

Mom enters, the sound of her heels on the hardwood announcing her presence before she arrives. When she spots me on the ground, she moves quickly and crouches down beside me. "Lewis, are you okay? What's going on?"

She's wearing a navy pantsuit, and her short brown hair is styled with so much hair spray it practically has its own force field. Mom's an anchor at the local news station, so she looks put together pretty much all the time, even when everyone else is a complete mess. Seriously. There are pictures in our family photo albums from Christmas morning where my hair is sticking up everywhere and Dad doesn't even have a shirt on, but Mom looks like she just walked out of a Norman Rockwell painting.

I flop my arm down over my eyes. "Don't look at me! Just pretend I'm not here."

She places her hand on my forehead, checking for a fever. "What happened, Lewis? You're burning up. Are you sick? Are you hurt?"

"I'm fine, Mom," I say, breathing hard. "I mean, I can't really feel my legs and the room seems tilted, but other than that, I'm fine. Does the room look tilted to you?"

"No, honey. You're sweating a lot. Are you sure you're okay?"

"Yeah, I just went running."

"Running? Where?"

"Outside." I cough.

"On purpose?"

"Um, should I be concerned about this?" I hear Dad ask. I peek out from under my arm and find him leaning in the doorway.

"Our son just went running, dear," Mom says, standing up.

"It went great. Can't you tell?" I pant.

"I didn't know you were . . . into that," Dad says, walking to the counter and then bending down to place the cup of water on the floor beside my head.

I lift myself just enough to take a drink. "Oh, you know I've always been into fitness." It's funny because it's clearly not true. Mom takes classes at the local gym four times a week, and Dad naturally has a lanky frame, but I've always been on the larger side. I'm that size where polite strangers affectionately refer to me as "Big Man" and ask questions like "I bet you play football, don't you?" You know, the kind of comments fat people are comfortable with. Well, for the most part, anyway. Still, I've learned there will always be bullies more than willing to make fun of the fat kid. (Mine's called Harold Lockner.) That's why I'm always the first to make a joke about my weight. If I can beat you to the punch line, I can at least hang on to some of my pride.

"Well, I think it's great you're trying something new," Mom says, pouring some coffee into her travel tumbler now that she's confident I won't die here on the floor. Probably. "It shows initiative and maturity."

"Yes, this is the height of dignity," I say, spreading my arms wide across the floor. Today I made the mistake of putting on some music and just running as hard as I could for as long as I could. I only made it to the second song on my '80s mix before my lungs were pounding against my chest and I was hunched over with my hands on my knees. I don't really know what a good running distance is, but I have a feeling when people say they ran a 5K, they aren't talking about five blocks. "I think I'm just going to lay here the rest of the day if that's okay," I moan.

"No, you're not," Mom says. "You have school."

I turn over onto my stomach with a groan. "There're still two days of summer left," I protest.

"Not for you," Mom says. "You and Cal agreed to help clean up the TV studio and get it ready for the new year, remember?"

I did remember, but that was before I made the mistake of scrolling through a couple of fitness Instagram accounts and convincing myself I was ready to try running. Now I think lying on the floor is the only thing holding back the rising tide of nausea.

"It's just sweeping and making sure all the equipment is working," I say into the kitchen tile. "I'm sure it can wait until the first day on Wednesday."

"No," Mom says. "You made a commitment, and you're going to stick to it."

"Because sticking to one's commitments shows initiative and maturity?" I mock. That gets a snort out of Dad, but he's quick to cover it with a cough when Mom shoots him a threatening look.

"Well, yes. But I was also going to say because extracurriculars look good on your college applications," Mom says. College is not a subject I particularly want to discuss, and I know fighting her on this is futile anyway. I'm senior producer in our TV studio this year, and it's the only sort of leadership position I've ever pursued at Groveland, so she's making sure I don't mess it up. Plus, I think it makes her a little happy to see her son possibly following in her television career footsteps.

I use the counter to pull myself to my feet, and Dad frowns at the floor. "You left a damp spot," he says.

He's right. There's an outline of my body in sweat. "It's like a snow angel, but gross," I say. He rolls his eyes and tosses me the paper towels.

On the way to Groveland, I stop to pick up my best friend, Cal, and my car groans a bit when he slides into the passenger seat. Not because he's overweight like me but because my car is old. I drive a 2003 Mazda hatchback. My parents say a seventeen-year-old doesn't deserve a nice car because I'll probably just wreck it.

I pull away from Cal's house, and he lifts my banana from the center console. "What's this?" he asks.

"You're about to start your senior year and you don't know what a banana is, Cal? The public school system has really failed you."

"Ha. Ha," he spits. "I'm just wondering why you're not having your normal breakfast of Pop-Tarts and Mountain Dew. You drink that stuff so much I figured you were trying to get them as a corporate sponsor for your funeral or something."

"I know you're just making a joke, but why would Mountain Dew sponsor my funeral? If I claimed I lost weight drinking Mountain Dew, *then* they might want to be my sponsor, but not if I died drinking it. Think through your material, man."

The real reason I'm not indulging in my normal breakfast is because I have big plans for this year. Not that I'm about to tell Cal that. The plan started with this weight-loss infomercial I saw last week. That sounds stupid, I know, but that's how it happened for me. I was watching a late-night showing of *Say Anything* on TV when, during a commercial break, some spray-tanned guy with weirdly white teeth and a microphone wrapped around his head started promising washboard abs if you bought his revolutionary exercise invention for three easy payments of $19.95.

They started showing pictures of former fatties who had supposedly gotten thin using the device. I was about to change the channel when they flashed a photo of a guy who looked like me. Like, *just* like me. He was large and pale and trying to appear relaxed in his Hawaiian swim trunks while standing next to a pool. His shoulders were slumping, and he had a tight, closed-mouth smile. Next, they showed what he looked like after supposedly using the device every day for three months. He was toned and standing on a beach, wearing aviator sunglasses and flexing like some Renaissance artist was about to chisel a marble statue of him. Just as I was biting into a s'mores Pop-Tart, the camera zoomed in on him, and he whipped off his sunglasses like a low-budget Tom Cruise. "I used to sit in my room all the time, staying up late and eating loads of junk food," he said. "Then I got this device, decided to have a little discipline, and now there are other reasons I'm staying up late at night." The camera panned back as a tiny blond woman wearing an even tinier bikini entered the frame and wrapped her arms around muscle me. It was honestly pretty gross, but even as I clicked off the TV, I couldn't help but wonder what it would feel like to be like him. Not frat-boy buff, necessarily, but confident. It's not like I suddenly pictured myself surrounded by models and piles of cash and a cheetah that I trained to fold my laundry, but maybe a girl would want to hold my hand. One girl in particular . . .

I didn't order the workout device, of course, but I kept thinking about what muscle me said about how his life changed when he decided to have a little discipline. So I woke up early and went running. Maybe this is the start of something, but since this was only my first day running and it was not particularly successful, I'm not exactly eager to tell Cal about all that. I've never been the type of person to set a goal and pursue it relentlessly, especially something physical, so I figure there's a good chance I'll fail. I don't want to give Cal a reason to mock me in a few months if I'm still the same idle self-deprecating fat ass I am today.

"Well, if you are giving up Mountain Dew, I support that decision," Cal says. "I heard it makes your testicles shrink. That's probably why you've never had the balls to ask out Rebecca."

Cal never misses a chance to remind me that I've had a crush on our friend Rebecca Woodruff for about five years now and I've never had the courage to tell her about my feelings.

"Number one, that's an urban legend," I say. "And number two, I have the balls to ask out Rebecca. I'm just waiting for the right moment, all right?"

"It's been years, man. I think the right moment has come and gone several times."

I can't think of a great rebuttal to that, so I just turn up the stereo.

Cal spends the rest of the ten-minute drive to Groveland pretending my banana is his penis and using it to do things like change the station on the radio and try to roll down the window. It's so unsettling that I can't even bring myself to eat the thing. I just toss it in the trash outside school.

It's a little weird being back inside Groveland after three months away, especially with no one else here. It's too quiet and too clean. All the shiny surfaces and the lingering smell of bleach are clear indications everything has recently been given a good scrubbing.

When we get down to the TV studio, Mrs. Hansen walks out, and Cal yells, "Hey, Mrs. H! How was your—" before faltering on the word "summer" as Groveland's own unintentional YouTube sensation Hayley Mills steps out of the studio behind her. Before this moment, if you had asked me to guess who I was going to see at school today, I would have listed Amelia Earhart or Bigfoot above Hayley Mills. I'm so surprised, I trip over my own feet and have to grab on to Cal's arm to steady myself.

"Hi, boys, good to see you again," Mrs. Hansen says, her Southern accent coming through strong. A lot of guys at Groveland have a crush on Mrs. Hansen. She's young and cute and pretty chill. Kind of like having Reese Witherspoon as a teacher. "Do you know Hayley?" she says, touching Hayley's shoulder. It's a ridiculous question because at this point I'm pretty sure the whole school and probably several schools in the surrounding counties know Hayley.

At the end of last year, she had some sort of mental breakdown and stopped her car at the main entrance into Groveland. She sat in the middle of the intersection for so long that it caused a major traffic jam, cars and school buses backed up for blocks. People started getting out of their vehicles to see what was going on, including me and Cal. A few concerned teachers tried to get her out of the car, but she had all the doors locked. I don't even think she acknowledged them as they tapped on her windshield and tried to open the doors; she just sat there with her hands at ten and two. By the time the police showed up, there was a traffic helicopter floating over the whole scene. The cops were able to pop her lock and open the door. One officer walked her over to the curb while another moved her car, and a few others started directing traffic. Kids had a field day with all the news and cell phone footage. For weeks there were new edits popping up on TikTok and YouTube every day with funny captions and goofy music. Hayley spent the last couple weeks of school taking all her finals alone in one of the small study rooms in the library. People thought she wasn't going to come back this year.

Hayley and I actually had history together our sophomore year, so I sort of knew her before. But I didn't even feel comfortable saying hello to her in the hall, let alone reaching out after her incident.

"Yeah, I know Hayley," I say. "We have history, uh, had history together. Mr. Rosco, right?"

"Right," Hayley says, giving me a tight-lipped smile.

"Hayley, Lewis is our senior producer this year. And Cal Raglin is one of our lead anchors. Boys, I was just giving Hayley a tour of the studio. She'll be joining our class this year."

"Why?" Cal blurts, cementing his position in the "Terrible at Social Cues" Hall of Fame. Even though he's asking the same question that's at the front of my mind. I have no idea why someone like Hayley would want to spend her senior year in TV Production, but I at least have the common sense to save my questions for a more appropriate moment. I give Cal a nudge.

"*Whhhyy*, that's great," he croaks in what is arguably the worst recovery of all time.

"I agree. It is great," Mrs. Hansen says before turning to Hayley. "Lewis and Cal generously agreed to help get the studio ready for the new school year. Boys, I'm going to walk Hayley out. Why don't you go in there and get started?"

Cal and I watch as they disappear up the stairs. When the large studio doors shut behind us, Cal shoves my arm. "Dude! What. The. Hell?" he exclaims, his eyebrows shooting up into the blond curls of his hair. "Hayley Mills is joining TV Production?"

I move toward the brooms in the corner. "I know. I was there beside you when Mrs. Hansen just told us."

"So how are you not freaking out about this?"

I shrug. "New people join TV Production every year." And while I'm very curious about why Hayley suddenly wants to be here, I saw enough posts about her over the summer to know we tipped the scales from playful hazing to outright cyberbullying long ago. Even I'm guilty of making a joke or two at her expense, but it doesn't feel funny anymore. "I'm sure it'll be fine."

"This isn't just some new person. It's *Messed-Up Mills*. She's a wild card, man. Did you see her hair?"

"C'mon, man, don't call her that. And what was wrong with her hair?" I ask, tossing Cal a broom.

"It was, like, three inches shorter than last year." He pauses like that should mean something to me. When I shrug, he sighs and forges ahead. "Girls only get dramatic haircuts like that when weird shit is rattling around in their head."

"Maybe it just got hot over the summer."

"No, no, no. You don't understand, man. Girls don't have the same relationship with hair that you and I do. It's different for girls." He waves his broom in front of him like the shittiest of wizards. "For them, it's something spiritual."

I snort. "I think you might be reading into it too much."

"You better hope so, senior producer. This is basically your studio this year. Your baby. And now Hayley Mills is loose in it. Anything could happen. You're going to have to keep her in check."

I walk over to Cal and place a hand on his shoulder. "Dude, relax. It's going to be fine. You and I are going to be partners just like last year, and we're going to keep making hilarious video segments that Mrs. Hansen loves, and she'll keep Hayley in check. Yeah, I'm senior producer, but she's still the teacher."

Cal relaxes a little. "Okay. You're probably right."

"Of course I'm right. We're basically Mrs. Hansen's favorites. She's not going to let anything bad happen. Nothing's going to be any different."

THREE

HAYLEY

There's one," Lucy says, pointing to the grocery store parking lot across the street.

"Oh no, does that one have a feather in the band?" I ask.

"That's how you know it's fancy, Hayley."

Lucy and I are currently sitting in our "mansion," which is what we affectionately call the tiny shaved ice stand where we've worked the past two summers. The space is barely big enough for both of us, but we have fun bumping into each other and joking that we're "going to recline in the parlor" or "going to relax in the library." The stand is owned by Lucy's neighbor, Mrs. Cambridge. We don't really know what she does on a day-to-day basis, but it keeps her away from the stand most of the time, so Lucy and I basically have free run of the place.

The stand is in the parking lot of a small shopping center containing a post office, a couple restaurants, and a second run movie theater. Sometimes we get a small rush of customers after a showing lets out, but we've never truly been busy. To pass the time, Lucy and I play people-watching games. Yesterday we looked for people walking animals other than dogs. Not many results there. We saw a middle-aged woman walking a fat orange cat and a man in a denim vest walking a ferret. At one point there was also an old man at the bus stop feeding oyster crackers to a bird on his shoulder, so we counted that, too.

Today's hunt is much easier; we're looking for people in straw fedoras. They're very common. We've been open for two hours, and we already have six tally marks in our notebook.

Lucy pushes the notebook aside and stretches her arms out into the ray of sun that's coming in through the serving window. She keeps them there and closes her eyes, enjoying the warmth on her brown skin. Summer has always been Lucy's favorite season. She says it's the only time of year that the bright colors and loud prints she likes to wear are socially acceptable. She usually looks like she just stepped out of a '90s sitcom. In the best way.

"Soak it up while you can," I say. "Last day."

"Quiet," Lucy responds. "We are not talking about the fact that school starts tomorrow, okay?"

I look out the window and spot Mallory Scott marching across the parking lot. It suddenly feels as if the shaved ice stand is even smaller, like the walls are closing in and the air is evaporating. "Oh no."

"What?" Lucy asks.

"Mallory's coming. I called her last night and told her I wasn't doing tennis this year. She basically lost it, hung up on me, and then called back ten minutes later to yell some more."

"And now she's come to harass you at your workplace? How lovely." Lucy slides open the window, and Mallory props her elbows on the counter. She gives us a big smile that's incredibly unsettling because the last time I saw her this happy was when she beat the captain of the boys' tennis team in a match by drilling a serve right into his crotch.

"Hi, guys!"

"Hi, Mallory," I say, my hands clasped in front of my own crotch in a subconscious defense position.

"What can we get you?" Lucy asks dryly.

"Actually, I just came to talk to Hayley," Mallory says.

"Sorry," Lucy responds. "Gotta keep the window free for customers."

Mallory turns around to look at the nobody behind her. "Seriously?"

Lucy gives her a silent grin, and it takes everything in me to not laugh. "Fine," Mallory relents. "I'll take . . . lime."

I take a couple steps to the rear of the hut, happy to be putting a little distance between Mallory and me as Lucy collects her money. I add a fresh block to Bertha, which is what we call the cantankerous machine that shaves down the ice. When I pull the lever, Bertha rumbles to life, shaking the whole counter.

"I think I owe you an apology, Hayley!" Mallory shouts over Bertha's moaning. The block of ice slowly vibrates down into the inner workings of the machine as I grab a cup and position it at the dispenser. "I may have overreacted a little last night when you told me you were quitting tennis," Mallory continues. "But I hope you can at least see where I was coming from. It was very jarring to find out less than two days before the start of the school year that we're losing one of our best players." The shavings quickly fill up the cup. I pass it off to Lucy, who shapes the top into a mound and begins pouring the green syrup.

"Yeah, I understand," I tell Mallory, handing her a spoon and a napkin. Even though it may sound like Mallory is here to make amends, I know this conversation is actually a minefield. The slightest misstep could be a disaster. "For what it's worth, I don't like the situation either."

"And I was hoping that after you'd slept on it, you might have reconsidered and decided to stick with tennis. I know the rest of the team will really, really miss you."

I have a flashback of lying in a sleeping bag on Mallory's bedroom floor, wiping tears of laughter from my face. Last December we did a team holiday gift exchange, and several of us slept over, spending most of the night talking and gossiping and laughing about things I can't even remember now. That memory alone is enough to give me second thoughts.

I'll miss everything about tennis. The satisfaction I get when I'm able to return a shot my opponent wasn't expecting, the buzzing in my arms and feet when I come from behind to take the lead, the van rides with my teammates where Coach would yell at us for being too rowdy.

But it's not like I'm going to become a professional tennis player. I'm good at Groveland, but not good enough to land a scholarship to any of the colleges in my top five. I'm going to earn my way based on academics. I can't sacrifice that for a game. Even a game I love.

Lucy hands Mallory her shaved ice. "Sorry," I say, not really able to meet Mallory's gaze. "I can't afford to drop my AT classes."

"I think you can," Mallory says, clearly working hard to keep her voice even. "I know you're thinking about college, but your transcript is already solid. Just get a good SAT score and you'll be fine."

"My schedule's already set, Mallory." Even before I'm done speaking, I can feel the click of the land mine beneath my feet as Mallory's face begins to contort. I try to counteract it by continuing to ramble. "I can still play with you guys sometimes, I just can't—"

Mallory slaps the counter, cutting me off. "Seriously? You're just going to abandon the team? You're going to regret this." Then she turns and marches away, dumping her untouched shaved ice in the garbage. Lucy and I watch her get back in her car and peel away.

"Damn," Lucy says. "That girl just needs a white cat to stroke and she'd be like a real-life movie villain. Who says, 'You're going to regret this' unironically?"

"She's definitely intense," I say, lifting my arms to air out the sweat I notice has started to gather there.

"Too intense. And about school sports no less."

"Says the girl who spends hours after school every day hanging out in the photo lab."

"Hey, I've never shunned someone over photography," Lucy says, doodling in our notebook. "Don't let it get to you. I'm sure she'll be over it before Halloween."

Lucy says it lightly, but my stomach grinds like Bertha's gears. That's part of my fear going into this year: that people won't ever be *over it.* That they'll never move on. I'm worried people will still be weird around me and only see me as the girl who had a nervous breakdown. Dr. Kim says I'm probably feeling this way because I'm too close to the situation. She thinks all my classmates have had three full months of new experiences and they're all too consumed with their own lives to be worried about me. She phrased it better, but it still came across a little like she didn't really remember what high school is like. I mean, I bring traffic to a screeching halt right in front of school and people will just forget? I doubt it.

Lucy and I finish the day with eleven straw fedora tally marks. She says eleven plus one because we saw a guy in a straw cowboy hat, which is "worth noting." As we're locking up, a white SUV cruises into the parking lot.

"Looks like your boyfriend's back in town," Lucy says.

I curse under my breath. I knew this day was coming, but I was hoping the first time Parker saw me once he got back would be under better circumstances. I may have been imagining some magical moment where I looked flawlessly elegant, my face and hair illuminated by the soft orange light of the setting sun. Guess I'll have to settle for standing in an asphalt parking lot while keeping my arms down to conceal my pit stains. "Ex-boyfriend," I say, quickly taking off my hat and raking my fingers through my hair a few times, hoping it doesn't look too matted.

"Yeah, we'll see how long that lasts," Lucy jokes.

Parker Murakami is in the Accelerated Track program with me, and we dated for around five months last year. I ended things back in March, about a month before my incident, because it started to feel like we were just constantly competing, seeing who could achieve more. At first I thought it was just part of the playful way we flirted, but soon I realized I had this small but very real flame of resentment inside of me each time he told me about another one of his accomplishments. It's like we were Mozart and Salieri if Mozart and Salieri liked kissing each other. I broke things off gently, and we're still something resembling friends. Lucy is convinced it's only a matter of time before we get back together.

He pulls up beside us with his windows down. "Hey, ladies. Need a ride?"

"Who is this international man of mystery?" Lucy asks, already starting to climb into the back seat. Parker spent most of the summer visiting his grandparents in Kyoto, Japan. We were all very jealous of his Instagram feed when he was posting photos of ornate temples while we were uploading pictures of our Starbucks run. Parker flashes us his big class president grin, a smile that reminds me just how different our summers have been. Because it seems like it takes nothing for him to produce something so wide and genuine, and most days I can barely muster a smirk. "I ate soooo much ramen," he says.

"I'm sure you did," I say, climbing into the passenger seat and adjusting one of the AC vents. It's a move that still feels surprisingly natural, even though we haven't been a couple for roughly six months. "When did you get back?"

"Just a few days ago. I've been trying to adjust to the time difference." A few days. Part of me wonders if Parker has also been planning how we might first see each other, and this was his plan, showing up casually cool right at closing time.

On the way to Lucy's house, Parker tells us all about his favorite sites from Japan, and then he drops her off and it's just me and him in the car. It suddenly feels stifling as I realize this is the first time we've been alone in close quarters since our breakup. Before, when we drove around, he would slide his hand over toward me, palm up, so I could lace my fingers through his. Now both of his hands remain firmly on the wheel, and I don't really know what to do with mine, so I slide them under my legs to keep from pushing open the door and rolling out into traffic to get away from this awkwardness. I desperately try to think of anything to say, and I'm about two seconds from asking Parker if he rode in a rickshaw during his trip when he says, "How was your summer? I assume you've been playing a ton of tennis."

"Oh, yeah. Some," I mutter, wondering if it's too late to jump into traffic. "I'm actually not doing tennis this year." I try to make it sound casual, like it's no big deal.

"Really?" he asks.

He glances over toward me, but I keep my eyes on the houses

moving past the passenger-side window. "I just didn't want to over-schedule my senior year, you know? I wanted to make sure I had some free time to just hang out and enjoy it."

He's quiet for a moment before finally nodding. "Yeah. I get that."

He doesn't get it. He can't possibly get it because it's the total opposite of the attitude we both had during our relationship—that he still has. But I can't open up to Parker about everything that's happened in the past couple of days. I couldn't even open up to him when he reached out after my incident. I just sent his calls to voicemail and ignored his texts until he was too busy in Japan to keep trying. I know if I told him about being forced to quit tennis, he would be sweet and supportive and it would just annoy me, because yeah, Mallory's reaction was excessive and borderline deranged, but I prefer her anger to the usual looks of pity I get so often these days.

"I just want to have more fun this year, you know? You know colleges mainly look at what you did during your junior year, so why not enjoy senior year, you know?" Oh God, how many times did I just say "you know"? This is pathetic.

"Sounds like a plan," Parker says, and in this moment I'm thankful he's my ex because he's clearly too uncomfortable to press into the messy details. "Well, having fun means coming to my annual First Friday party, right?" he asks, shifting the subject to something lighter. Unlike me, Parker is able to successfully balance a rigorous academic schedule and a thriving social life, and he always hosts a party at his place at the end of the first week of school.

"Yeah, I'm sure Lucy and I will be there," I say as he pulls up to the curb outside my house. I open the door before he even comes to a complete stop, eager to make my escape. Part of me is secretly hoping I come down with pneumonia or a bad case of food poisoning before Parker's party. Apparently I'm at the point in my life where diarrhea is preferable to social engagements.

FOUR

LEWIS

C al takes a bite of his burger, and a large glob of ketchup and mayonnaise lands on the foil wrapper in front of him. Normally food that oozes and drips kind of disgusts me, but today it's different. Today I'd give my left leg for it. Well, maybe not my whole leg, but at least one of my less important toes. We're sitting at our regular picnic table outside Graze Daze, and while Cal is diving into one of their famous double bacon cheeseburgers, I'm attempting to enjoy a grilled chicken salad.

After Cal's comment about drinking Mountain Dew yesterday, I decided to reevaluate my diet and do a little research. Most dudes would be embarrassed by their internet search history because it's full of porn. I'm embarrassed of mine because it's full of questions like "What is a calorie?" and "Why are carbs bad?" I even stumbled across a fitness blog where a muscular guy wearing nothing but a towel was talking about how his body doesn't even crave sugar anymore because he detoxed and now he craves quinoa and brussels sprouts, and he can't even remember what a doughnut looks like because he spends all of his free time mountain biking with swimsuit models who shove crystals up their butts to cleanse their auras or something. It was terrible, but I'm trying to make some smarter food choices. I stab a mushy forkful into my mouth and try to imagine it's a burger.

Rebecca slides onto the bench beside me and places a chocolate milkshake on the table. "The paychecks are great, but the free milkshakes might actually be the best part of working here," she says. "That and the lasting smell of french fries I can't ever seem to get out of my hair."

"Truly intoxicating," I say.

She flips her brown curls into my face. "Girls spend so much money on products that make their hair smell like coconut or eucalyptus, and what's the point?"

"Maybe she's born with it. Maybe it's fry oil," I joke.

Okay, so let's get real. It's her. Rebecca is the main reason I'm trying to change things up this year. Lose some weight, gain some confidence, get the girl.

Rebecca Woodruff has been one of my closest friends since sixth grade. That's when she and her parents moved here from New Zealand. During her first week, we got paired up as scene partners in drama class. We were assigned a scene that involved two teenagers from the Bronx, so we kept trying to do New York accents. It was particularly funny to listen to Rebecca attempt it. "How about you just try to sound less like Steve Irwin?" I joked. That earned me an earful on the difference between New Zealand and Australia. We've been pals ever since, even after her dad left and she and her mom had to move into a new apartment in another school district.

She's been working here at Graze Daze since last November. It was already one of our regular hangout spots before she got the job, but now we spend more time here than ever. Not a week of summer has gone by where we haven't spent some time sipping shakes at these outdoor picnic tables.

"I thought people usually stopped enjoying the food from a restaurant when they started working there," Cal says.

"Not me," Rebecca responds. "If anything, working here has only rejuvenated my love of burgers."

"So it's clean back in that kitchen? Because I've had some concerns," Cal says, stuffing several fries into his mouth.

"Oh yeah, you clearly look like you have reservations." Rebecca laughs.

I don't think Rebecca loves working in fast food, but she talks like it's not too bad. I know she feels a certain level of responsibility for helping out at home now that her dad is out of the picture. She pulls off her work shirt so she's just in a tank top and slips a pair of sunglasses onto her face. Then she shifts and lies across the bench seat, her head resting on my leg and her hair pooling in my lap. Something lights up in my gut.

"So what's the plan for tonight, boys?" she asks. "Another movie night?"

"I'm actually supposed to go to the mall," I say. "My mom wants me to get some new clothes for school."

"Wow. I can't believe she doesn't appreciate that half of your shirts have slogans from eighties movies printed on them," Cal mocks.

Rebecca sits up. "Hey now. That's *The Breakfast Club*, Cal," she says, pointing to my shirt. "They were strangers before an afternoon in detention changed their lives forever. Respect the journey."

"I do! I'm the one who introduced you to *The Breakfast Club*!"

He's not lying. Our journey into '80s movies started last summer. One day my neighbor was having a yard sale where there was a box of dollar DVDs. When Cal was digging through it, he found a copy of *The Goonies*, and Rebecca said she had never seen it. Cal was shocked.

"You've never seen *The Goonies*?"

"No, is it good?" Rebecca asked.

"So you have no idea what the Truffle Shuffle is?"

"Is this some kind of weird American thing?"

"Uh, is adventure a weird American thing? Is friendship a weird American thing? Lew, help me out. Tell Rebecca she's missing out."

"How old is this movie?" Rebecca asked, taking the case from Cal's hand and examining the back. "I don't think I should be judged for not knowing about movies that were made decades before I was born."

"But what about all the other great eighties movies?" Cal asked.

"Like what?" Rebecca asked.

Cal and I started listing them in quick succession: *Ferris Bueller's Day Off*, *Fast Times at Ridgemont High*, *Risky Business*, *Ghostbusters*, *Die Hard*. Rebecca shook her head at each one, only admitting that she had seen part of *E.T.* on TV once.

That's how we ended up watching at least two '80s movies every week for the rest of the summer, upon Cal's insistence. He got kind of fanatical about it honestly, constantly shopping for new ones online and digging through the discount bins at big-box stores. He even started creating themes for each week. There was "Lovable Misfits" week where we watched *The Breakfast Club* and *Stand By Me*, and "Cyborg Week" where we watched *The Terminator* and *RoboCop*. Even though Cal was more passionate about the whole thing than I was, I never complained because his project gave me multiple hours a week in his dim basement with Rebecca by my side. Each time she would lay her head in my lap or her fingers would find their way close to mine, something electric pulsed over my skin. After a while, Rebecca actually got into it herself and started doing her own research on '80s films. At one point, she demanded we have "Molly Ringwald Week," which meant watching *Pretty in Pink* and *Sixteen Candles*.

Ever since then, '80s-related stuff has just been part of our friendship. I gave Rebecca and Cal an '80s mix for our first day of school last year, and back in December, Rebecca gave us '80s-themed Christmas presents. She gave me my Mr. T T-shirt and gave Cal a *Say Anything* poster with John Cusack holding his boom box over his head. Cal promptly tacked it up next to the foosball table in his basement.

I take a sip of Rebecca's milkshake. (I mean, if I'm eating a salad, I should at least wash it down with some chocolate ice cream, right? Balance is important.) "Well, I was thinking of just going to the mall and blowing all the money my mom gave me on fifty soft pretzels, but I guess I could buy some actual clothes," I say. "You guys want to come along?"

Rebecca stands up and grabs her milkshake. "Sure. What are friends for?"

The word "friend" catches in my mind. Part of me has always thought—or at least hoped—Rebecca and I would end up together. It sort of feels like we're always circling each other, waiting for our orbits to sync. Now I'm finally realizing that if we are ever going to get together, something is going to have to be different. I can't keep creating excuses or hoping she'll make the first move. Maybe this year can be different. If I can be more disciplined about what I eat, and intentional about exercise, maybe I can be more intentional about Rebecca, too.

At the mall, Cal quickly gets distracted by the sports equipment, leaving Rebecca and me to dig through the racks of clothes on our own.

"Oh yes, I've found the one," Rebecca says, holding up a short-sleeved button-up.

"Is a shirt supposed to have stripes *and* polka dots?" I ask.

"Only the best ones," she says, her mouth twisting into a mischievous grin.

"You're supposed to be helping me. Not sabotaging me," I say.

Rebecca slides the shirt back onto the hanger. "Sorry for trying to broaden your horizons," she says sarcastically. "I just thought you might want to be a little adventurous."

We keep fishing through the rack together, and after a few moments of silence I say, "So what kind of clothes do you like to see on a guy?" Super subtle, Lewis. Really great.

"Hmm, I don't know," Rebecca says. She takes a step back and places her hands on her hips to look at me. "For you, I see a more classic wardrobe. You're not a trendy guy."

"Thank you?"

"I just mean you need items that are going to be more timeless. Not things you're going to look back on in five years and be embarrassed about. Here, you go to the dressing room and I'll find some stuff."

I follow Rebecca's command and head to the small hall of dressing rooms in the corner. Since it's the middle of the day on a Tuesday, we're the only people in the entire men's department. I take a seat in one of the chairs, and after a few moments Rebecca appears with armfuls of jeans and khakis and collared shirts.

For the next twenty minutes, I try on all the clothes, emerging from behind the curtain time and time again like a movie montage so Rebecca can give her opinion on each look. There are a lot of items that I like, but Rebecca makes sure to slip in a few nonsensical ones too, like a purple spandex turtleneck. She laughs when I put it on. I hate the way the material hugs the roundness of my stomach and chest, but if it makes Rebecca laugh, I'd wear this every day.

Just as we're finishing up, Rebecca brings over a gray blazer. "Wait, you need a jacket," she says, holding it up so I can slip my arms in. Once it's on, I step onto the raised platform surrounded by mirrors and button one of the front buttons. "What do you think?" I ask.

Rebecca steps up onto the platform behind me. "Here," she says, twisting my shoulders so that I'm facing her. She brings her arms up and adjusts the collar behind my neck, getting it to lie flat. Then she runs her hands along the length of the lapel, smoothing any wrinkles. I'm suddenly aware of how close we are, and I swallow hard. She looks up at me, and I try to read her expression. What is she expecting? What is she noticing about me?

There's a tension building in the silence, and I know something has to happen. If this were an '80s movie, the piano music would swell and I would take Rebecca's face in my hands, pulling her closer to me. Her lips would part and our mouths would meet as the camera pulls back and the picture goes soft on the edges.

But that's not what happens.

"Do you think this coat will look good with that spandex turtleneck?" I ask.

Rebecca smiles, then presses her forehead against my chest, shaking her head. After a moment she turns and steps off the platform. "It looks good. You should get it," she says, moving back toward our pile of clothes.

I feel more stupid now than I did in that purple spandex. I'm mad that I'm the one who broke the tension, but it's something I've been doing all my life—using humor to sidestep sincere moments of vulnerability.

"Should I wear it on the first day?" I ask.

"It's the first day of school, Lew. Not a job interview."

"Not just any first day. The first day of senior year," I chime. "Anything could happen."

I think I'm half trying to convince myself because I'm hoping something big actually *will* happen, like me finally making my move with Rebecca. "I could end up on the cover of GQ. You could become a manager at Graze Daze."

Rebecca leans against the wall and crosses her arms. "So in your senior year fantasy, you become a cover model and I only rise to the rank of fast food restaurant manager?"

"Hey, the world needs little people like you to appreciate the beautiful people like me."

"Oh God," she says, tossing a sweater at my face. "Come on, let's pay for your clothes and get out of here. You said something about soft pretzels, right?"

FIVE

HAYLEY

I have a standing appointment with Dr. Kim every Tuesday evening, and I'm still trying to decide if I like her office. It kind of looks like Coachella got relocated to an IKEA. The furniture is simple, all clean lines and right angles, but with colorful linens draped over them. There are lots of plants and little potted cacti, and something called a Himalayan salt lamp sits on the corner of her desk. I appreciate that it's not a sterile room with big bookshelves and stiff leather couches, but she might be leaning a little too heavily into the bohemian coffee shop vibe. If she starts putting up weird abstract art that looks suspiciously like vaginas, I'll probably have to find a new therapist.

"Hayley, welcome," Dr. Kim says. She's wearing gray capris and a crisp white collared shirt. Today her black hair is down, parted in the middle so that it brushes against the frames of her glasses and gathers on her shoulders. Her decorating style might be kind of weird, but on the fashion front she always looks incredibly put together. "Hazelnut or vanilla today?"

"Vanilla," I say. Dr. Kim takes a pod and places it in the Keurig machine on her credenza. She presses a button and positions a yellow mug beneath the spout while I settle into a plush green chair. After a moment she hands me a steaming mug and takes a seat in the identical chair across from me.

"So what's new?" she asks, setting a notepad and pen on the arm of her chair. This is how Dr. Kim opens most of our sessions, and it's a bit of a tricky question. I know she wants to get to know me, but I don't need a new best friend. I just need her to give me a few tips and tricks for dealing with my stress, fix whatever it is that made me stop my car in front of Groveland, and then I can go on my merry way. "You had that meeting with your school administrators this week, right?"

"I did. They decided I need to give up all my extracurriculars this year. Including tennis. Said they don't want me feeling overwhelmed." I take a sip of my coffee, and it scalds my tongue.

Dr. Kim leans back in her seat. "I'm sorry to hear that. But there's nothing wrong with not pushing yourself to the limit all the time, Hayley. It's okay to take a step back, especially if it's going to keep you healthy."

I don't like stepping back; I like moving forward. In sixth grade there was a reading challenge at my school. Every kid who read twenty-five books or more by the end of the year got an award. They made a special plaque for me because I read seventy-nine books, easily lapping the other kids in my class. At the awards assembly, the principal slapped my shoulder and said, "This girl's got ambition." That's who I've always been, a girl with ambition. "I don't want to slow down too much," I say. "The early bird gets the worm, you know?"

"Yeah, but the second mouse gets the cheese," Dr. Kim says. And she's smiling like that's just brilliant and not something she probably stole from an unoriginal positivity blogger.

I don't particularly feel like exchanging more animal metaphors, so I change the subject. "They're making me take TV Production."

"And you're not excited about that?"

"It's just not interesting to me." I slump a little deeper into my chair. "It'll probably be full of potheads. If I walk in and see more than one white guy with dreads, I'm getting a transfer slip."

Dr. Kim laughs a little. "Maybe it'll be better than you think."

My recent history at Groveland has given me very few reasons to believe anything will be better than I think. "It feels like things are slipping through my fingers. I can't even control my own schedule."

"Let's try an exercise," Dr. Kim says, rising out of her chair. She walks behind her desk and pulls up an easel and a large white pad of paper and starts writing on it. When she steps away I see that she's drawn a line down the center. One half of the paper is labeled "Things I Can Control" and the other is labeled "Things I Can't Control."

"We're never going to have as much control as we want in life, Hayley." Dr. Kim tosses me the black Sharpie. "I think part of your worry stems from the fact that you're trying to hold on to things so tightly. So let's make a list and get it all out. Sometimes it helps to look at it in black-and-white rather than having it all bouncing around inside."

I'm doubtful this will help, but she's right. I am worried. Anxious thoughts have started moving in and pushing my confidence to the corner. My ambition is starting to feel less like a medal on my chest and more like a weight tied around my neck. Not that I'd ever admit that out loud.

I make quick work of the "Things I Can't Control" side, writing down the weather, how much homework is assigned, what people say or think about me, if people like me, my nervousness.

"Great," Dr. Kim says, "now let's see what you can control."

I squeeze the marker in my hand and stare at the blank side.

"Write down anything that comes to mind."

I write "what I wear" and "how I engage in class." The answers feel shallow and wrong, and I cringe as I step away to reveal them to Dr. Kim.

"Okay. Good. Now what about the social aspect of school?" Dr. Kim prompts. She's leaning against the arm of her chair and giving me an expectant smile. I do some quick math in my brain to determine how long it's been since she's been in high school. She's what, in her late thirties? So probably twenty years, give or take a few.

"If there were parts of that I controlled, I'd probably be less nervous," I say.

"Being social with someone is a mutual interaction. You control half of the equation."

I write down "what I say to people," "how I treat people," and "how I label people."

When I turn around, Dr. Kim is smiling even more. Her teeth look huge. "There you go. I understand high school isn't easy. There's academic pressure and social pressure, but look at that board. You have power, Hayley. The same power you've always had is still inside you. If you don't like the way the system operates, you have the power to be a source of change."

"Yeah, maybe," I say reluctantly.

"Have you thought any more about going to the support group at State? I really think you'd benefit from it. See how others have found that power themselves."

I move toward my coffee and take a drink to give myself time to try to think of a good excuse. Dr. Kim brings up this support group every couple of sessions, and I really don't understand why. I can barely get a handle on my own mental and emotional state—I don't really have the bandwidth to handle anyone else's, let alone a whole group's. I usually tell her I'm working or something, but today I just say, "I'll think about it."

We spend the rest of my appointment talking about things I can do when I feel anxiety creeping in. Despite my hesitance regarding Dr. Kim's methods, I do leave feeling better than when I arrived.

For homework, Dr. Kim says I should make a list of what I want to accomplish during my senior year because it might help me feel a little more in control. Clearly the woman loves lists. As I sit in bed with my notebook, the first items come easily.

1. Get accepted to a good college

2. Graduate

The list of goals for one's senior year is kind of a no-brainer. Underneath "Graduate" I write "3. DON'T GO CRAZY" in big bold letters. Dr. Kim won't like that. She says "crazy" is a derogatory and dismissive term that gets used too flippantly, so I scratch it all out and replace it with "Stay healthy." But I don't like that either because it kind of seems like I want to start off each morning with some cardio and a kale smoothie, even though I haven't been able to stomach a green smoothie since biology class last year.

As part of an experiment, our teacher Ms. Julian had all of us put on gloves and stuff nasty swamp mud into empty two-liter bottles. It was disgusting, and we literally spent a full class doing it. Then we screwed the tops back on the bottles and placed them on a shelf in the corner of a room. As time passed, the experiment was supposed to teach us about the ecosystem of a swamp or something, but we never got that far because it went horribly wrong about a week after we packed the bottles. Ms. Julian was in the middle of a lecture when we heard it.

POP.

POP.

POP. POP.

Suddenly, there was the sound of splattering and a couple of students in the back of the class were screaming. When the rest of us turned around, there were large chucks of mud smeared across the cabinets and ceiling.

"It's the bottles!" someone yelled. "They're exploding!"

That sent the whole class into a panic. People were up and running, diving over desks and moving toward the door as fast as possible. Ms. Julian kept yelling at us to calm down, but it was too late. Everyone was shoving like we were trying to be the first inside Walmart on Black Friday.

In the end, no one was hurt, but there was mud everywhere. The cabinets, the ceiling, the dry-erase board. When we returned to class two days later, the room was clean, but there was a lingering stench of pond scum. For more than a week we had all the windows open and box fans whirling in the corner, but even then, being in the room for an hour was torture.

Staring at the somewhat pathetic list in front of me, I start to think how I'm kind of like those bottles of mud. The mounting pressure, the explosion, the residual odor . . . I didn't exactly explode last year, but the pressure of my life definitely created an event with a lasting stink. On the list I write:

3. Don't be the pond scum

Suddenly a foam arrow hits the side of my head, and I turn to find my little brother, Tanner, standing in my doorway. His mouth is hanging open in a large grin, the Nerf gun dangling by his side. Even though he's four years younger than me, he's only a few inches shorter and rapidly approaching a time when I will have to look up to make eye contact with him. "Would you believe I was aiming for your shoulder?" he says.

"No. No, I wouldn't," I say, tossing one of my pillows at him. He catches it and steps into my room.

"What were you doing?" he asks. "Talking to yourself?"

"Just thinking," I say, stuffing my notebook beneath my bedsheet.

"Mom says you're getting ready for school tomorrow and I shouldn't bother you."

"And you thought shooting a Nerf gun at my face wasn't bothering me?"

He turns to the dresser in the corner of my room. The top is lined with tennis trophies and perfect attendance awards and honor roll plaques. Above them, there's a corkboard mounted to the wall where even more monuments to my accomplishments hang. Ribbons and certificates. Seems like the best I can hope for this year will be a sorry participation ribbon.

"You're still going to Groveland?" Tanner asks.

"Of course. Why wouldn't I go to Groveland?"

"You know, because of . . ." He taps his Nerf gun against the side of his head and trails off.

I've been wondering how much of my incident Tanner really knows about. He has obviously picked up on some things, but he's never been present for any of the big conversations I've had with Mom and Dad, and I've never asked them what they've told him.

"Yes, I'm going to Groveland. Everything's going to be the same," I say, knowing full well it's not true. Instead of feeling excited about my senior year, I'm making a list that will hopefully keep me from having another breakdown.

"So you're going to drive and everything?" Tanner asks.

"Yep," I say, leaving out that I've already plotted an alternate route so I can get to the student parking lot through the backstreets; that way I won't have to face Groveland's main entrance. "What happened to me was . . . not a big deal. It was just a little accident. Everybody has accidents in cars sometimes. That's why people have insurance. Everything's going to be fine."

"But you had to have a special meeting?"

Yep, he's clearly picking up on some things around here. "Just making sure I'm ready for senior year. It's very important, you know?"

"I know; I'm going to be a senior too." He lifts up his gun and shoots the mirror hanging beside my closet.

"That's true. You're going to be the king of middle school," I say.

"I know you're saying that in a mean way, but it's true." He pivots and points his gun.

"If you shoot me with that gun, you're really going to see mean."

He squints and I hold his gaze, letting him know I'm serious. I watch him shift his weight to his left leg, already planning his escape. Then he smiles and pulls the trigger.

SIX

LEWIS

The first day of school is a lot like New Year's Eve. There's a big build up and some celebration, but it doesn't take long for everyone to realize that they're surrounded by the same people they spent last year with, and nothing has truly changed. Well, there are surface-level changes. Harold Lockner got a new car. Some sort of blue sports thing. When Cal and I walk by in the parking lot, he's leaning up against it with the rest of his soccer team bros like he's auditioning for the next *Fast & Furious* movie. Michelle Peppercorn got her braces off, so she's smiling at *everyone*, and Marcus McNally somehow had a growth spurt at the age of seventeen and now he's at least four inches taller. As I catch my reflection in the guidance office windows, I can't help but notice the only thing different about me is this dark green button-up Rebecca helped me pick out yesterday.

When Cal and I walk into Mrs. Hansen's room a few minutes before the eight-thirty bell, she's standing by the door greeting everyone. "Hello, Lewis. Cal. So good to see you again."

"Mrs. Hansen, did you miss us?" I ask.

"Since two days ago? Of course."

"This is our last year together," Cal says. "You should really cherish it."

She rolls her eyes. "Yes, what fleeting precious moments these are."

Cal drops his stuff on a desk in the third row, and I take a seat behind him. As I slide into my chair, we have a nonverbal conversation with our eyes. I'll provide translations for the sake of clarity.

First, Cal widens his eyes at me and gives the slightest nod to his left: *Check this out.*

When I look, I realize Hayley is sitting at the desk next to me hunched over a notebook. I give Cal a slight shoulder raise: *So?*

He nods toward me and then quickly at Hayley: *You should talk to her.*

I narrow my eyes and frown: *Why?*

Cal drops his chin and smirks: *Because it might be funny, and I would like to see it.*

I raise my middle finger at him, a form of nonverbal communication everyone understands. As he turns around in his chair, Mrs. Hansen steps to the front of the room.

"Welcome back, everyone," she says. "And welcome to TV Production, which will also serve as your homeroom every other day this year. Now, let's get the first day stuff out of the way so we can get to the fun stuff."

The first half hour of school is basically the same every year: a deluge of paperwork that doesn't really seem important. In a file somewhere there are four years of forms with my signature saying I won't simulate any sexual acts during school dances. Mrs. Hansen distributes the student handbook, which always makes for a fascinating read. Things not allowed on school grounds: guns, drugs, women with bare shoulders. You know, anything that threatens a safe learning environment. I'm flipping through the pages when Hayley mumbles, "Oh, come on."

When I look over, she's holding a pen that has exploded, leaving her hand and part of her new Groveland handbook covered in black ink. She catches me staring and says, "You don't happen to have a napkin or something, do you?"

Her hair is dangling over the top of her glasses, and she's holding her hands stiffly in front of her like she's scared to touch anything. She's wearing a striped T-shirt under a pair of short overalls, and I can't help but notice how toned her legs are.

"I, uh . . . I don't . . ." Somewhere in my brain the team in charge of building sentences has gone into panic mode. There are sirens blaring, and a supervisor in a hard hat is yelling into a walkie-talkie, "We need a noun down here, stat!"

"So . . . no?" she says, leaning her head down to catch my gaze.

Once I snap out of it, I pull my backpack to my lap and start frantically digging through it. "Uh. No napkins, but here." I hand her an unopened pack of travel tissues. "My mom always buys, like, twelve of these for me at the start of every year, which means I usually finish the school year with ten or eleven spares."

Hayley opens the pack and starts wiping down her hands. "Thanks. And thank your mom for me."

"I will. She, uh, she really goes overboard with health and safety stuff. You should see the first aid kit she made me get for my car when I started driving. I'm pretty sure it has morphine and a needle and thread in it so I can bind open wounds like a World War II medic."

Mrs. Hansen claps her hands together. "Lewis. You want to focus for me?"

I spin forward in my seat. "Uh, yeah. I'm . . . what?"

Cal is turned around, giving me a grin that I'm dying to smack off his face, but I pretend not to notice and instead focus on Mrs. Hansen. "I was about to start talking about TV Production this year. That okay with you?" she asks.

"Please," I say, smiling, but feeling the heat of embarrassment creep up under my collar.

"All right," she says, "I see a nice mix of old and new faces here this year, and I'm very excited about that because this year we're trying something new." Uh-oh.

Mrs. Hansen continues, "I know this class is a lot of fun, but I want you to know that the skills you're gaining here are actually very useful. You're learning about research and gathering information and finding sources. You may think of this as a place where you get to make goofy clips about powder-puff football and spring break, but you are all journalists. Start thinking of yourselves that way. Don't be afraid to dive into something deep and meaningful."

She pulls up a news clip about a group of high school newspaper editors who discovered their new incoming principal had fabricated a portion of her résumé and touted a fake degree. Their investigation ultimately led to the principal resigning before she even officially started. Rebecca actually showed Cal and me this story when it originally broke. It's the type of important work she tries to do as newspaper editor at her school across town.

"Believe it or not, these are the kinds of things we can accomplish with our program here," Mrs. Hansen says. "I'm not saying you'll discover a conspiracy like this, and I don't want all of you rushing to the front office demanding to see Principal Wexler's qualifications, but you can have a positive impact. I know there are things you all want to change about this school, and every morning you have a voice. Don't throw that away.

"So this year, I want you to really think about the clips you make because every clip will have to be personally approved by me." Cal's shoulders slump. One of the things we've relished about this elective is the minimal supervision, and we've already spent time this summer brainstorming funny clips we could make, some of which are thinly veiled excuses to leave campus under the guise of classwork. "And just to make all you returning students a little more miserable, I'm going to mix up your partners," Mrs. Hansen says. Then she counts off the rows in ones and twos. "Ones, your partner will be the person on your right. Twos, your partner will be the person on your left."

Hayley extends an inky hand to me. "Hi, partner." I shake it and look at the clock over Mrs. Hansen's head—9:20. We're less than an hour into the first day, and my plans for senior year are already falling apart. Cal gives me a wild-eyed look that I know means he wants to fight this. Maybe we can convince Mrs. Hansen to let us be the exception to this new-partners thing. I mean, we helped clean the studio. She kind of owes us.

"Also, because the school district is still overcrowded, everyone will be sharing lockers again this year. And though I can't force you to share a locker with your new partner, I think it's a nice idea for you all to break out of your usual social circles. If you do share a locker with your partner, I will add two whole points to your grade at the end of the semester."

"What do you think?" Hayley asks. "Want to share a locker?"

I force a smile. "Only if you let me hang my collection of Justin Timberlake posters."

"Since we have so many new students this year," Mrs. Hansen continues, "I think it would be a good idea for some of you returning students to show them around the studio. It's unlocked, so feel free to make your way across the hall." As everyone files out, Cal and I hang back to talk to Mrs. Hansen. She shouts after the class as they disappear into the studio. "Past students, be nice to the newbies. This is not a fraternity. No hazing!"

I know if Cal and I are going to convince Mrs. Hansen to let us remain partners this year, we're going to have to approach the situation in a mature and diplomatic way. Too bad before I can say anything, Cal blurts, "What kind of sick game are you playing, Mrs. H?"

Mrs. Hansen lets out a short laugh and walks back toward her desk.

Cal's about to say something else, but I elbow him out of the way. "Mrs. Hansen, I get what you're doing. Mixing it up this year. Encouraging a serious approach to journalism. I appreciate that. I support it." I touch Cal on the shoulder. "We both do."

"I'm glad to hear it," Mrs. Hansen says, leaning back in her chair.

"We were actually thinking the same thing over the summer," I say.

"We recognize that in the past, Cal and I have made some . . . questionable video clips that didn't necessarily have a lot of journalistic value, per se."

"I seem to recall your final project last year was a ten-minute tour of Mr. Keith's office. Most of which was all of you 'jamming' with his rainsticks. You called it your magnum opus."

"Yes, but you see, we've had a change of heart. That's why over the summer we spent a lot of time brainstorming about more interesting clips. Clips that you'll like. Meaningful stuff."

Mrs. Hansen crosses her arms. "Such as?"

"Like why the cafeteria chili makes so many people fart," Cal blurts. I bury my head in my hand as Mrs. Hansen's smile grows wider. "What? That's investigative journalism."

"Look, I appreciate that you've clearly put some thought into this," Mrs. Hansen says, "but I want you to really challenge yourselves this year."

"Come on, Mrs. H! It's our senior year," Cal begs.

"Get to know some new people, boys. Open yourselves up to some new experiences. I think it will be good for you."

"But it's unfair," I say, unable to hold in my frustration. "My partner's Hayley Mills. She doesn't know anything about TV Production. I'm basically going to have to carry her."

"From what I know about Hayley, she's a very capable student. I'm sure she's a quick learner. You will not have to carry her."

"What if she doesn't pick it up? What if it stresses her out? You know what stress has done to that girl, right? There's a chance she could snap."

Mrs. Hansen looks over my shoulder, and when I turn, Hayley is standing in the doorframe staring us down. "Sorry to interrupt," she says. "Just wanted to see if my new locker buddy wanted to go find our locker."

SEVEN

HAYLEY

One class period. One. That's how long it took for it to become abundantly clear that Dr. Kim was wrong when she said people will have forgotten about my incident. I've had a perfect GPA since I knew what the letters GPA stood for, and now Lewis Holbrook is concerned that he's going to have to *carry me* in TV Production? Are you kidding? Sure, Lewis. I'll definitely need your help figuring out how to work those cameras with all the complicated buttons. This big red one labeled RECORD, what does that do?

I'm fuming so much that I nearly march past our locker. When I come to an abrupt stop, Lewis knocks into me. "Sorry," he mutters.

"That's us, 257," I say, pointing. Sharing lockers at Groveland is pretty unpleasant because they're not even full-size lockers. They're half lockers.

Lewis must be thinking about the same thing because he says, "At least we're on the top row." He smiles at me, and when I don't say anything back, he trudges on. "When I was a freshman, I had a locker on the bottom row, and every time I needed a book, it meant having to put my face weirdly close to someone's crotch."

I bend down and pull a small foldable shelf and a combination lock from my backpack.

"Wow, you really came prepared," Lewis says. "If my mom's the queen of health and safety supplies, you must be the queen of locker swag. Yaaas, queen."

I look up at him, my mouth a straight line.

"I'm sorry. I shouldn't have done that. I immediately regret it."

Normally I would find this awkward-attempt-at-humor thing kind of endearing, but I can tell Lewis is just being overly friendly because I caught him bad-mouthing me to Mrs. Hansen. I set up the portable shelf in our locker and shove the silver lock into his palm. "Combination's on the back. Once you have it memorized, rip off the sticker and lock up. I'll see you later." Then I march down the hall without looking back.

When I walk into AP European History, Mr. Litzner grunts that there are assigned seats, and I move along the rows until I find one with an index card labeled H. MILLS. As soon as the bell rings, Litzner shuts the door and distributes his four-page syllabus without even saying "hello" or "good morning." He starts droning on about the substantial amount of reading and weekly quizzes, and ten minutes later, I already feel myself fading. I'm trying desperately to stay awake by taking notes in the margins of my syllabus when a ball of paper hits me in the shoulder.

I turn around and spot Parker a couple of rows behind me. He smiles and holds a piece of notebook paper over his head. On it, he's drawn a thought bubble containing several Zs. I smile as he closes his eyes and pretends to sleep.

After twenty minutes, Mr. Litzner has moved on to explain how we should format all of our papers when someone knocks on the door. Lucy sticks her head inside the classroom. "Hi, Mr. Litzner. Mr. Keith needs to see Hayley Mills up in his office." Mr. Litzner looks at his class, clearly trying to remember which one of us is Hayley. I lift my hand, and he waves me out.

"Does Mr. Keith really want to see me?" I ask Lucy once the door is shut behind us.

"No," she laughs. "I'm not even an office aide, but Mr. Litzner doesn't know that." She hands me a small carton of chocolate milk from the cafeteria. "I just thought you might want a break. Check out the side. There's a joke."

I turn the carton in my hands. "'Why did the cow cross the road?'"

"I don't know. Why?"

"'To get to the udder side.'"

"Oh boy. Well, these things are only seventy-five cents," Lucy says, opening her milk. "I guess they can't afford much of a joke-writing staff. How was your morning?"

"Pretty bad," I mutter. "My parents were doing their overly cheerful and optimistic act before school. My dad made a smiley face out of eggs and bacon, which I'm pretty sure he's never done ever. Even Tanner noticed how weird it was."

"Wow, your super supportive parents made you a nice breakfast? How do you even keep it together?"

Lucy has a point. "I appreciate the breakfast; I just wish they were actually acting like themselves. They're still treating me like I'm fragile. Then I got to school and saw Mallory. She just blew right past me like I'm invisible, which is maybe the best I can hope for. Then there was TV Production, where I got assigned my new partner and locker buddy, Lewis Holbrook."

"Lewis who?"

"Holbrook. You'd know him if you saw him. Bigger guy. Brown hair."

"Oh yeah, I think I know who you're talking about. He seems nice, right?"

"I thought so, but then I heard him talking to our teacher, trying to get out of being my partner. He said he was worried the class would be too stressful for me and I might snap."

"Okay. So actually not a nice person at all," Lucy scoffs.

"I don't know. Maybe I can't blame him. He's the senior producer this year. TV Production is, like, his thing. And now I'm the project that got dumped in his lap."

"Forget that noise," Lucy says. "You're hardly a project, Hay. You carry projects. You're the supersmart girl that everyone is superexcited to get put in a group project with because they know you're going to do a majority of the work."

"Maybe not completely a compliment there, but I think I get what you're saying."

Lucy steps in front of me and swings her arms wide. "I'm saying don't let anyone make you question your worth. If TV Production's going to be a year of gaslighting nonsense, you shouldn't put up with it. Get out of there." She taps her milk against mine, and I take a long swig.

At the start of my lunch, period I head to the front office instead of the cafeteria. An older woman wearing a frown and a golden brooch of a cat playing with a ball of yarn sits behind the desk. I approach cautiously, worried Mr. Keith or Principal Wexler might appear at any moment. Who knows what they'd do if they knew I was about to change my schedule. "Excuse me, I'd like to get a class drop sheet," I say, my voice barely above a whisper.

"Name," the woman barks, not even taking her eyes off her computer.

"Hayley." She turns and silently glares at me over the brim of her glasses. "Mills," I mutter. "Sorry."

She sucks in a loud breath and taps firmly on her keyboard. "Hayley Mills." I'm certain her voice is echoing through the entire hall. "There's a hold on your schedule."

"What?"

"A hold on your schedule," she repeats, taking her time to enunciate each syllable. She turns her computer monitor so that I can see the red banner running across the screen: SCHEDULE HOLD. "Can't change any of your classes without meeting with your counselor first. They have to sign off on any changes." This figures. I should've known Wexler and

Mr. Keith would make sure I'm not able to circumvent their plan. I nod, and the woman pulls the screen back to its original position. "Would you like me to set up an appointment with Mr. Keith for you?" She sighs, clearly not wanting to put in the effort.

"Uh, no. It's fine. I'll figure it out. Thanks." I hoist my backpack and sulk off toward the vending machines.

EIGHT

LEWIS

After third period, Cal and I meet up for lunch. By the time we get to the cafeteria, the line to buy food is already stretching out into the hall.

"How do we have three separate lunch periods and the line is still this long?" Cal asks. He cups his mouth and shouts at a freshman lingering around the hot bar. "Hey! Bowl cut! Tater tots or corn. It's not that hard. There are people behind you!"

After several moments, we move up a few places to where we can finally pick up our trays. "So, Hayley already hates me," I say.

"Yeah? She definitely heard that stuff you said to Mrs. Hansen, huh?"

"Yyyyyep. At least we only have TV Production class every *other* day. But wait. We're locker buddies, too. So I guess it'll just be awkward all the time. What a great senior year."

"Damn," Cal says. "That's going to be rough. I just hope your locker's big enough because you're not just sharing it with Messed-Up Mills. You're also sharing it with all the voices in her head."

I groan. "Again, you got to think through your jokes, man. Why would the voices in her head take up space in our locker? If you're gonna be a dick, at least be a logical one. You should've said, 'I hope it's big enough because that chick has a lot of baggage.'"

"Oh shit, you're right. That is better. Do you have a nickel or something I can whip at this kid?" He raises his voice again. "Yo! Everything up there is a shade of brown! Just pick something and move on!"

When Cal and I finally exit the line with our food, we nearly run straight into Harold Lockner. Harold is the captain of Groveland's soccer team, so he's all lean muscle and sharp elbows. He's also several inches taller than I am, so I feel like a toddler when I look up at him as he separates us by placing his hands on my shoulders, pretending to steady himself. "Whoa, watch it there, Cheese Fries. No need to be in such a rush."

During our freshman year, Harold saw me carrying a cafeteria tray with two orders of cheese fries. One was for me and the other was for Cal, but given my size, Harold assumed I was going to devour both and took it as an opportunity to give me a new nickname. He made sure all the soccer bros at his table took notice, and he's been saying it ever since. A joke like that, with so many layers and such clever wordplay, obviously never gets old.

"Sorry," I mutter, trying to push past him, but he keeps a firm grip on my shoulders. His eyes wander down to my tray, which contains a side salad, a scoop of tuna, a few crackers, and an apple. He picks up the apple and tosses it in his hand. "What's this, Cheese Fries? I figured you only eat apples when they're covered in caramel." A couple of his teammates chuckle, and I try not to die inside. "You tryin' to slim down?" Harold asks, giving my stomach a slap with the back of his hand. "Maybe I could train you. When's the last time you broke a sweat that wasn't related to masturbating?"

I stare back at him, desperately trying to think of some clever and devastating retort. The sentence-building construction crew in my mind is clearly at lunch too, because I'm coming up empty. If this is anything like other run-ins I've had with Harold, I'll come up with the perfect response three days from now in the shower.

"Can I just get by, please?" I say, working hard not to break eye contact.

Harold shifts sideways, and I move past him. "Good luck out there, champ," he says, dropping the apple back on my tray before slapping me on the butt. His boys snicker and follow him as he heads out into the hall.

Once we find a table, Cal says, "Dude, you got to stick up for yourself. Otherwise he's just going to mess with you all year again."

"Well, you were definitely a big help. I appreciate your support back there."

We're silent for several moments before Cal says, "So really. What is the deal, man?" He gestures toward my tray of tuna and fruit.

I play dumb. "What?" This is definitely not a conversation I want to have after what just went down.

"What's going on with your eating?" Cal persists. "No more soda, no more Graze Daze burgers. You didn't even look at the tater tots back there, which is arguably the only thing served in this cafeteria that actually tastes like what it's supposed to. Are you trying to lose weight, like Harold said?"

I slam my utensils down, but they're plastic, so it doesn't have the effect I was hoping for. "Yeah. I'm trying to lose weight, okay? I've spent the past three years getting progressively fatter, and I'm tired of it. I'm tired of Harold making fun of me. I'm tired of Rebecca not showing any interest in me. So I'm doing something about it. We don't need to discuss it or have some heart-to-heart. It's just something that I'm doing, and I would appreciate it if you just never brought it up again until I become devastatingly handsome."

After an awkward moment of silence, Cal says, "You think the thing keeping you from Rebecca is your weight?"

I swallow down a dressing-less bite of salad. "Girls aren't interested in the funny chubby guy, Cal."

"Some girls are."

"Okay," I scoff.

"I'm serious," he says. "You like Rebecca, right? Why?"

"Why do I like her? I don't know—she's nice and she cares about people and she makes me laugh and we get along well and . . ." I stop because Cal is smiling and nodding a lot.

"Yeah. Those are all the reasons Rebecca likes you, too, idiot," he says. "Notice how you just listed off a bunch of things in rapid succession and none of them had anything to do with her looks?"

The construction crew in my mind perks up. "You think Rebecca likes me? Seriously?"

Cal rolls his eyes in exasperation. "Dude, how do you not see it? The way she looks at you. The way you guys joke. It's like you're already a couple half the time. I've been the third wheel for, like, ever."

"So, why aren't we together, then?"

Cal smiles and points his fork. "Because you're having this conversation with me and not her."

Ugh. I hate when Cal makes a good point.

During the last half of the school day, I keep thinking about what Cal said. Maybe he's right. Maybe I've been so focused on my weight because I wanted a simple solution. But when I really examine my life, I'm not missing out on things I want because I enjoy french fries and milkshakes. I'm missing out on things because I'm scared. When Rebecca and I were in that dressing room together, it wasn't my weight that was holding me back. She was right there in front of me. All I had to do was lean in and *do something*, but I didn't. I was a coward. If I want this year to be different, I have to take some risks.

I have to become the leading man of my own life. I can't just settle for being the funny sidekick and expect great things to happen to me. I have to actually make things happen.

NINE

HAYLEY

On Friday night, Lucy and I find ourselves at Parker's party. After spending the past two days coming to terms with the fact that I'm stuck with TV Production and largely avoiding Lewis, I'm hoping this can actually be an enjoyable evening. As expected, the place is packed. As senior class president, Parker's popularity defies normal high school cliques. He has a natural charisma that allows him to make friends easily, and he never turns people away. I once heard someone call him "Asian Jesus." Can't imagine why I found dating him intimidating. Because of his Christlike ability to bring people together, his party is a mixture of every school subgroup. There are goths throwing ice cubes at each other in the kitchen. There are theater geeks playing charades in the living room. In the basement, half of the football team is engaged in a Ping-Pong tournament, while not far from them, a group of guys is crowded around the big screen playing some sort of cartoonishly violent video game. We're all still mostly segregated, but maybe separately together is the best you can hope for when it comes to high school.

Lucy and I end up at one of my favorite spots in Parker's house, the plush wicker chairs on the second-floor balcony that overlooks the pool and the rest of the backyard.

"Parker made the guac," Lucy says. "It's so good. Is there anything that kid can't do?" She extends her plate of chips toward me, and I take one.

"It *is* good."

"Told you. I haven't even mastered peanut butter and jelly, and this guy has already moved on to international cuisine."

"It's mashing avocados, Luce. It's not a soufflé."

"Still." She shrugs, scooping up another mouthful.

"I should've known I'd find you guys out here."

I turn to see Parker making his way through the sliding glass door. He has three red Solo cups in his hands, and he places them on the small glass table between Lucy and me. "Thought you might be thirsty."

Lucy picks up one of the cups and takes a swig. "Oh my gosh," she says with mock indignation. "Is there alcohol in this? You better be twenty-one, sir. Do you have any ID on you?"

Parker digs his hand into his front pocket. "Yeah, actually, I do. It's right here," he says, pulling his hand free and showing Lucy nothing but his raised middle finger. Parker nudges me with his knee. "You good?"

"Yeah, I'm fine," I say, tapping the bottled water in my lap.

Despite the various alcohol options that are always available at Parker's parties, I've still never had a drink. I have this irrational fear that as soon as I take a sip from a red Solo cup, the police will barge in and arrest me, and then my parents and the ghost of my dead grandfather will show up and tell me how ashamed they are.

Last year, on a tennis trip, Mallory snuck some vodka into the hotel room, and all the girls took turns passing the bottle around. Even though half the team played terribly the next morning because they were hungover, I still felt like a loser for not joining in.

Suddenly there's the sound of screaming and splashing from below us. We move toward the railing where we see that Harold Lockner has taken off his shirt to reveal that he's written "Pool Party Police" across his chest in thick black marker. He's wearing aviator sunglasses and waving a plastic gold badge.

"What the hell, Harold?" comes a cry from the pool. A fully clothed girl floats in the deep end. She pushes her wet matted hair from her eyes as she doggie-paddles in place.

"It's time to get the pool party started!" Harold yells.

"You're lucky I didn't have my phone on me, jackass!" the girl yells back. There's also another fully clothed girl standing in the shallow end, but she seems too stunned to speak.

"You be quiet before I hold you in contempt," Harold shouts.

"I'm confused," Lucy says. "Is he a cop or a judge?"

"I think he's just repeating words he's heard on *Law & Order*," I say. "You would think if he put all the effort into bringing props, he would've planned this out better."

Parker rolls his eyes. "Guess I better go deal with this now," he says, making his way back into the house.

Harold begins stalking around the pool, tossing other partygoers into the glowing blue water. He starts with smaller underclassmen, then moves on to the girls who haven't already fled inside. For several moments, it seems like Harold might bring the party to a crashing halt. Some people are starting to climb out of the pool uneasily due to the weight of their now-soaked jeans, and they don't look happy. Others are frantically splashing at Harold, who is remarkably dry considering this pool party was his idea. He's lumbering toward the pool with a wiggling blonde in his arms while her friend jumps up toward his shoulders in protest when Parker emerges into the backyard. He's wearing a pair of floral swim trunks and a white T-shirt. Around his waist is a bright yellow duck float. He has a snorkel mask over his eyes, and each arm is decked with one of his little sister's pink floaties that are so small, Parker can't even get them past his elbows.

"Hey," Parker calls out. "I just got an APB that the Pool Party Police might need some backup." He hoists up his duck float and charges for the pool.

Harold lets out a victory yelp as Parker springs off the diving board and into the deep end. When he surfaces, with the snorkel now lopsided on his face, there is laughter and a round of applause. Suddenly, everyone's anger toward Harold dissipates, like they're taking their cue from Parker. Harold, still holding the blonde, falls backward into the pool, and her protesting friend dives in after them. More people run from inside the house and leap into the water, tossing their clothes, keys, and phones onto the nearby deck chairs. In no time, there are at least thirty people in the pool.

Without warning, a stream of water hits Lucy and me across the chest. We scream and duck beneath the balcony railing. Between the slats I spot Parker sitting on the steps in the shallow end pumping a water gun. He's wearing Harold's aviators and looking up at us.

"Hey, no onlookers!" he yells as he sends another blast of water over our heads. "You're either in or you're out!"

"Who's hiding up there?" Harold calls out. Lucy and I stand and make our way to the railing. "The party's down here, ladies. Come on, always room for two more," he continues.

"Yeah, just jump in!" someone shouts. Then there's a chorus. "Jump! Jump! Jump!"

Parker climbs out of the pool and comes to stand directly under us. "Don't jump," he says sternly, breaking his party animal bravado. I look down from the deck to judge the distance to the pool. It's a distance someone could likely clear, but not one I'm comfortable attempting.

"Come on, Murakami. It's a party!" Harold says.

"Yeah, you're right," Parker replies. "And nothing ruins a party faster than a broken leg or blood in the pool. No one's jumping off the balcony, Harold. That's crazy."

"Hey, it wouldn't be the first crazy thing Hayley Mills has ever done, right?" Harold says it so casually that at first I'm almost convinced I misheard him. But then people in the pool are laughing, and a chill spreads over my skin. Lucy moves her hand on top of mine.

"Harold," Parker hisses, sending a blast from the water gun at his face.

"What?" Harold says. "I think it's kind of cool Messed-Up Mills is a little off in the head. Come on, Hayley! Don't bring this party to a screeching halt like you did with traffic."

The pool falls weirdly quiet, and I'm frozen at the railing, staring down at no one in particular. The image starts to blur. I can't move, and my tongue feels too big for my mouth. It's not like I haven't seen the sideways glances at school or heard the hushed whispers in the hall, but no one has ever thrown my breakdown in my face so publicly.

Lucy figures out the proper response before I do. "Hey, Harold, why don't you come up here and jump yourself if you want someone to do it so bad? Or do you need a girl to show you how because your balls and your brain are roughly the same size?"

This elicits a round of laughs from the pool crowd. I find my legs and back away from the railing. Harold shouts something else, but I don't hear it because I'm moving back through the room and heading toward the stairs. I know Lucy's close behind, but my mind is focused on getting out of Parker's house and away from this party. Parker meets me at the bottom of the stairs, still holding the water gun, his trunks dripping onto the hardwood.

"Hayley," he says. "I'm sorry about that. Just ignore Harold. He's an idiot."

"Yeah," Lucy says, quickly descending the stairs behind me. "You know that chart that shows a monkey evolving into a man? Harold's like the third one from the left on that chart."

"It's fine," I say, watching the puddle forming around Parker's feet. I can't look either of them in the face right now.

"No, it's not," Parker says. "Lucy's right. Harold has, like, a fifth-grade reading level, so there's no way he has a decent grasp on something as complex as empathy."

"I'm just going to go," I mutter.

"You don't have to do that," Parker says, trying to be reassuring. But he's wrong. I do have to go, because just getting through this conversation is exhausting. I'm only a few feet from the front door, and I need to get on the other side.

"I can guarantee you all those people in the pool are giving Harold shit over what he just did," Lucy says.

"It's true," Parker adds. But I know all those people have had the same thoughts as Harold. They just have enough social grace not to say them to my face. Parker reaches for my hand. "Please don't go."

I try to imagine staying at the party and going to the pool now. I wouldn't have the strength to confront Harold to his face, so I would just end up splashing around, trying not to look defeated as people sneak glances, feeling sorry for the mentally unstable girl.

I pull away from Parker. "Thanks, guys, but I'm just going to walk home."

"I'll walk with you," Lucy immediately volunteers, just as I expected she would.

"No, you stay," I say. "I think I just need to be alone right now."

Lucy hesitates, and I can see Parker trying to work out in his mind the best way to handle this situation. He looks at Lucy, then at me, then back at Lucy. Both of them are clearly uneasy with the idea of me leaving alone.

"Guys, I live four blocks from here. You don't have to worry," I say.

When they don't respond, I turn and open the front door. Lucy steps forward to give me a quick hug. "I'll see you at work tomorrow," she says. Once I step outside, I turn and give Parker a small wave as I shut the door. They both stand there looking at me like I'm an astronaut who has bravely volunteered to step out onto a new planet to see if the air is breathable.

Once I'm a block away, the noise from the party fades and gives way to the summer night. The air is warm, and an occasional firefly blinks past. I try to remember what Dr. Kim said about dealing with anxiety and stressful situations. I pause and take a few deep breaths and remind myself that I don't have to dwell on my anxious thoughts, but it's hard.

What I feared all summer is actually coming true. Despite what Dr. Kim said about the passage of time, about everyone having their own life to worry about, the past few days have made it abundantly clear that everyone at Groveland still sees me as the girl who snapped, the girl who couldn't handle the pressure of eleventh grade. How can I possibly excel in a premed program at a prestigious college when I can't even handle homework and the PSATs at the same time?

What if this is how things will always be? As much as I've committed to recovery and better stress management, maybe I'll never get better. Maybe there's a fault line running through my brain that I have no control over, and every few years it will shift, causing a catastrophic earthquake that will eventually bring things crumbling down around me.

TEN

LEWIS

Night running is best, once the temperature has dropped a little and the noise of the neighborhood has dropped with it. I tried to stick with running first thing in the morning for a few days, but that quickly fell apart. I always felt sleepy and sluggish, and there were weird dads in bathrobes out watering their lawn. Nights are better. Just the sound of distant traffic and the steady beat of my shoes against the pavement.

I watched some YouTube videos, and now I know how to pace myself, so I don't feel like I'm going to pass out after only a few minutes, but it's hard. I try to keep my mind occupied as a distraction. When I first started running, I just kept thinking, "This is running. I'm exercising now. How far have I gone? Half a mile? I should keep going. My side hurts. I'm thirsty. Is that person watching me?" You can't think about running when you're running. You have to focus on something more pleasant, like dental work or falling naked into a bushel of cacti.

Tonight I'm thinking about what Cal said to me the other day. It's taken a while to fully seep in, but now I can't deny how true it is. My weight isn't the thing that's holding me back from having the life I want; it's my attitude. My whole life I've been content with being a guy who just sort of blends into the background, only surfacing to make a joke or two and then disappearing again. Just going with the flow and never trying too hard at anything.

Even Mrs. Hansen can see I need to change, so she's pushing me out of my comfort zone. She wouldn't let me keep being partners with Cal this year because she wants me to actually apply myself as senior producer. Or at least that's my guess. That's why I'm going to keep running, too. It's uncomfortable, but maybe I need some discomfort right now.

I'm thankful to be doing something physical tonight since the first week of school was so mentally exhausting. I haven't even had a chance to apologize to Hayley because I've hardly said two words to her since our disastrous first day. Mrs. Hansen has been dealing with the new students herself, showing them how to work some of the equipment while the rest of us have been getting the studio prepped for our first broadcast Monday morning. I had to set the anchor rotation, figure out the tech booth schedule, and edit a new opening montage.

Young MC's "Bust a Move" comes up on my '80s mix, and I tap the volume up a couple notches. My strides increase in length, the ground solid beneath my foot for an instant before connecting with the other. Again and again. Footfall after footfall. When I'm running, it's easy to imagine myself as the leading man I want to be (even when I'm feeling like I'm about to pass out). I picture the camera panning along beside me as the soundtrack builds. Maybe I'm running to stop Rebecca from marrying the wrong man and I'll burst into the chapel at just the right moment, or maybe I'm running to save all the children from a burning orphanage, and Rebecca the nun is so moved by my bravery that she gives up her vow of celibacy and we run off into the sunset together. It's a different fantasy each night that keeps me pumping my arms and sucking air into my lungs.

As I round the corner, I see a figure moving down the street toward me. She moves through a streetlight and I catch a flash of red hair. *Hayley?*

She's walking slowly, her gaze on her sandals. This has to be a sign, right? Now is my chance to apologize, outside of school where we can really talk. I move to cross the street but hesitate. This isn't some movie where I get to direct what happens. It's real life, and real life is messy. Maybe Hayley has no interest in talking to me. What if I approach her and just freeze up like I did when she first talked to me in class? This is a bad idea. The more I mull it over, the worse it seems. I mean, I've just run more than a mile, and my shirt is covered in sweat. What girl wants to be surprised by a large smelly man emerging from the shadows to pant an apology at her?

So instead of going to talk to Hayley, I dart up into some stranger's yard and crouch behind some bushes until she passes, telling myself it's the right thing to do. Some leading man I am.

ELEVEN

HAYLEY

When I make my way up my driveway and round the back of the house, I find my brother shooting hoops on the goal our dad cemented into the ground four summers ago. It's not unusual to find Tanner playing well into the night. He's on the basketball team at his middle school, and he loves the game. For a moment, I stand by the corner of the garage watching him practice his free throws. The ball usually slips almost silently through the net, and then he runs to grab it before hurrying back to the same spot on the driveway.

"Hey," I say, stepping out into the yellow glow of the light hanging above the garage.

Tanner turns and pulls out one of his earbuds, letting it dangle against his sweatshirt. "Hey."

"Another late-night practice?" I ask.

"Yeah, well, I'm hoping we win more than four games this year, so . . ."

"Dare to dream."

Tanner tosses me the ball. Despite the fact that we've had this hoop for years, I'm still not very good. Put a tennis racquet in my hands and I can do some damage, but a basketball, not so much. My shot bounces off the side of the rim, and Tanner grabs it for a quick layup.

"So, how was your first week of eighth grade?" I ask.

"Okay. Yesterday my friend Brandon stood against the wall in the locker room and pissed into the urinal on the other wall. It's, like, seven feet!" God, middle school boys are disgusting.

"Give my congrats to Brandon," I say.

"I thought you were going to a party tonight," Tanner says, sinking another shot from the edge of the driveway.

"Eh, wasn't really my scene," I say. Part of me wants to stay and shoot around with Tanner for a while, but I just don't have the energy. Plus, he probably doesn't even want his moody older sister inserting herself into his practice session. "I'm gonna turn in. Good night."

Up in my room, I collapse onto my bed and pull my phone from my pocket. There's a text from Lucy.

Hope you made it home OK. Sorry the party sucked. See you at work tomorrow!

The text is more than half an hour old, and I feel bad about my delay in response because it means she's probably been worried about me. I write her back.

Got home fine. Thanks for looking out for me. See you tomorrow.

Before I turn off my light, I can't resist one final scroll through my social feeds. I'm immediately met with a wave of photos from Parker's party. There are selfies from the balcony and videos of people being tossed into the pool. In the background of one, I spot Lucy riding on Parker's shoulders, her hands locked with another girl's in a game of chicken. There's a twist in my gut, a mix of annoyance and jealousy. Clearly they weren't so concerned about me that it kept them from having a good time. In another photo Harold is sitting on the edge of the pool holding a water gun, the black writing on his chest starting to run down his stomach. There's a brunette beside him, laughing and touching his thigh. A boulder inside of me cracks and gives way.

Even after he was a total dick to me, Parker let Harold stay at the party. He didn't even kick him out.

Now I'm mad at myself. Why am I letting people who don't even care about me have so much control over my life? I pull my notebook from the drawer in my bedside table and open it to my "Goals for Senior Year" list.

1. Get into a good college

2. Graduate

3. Don't be the pond scum

I stare down at the last item on the list. It stands out the most because it's the only item that's a "Don't." The others are about actually achieving something. Number three is about keeping people from noticing me. Suddenly it strikes me as timid and meek. I hate that I ever wrote it. Frustrated, I fling my notebook across the room where it knocks against my dresser, sending one of my tennis trophies tumbling to the carpet.

When I get out of bed and place it back on the ledge, I suddenly realize how misguided I've been. I keep letting everyone else's perceptions of me define me instead of being the Hayley that earned all these trophies. It's time to turn this whole thing around. If Wexler and Mr. Keith think I need TV Production to offset the stress of being in the AT program, I'm going to show them that I can dominate my AP courses and elevate TV Production to something they've never seen before. If Lewis thinks I'm on the verge of another breakdown, I'm going to prove to him exactly what it means to have Hayley Mills as a partner. And if the Harolds of the world think I'm just some crazy girl who can't have fun or be daring, well, they've got another thought coming too.

I'm about to make some noise. I'm about to be the fucking pond scum.

TWELVE

LEWIS

On Monday morning, Hayley is already at our locker when I approach, taking items out of her backpack and placing them on the top half of the plastic shelf she installed. I know I can't spend the rest of the year avoiding my own locker buddy. There won't always be convenient bushes to duck behind. I need to actually talk to Hayley.

"Hey, I, uh, I made you a card," I say, approaching cautiously.

She stops what she's doing and turns her head toward me. "You did what?"

"I made you a card," I repeat, extending the folded paper toward her. "I feel really bad about that stuff I said last week, and I wanted to apologize."

Hayley takes the card. On the front are two stick figures, one of which is saying "I'm sorry" in big, bold letters. "That's us," I say. "You can tell that's you because I used a red pen for your hair and gave you glasses."

"I see that," Hayley says, slowly opening the card. On the inside it's the same stick figures, except now they're jumping together and smiling. "That's us after you've forgiven me," I say. "We're celebrating. That's why I drew some balloons."

"And what are we holding?" Hayley asks. "Coffee cups?"

"No, those are supposed to be video cameras. Representative of the fact that we're such great partners in TV Production."

"Ah," Hayley says. And I think I catch just the slightest bit of a smirk sneaking into her expression.

I consider that a positive sign and jump into the speech I've been practicing since last night: "In all seriousness, what I said last week was messed up. I don't know why I said it. I was just having a bad morning, and I know that's not a good excuse, but—"

"Lewis," Hayley says, thankfully cutting me off just as I was ramping up to what was bound to be a long, rambling apology. "It's okay."

"Really?"

"Well, no, it's not okay. But this very weird card is actually kind of nice. I didn't have the best first week either, so maybe we can just put the whole thing behind us and start fresh."

"Yes! Fresh start. Perfect. I love fresh starts."

"Great," Hayley says, tacking the card up to the inside of our locker door with a small magnet. She pushes one of her books into place, and when she does, a small silver object falls off the back of the shelf and clanks against the bottom of our locker.

"Wow, already trying to put stuff on my half of the locker," I tease, reaching to pick up the object.

"Sorry, I'll get that. You don't need to . . ." Hayley is speaking so quickly that all of her words are running together as I retrieve her . . . flask. I stare at it in my hand, trying to process what I'm seeing.

"Oh, th-this is—" I stammer.

"Yeah . . . ," Hayley says quietly, placing her hand on the flask.

It suddenly dawns on me that I don't really know anything about Hayley. Maybe she always carries a flask. Maybe she drinks all the time. Maybe she was drinking the day of her breakdown. Maybe she runs an underground casino and cuts off fingers when people can't pay their gambling debt. Okay, that one's probably not true, but how can I be sure?

"Mr. Holbrook. Ms. Mills."

I snap out of my trance, and Hayley's eyes meet mine. We both look over at our sophomore history teacher, Mr. Rosco, who is standing with his hands on his hips. For a man who's only a couple inches taller than me and happens to be wearing a tie embroidered with little horses, Mr. Rosco suddenly seems quite intimidating. He's scowling hard. "Care to share with me what you're holding?" he says.

I realize that both Hayley and I have one hand on her flask, and I quickly drop mine like the thing is on fire. Hayley holds it steady, seemingly frozen as Mr. Rosco reaches out and takes it from her. "Ah, I was afraid that's what it was," he says, untwisting the cap. He sniffs at the open top and then shifts his glance, momentarily looking both of us in the eye.

Then he turns the flask over.

Nothing pours out. The knot in my stomach relaxes a bit and then clenches back.

"There's nothing in it," Hayley blurts, as if that wasn't already apparent.

"I can see that," Mr. Rosco says.

"I mean it's always been empty," Hayley says. "It was a gag gift. My friend gave it to me." Most of the color has drained from her face. Three guys step out of the room across the hall, laughing among themselves. One notices Mr. Rosco standing there and nudges his friends, who both look our way.

The scene crystalizes in my mind, and I can see it playing out in an '80s movie. The camera moves from a close-up of the flask to settle on Mr. Rosco's angry face. The sound drops out, and Queen's "Under Pressure" builds as the shot pulls out to reveal the hall filling up with students, all of them pointing and whispering. The camera pans back to Hayley. She's wide-eyed and swallows hard. Then the camera moves to me, where a single bead of sweat rolls down the side of my face. This is a crucial scene. One where the leading man steps up.

"It's mine," I blurt. The knot in my stomach clenches tighter than before, and I hear Freddie Mercury's voice crescendo in my mind. "Hayley's just trying to protect me, sir. I was showing it to her because I thought it was cool." The construction crew in my mind has gone into panic mode. I can hear the foreman shouting orders. *He's lying, people! We need a believable story, now. Details! Someone bring me some details!* "My dad gave it to me," I say before Mr. Rosco can press me. "We went camping this weekend. He said it was an incentive for me to have a successful senior year. He said when I graduate, we'll share our first drink together." I shut up, and the silence seems sharp and sudden.

Mr. Rosco turns the flask around to reveal the front, which I had totally missed. "Your dad bought you a flask that says 'Slut in Training' in pink rhinestones?"

I try my best to keep my face from showing any shock, but I can feel my eyes widening. "My father has a very weird sense of humor, sir."

"And did your father tell you to bring this to school?" Mr. Rosco asks.

"No. It was dumb. I'm sorry. I shouldn't have," I say.

"He's lying," Hayley says. "It's really mine. He's just trying to protect me."

"No, it's the other way around," I interrupt. "I'm the slut in training, Mr. Rosco."

"Lewis, just shut up," she says, her voice filled with a surprising amount of confidence.

Hayley and I both start talking over each other until Mr. Rosco cuts us off. "All right. Enough," he says, clearly annoyed that this conversation has gotten away from him. "Since you're both so eager to claim ownership, you can both come see me in my classroom after school. If you aren't there at three forty sharp, I can assure you this will get much worse. Am I understood?" Hayley and I both nod, and Mr. Rosco walks off toward his classroom.

When he's out of listening distance, I turn to Hayley. "Well, that was . . . something," I say. But she doesn't look at me. Just turns her attention back to our locker, tosses her bag inside, grabs a book, and slams the door. Then she walks away without a word. How does every interaction I have with Hayley Mills end with her storming off?

I don't have any time to dwell on the question because I'm already late getting to the TV studio. We don't have class today, but we still have to broadcast the announcements. Thankfully, when I arrive, everyone is already in place. The anchors are at the desk reviewing their scripts, the camera operators are in position, and the sound booth students are ready for my cue. At eight thirty, I give a five-second countdown, and then we roll the intro, broadcasting across every TV in the building. Since it's the first week of programming, only experienced seniors are in the studio. I don't have to babysit, which is good because I'm only half present. Mainly I'm worried about Hayley. I try to keep her out of trouble, and now she's mad at me? That doesn't make any sense.

The rest of the school day creeps by. After every class, I sprint to our locker, hoping for a chance to talk to Hayley, but she never shows. Even at the end of the day, there's no sign of her. By 3:38, the hallway's mostly empty, so I take the stairs two at a time in order to make it to Mr. Rosco's room by 3:40.

When I arrive, Mr. Rosco is seated at his desk reading a newspaper, and Hayley is sitting at a desk near the window. "Mr. Holbrook. Nice of you to join us," Mr. Rosco says, folding down his paper and pulling the flask from his top desk drawer. "Shall we cut to the chase?" He stares at me for a moment and then shifts his attention to Hayley, who has now twisted in her seat so that she's facing him. "I'm guessing we're still not in agreement about who this belongs to."

Hayley nods, and I say, "Mr. Rosco, it really is mi—"

Mr. Rosco raises his hand to cut me off. "Mr. Holbrook, I really don't want to get into this again. I'm not going to try to play detective to figure this out, and I'm not going to listen to you two fighting. For now, I'm just going to treat this like it belongs to both of you. As

I'm sure you're aware, this sort of paraphernalia is strictly prohibited on school grounds. Luckily, for both of you, this was empty." He picks the flask up by the cap and gives it a little shake, using just his thumb and forefinger. Even though he just said he's not going to play detective, he's acting like he might dust the thing for prints later.

I do my best to steel my resolve, but each sentence seems to be taking ten minutes. It's like he's stretching this whole thing out for as long as possible just to watch us sweat. *Just get to the punishment,* I want to scream.

"I have decided not to escalate this incident up the chain of command. For now I will not tell the administration, and I will not contact your parents."

My mind explodes in relief.

"However, that does not mean you'll be getting off scot-free. Do you see those bookshelves over there?" One wall of Mr. Rosco's room is entirely bookshelves. Each one is at least seven feet tall, and they're all covered in books. Some books are stacked upright, and others are lying on their side. Some are lined in rows, and others are stacked on top of the rows or placed in front. In short, it's a mess. "I have a department meeting now, and while I'm away, you two are going to organize those books for me," Mr. Rosco says. "Place the classroom collections together and then alphabetize the others by title. Do you think you can handle that?"

"Yes, sir," Hayley and I both say.

"Great. You can leave when you're done, but I will be checking your work when I get back," Mr. Rosco says, sweeping the flask back into his desk drawer. "You're both smart kids, so I'm going to skip the lecture on the dangers of teenage drinking, but rest assured this is not something I take lightly. I will be keeping an eye on both of you for the rest of the year."

THIRTEEN

HAYLEY

When Lucy first gave me that silver flask, I thought it was funny. Her parents took her to Daytona Beach last year for spring break to visit her grandparents at a retirement community where people drive around in golf carts and spend hours playing shuffleboard. It sounded kind of nice to me, but Lucy acted like it was basically torture.

"My grandmother cans things as a hobby, Hay," she said. "Do you know what canning is? It's just hours and hours of putting vegetables in jars. That's it."

Her only relief was that her grandparents went to bed early every night, and Lucy was allowed to go explore. There was a boardwalk with souvenir shops within walking distance. The night she got back from Florida, she showed up at my front door with a wrapped gift. "I guess I could've gotten you a key chain or something, but I thought this was better," she said. I laughed when I saw the rhinestones because Lucy and I both know I'm hardly the scandalous type. Last summer, she came with my family to Gatlinburg, Tennessee, for a week and the only trouble we got in was when a go-kart track attendant banned us for the day because we kept intentionally spinning out my brother.

I realize I'm smiling just thinking about the memory, and I quickly shut my mouth, hoping Lewis didn't notice. He's crouching at the lowest shelf, removing books and stacking them in little piles on the floor. Why would he pretend that dumb flask was his?

Bringing the flask to school was a spontaneous decision. After I decided to "be the pond scum" on Friday night, I spent all weekend trying to figure out what that really means. It's easy to decide to be a metaphor; it's a little harder to break that idea down into actionable steps. When I saw the flask tucked into my dresser drawer, I had an idea. Lucy has been known to occasionally sneak sips from her dad's liquor stash, and I figured if I'm going to show people that I can still be smart and fun, maybe I should actually try drinking. Maybe it would help me loosen up and not leave parties on the brink of tears. So I threw the flask into my backpack, thinking it might be a fun way to surprise Lucy and get her on board with my idea.

I pull my phone out and shoot her a quick text.

Got detention. Long story. I'll call when I'm free.

I'm watching my phone for a response when Lewis says, "You think I'm more of a Judd Nelson or an Anthony Michael Hall?" His voice seems loud, but it's probably just because we've been silent for more than half an hour. I don't look away from my phone. "*The Breakfast Club.* You've seen that movie, right?" he continues. "Bunch of lovable misfits get thrown into detention together. Judd Nelson's the tough loner. Anthony Michael Hall is the scrawny geek. I know I'm not Emilio Estevez. He was the jock."

He pauses, giving me the opportunity to speak, but I don't. I just want to organize the books in silence and get out of here. Why would he pull my flask out of our locker and just stand there with it in his hand on display for the entire hallway?

"I guess I'm a mix of Nelson and Hall," Lewis says, seemingly undeterred by the fact that I haven't even looked at him. "Hall's character got thrown in detention because he had a flare gun in his locker. That's kind of like us, huh? Contraband in the locker and all." Is he seriously making a joke about this? All day I've been walking around hardly able to form complete sentences because I was so worried about what Mr. Rosco was going to do to us, and Lewis is acting like this is just some old movie.

"Maybe we should get high and dance like they did," he says. Yep, he's definitely already joking about this. "More movies really need dance scenes, if you ask me," he continues. "That's why I like eighties movies. The parade scene in *Ferris Bueller*? That's one of my favorites. Ferris is great, but I think personally I'm more of a John Cusack. *Better Off Dead* Cusack, not *Say Anything* Cusack. Have you seen those? I like eighties movies."

For the first time since he started talking, I peek in his direction. Hearing Lewis talk about his favorite movies makes me realize we've been at Groveland together for more than three years and all I really know about him is that he's into TV Production and drives a run-down car. When you're around the same people day after day, you tend to think you know who they are even if you don't really know them at all. This past week, I've just been hoping people will forget about my incident and get to know who I really am. Maybe Lewis deserves the same chance.

"Am I rambling?" Lewis asks. "I tend to do that sometimes when—"

"There's (500) *Days of Summer*," I say.

"What?" he asks, looking up from the books.

"Movies with dance scenes—(500) *Days of Summer* has a great one. The main guy dances with all these people on his way to work, and a marching band comes out of nowhere. It's a lot of fun. It's from the two thousands, though, so not sure if it's your thing."

"I'll have to check it out," he says, sitting another pile of books on the floor and then looking up at my face. "Look, about this morning. I wasn't trying to be intrusive or rude. I'm sorry."

"You seem to be apologizing to me a lot."

"Yeah, I've noticed that too. So much for trying to help."

Annoyance rises up in me, and I let the books in my hand fall back to the floor. "What?"

"I mean I just tried to help you this morning," Lewis says, clearly confused by my anger. "And look where it got us."

"I don't recall asking for your help."

"I was trying to be nice."

"So why did you just apologize?"

"I don't know!" Lewis slams several books into place. "You're obviously mad. So I guess I was trying to be nice. Again."

"I don't need you to be nice to me, Lewis. Everyone seems to think I'm incapable of taking care of myself these days, so they make decisions for me under the guise of 'being nice,' and it sucks. God, you have one little mental snap and suddenly everyone treats you like a baby."

Lewis isn't looking at me anymore. The clock ticks off a passing minute and then another as we organize the books in silence.

"I feel like I should say 'sorry' again, but you don't seem to like that," Lewis eventually says. It comes out so soft that I barely hear it.

"It's fine," I say, the words coming out clipped and hard. "You know, I got an A in every class last semester?" I sit cross-legged on the floor, and Lewis pivots toward me. "I mean, I already had mostly As, but still. Before the incident, I had a solid B-minus in Spanish III. Then Señora Rosell refused to let me take the final. I didn't know what to make of that, but then final grades came out and I had a ninety-two for the semester. You tell me how that happens."

"Damn. Maybe I should have a breakdown."

"I don't need people handing me sympathy As, Lewis. I don't need people standing up for me or trying to take blame for me. Especially if it's just an act. I know the way people talk when I'm not around."

"I wasn't acting," Lewis protests. "I was doing it because . . . God, this sounds so stupid. I thought it would make me feel brave."

That surprises me. "What?"

Lewis hides his face behind his hands with a groan. "I thought it would make me feel brave. Maybe part of me was trying to rescue you, sure, but I was also just trying to feel something."

"So . . . what did you feel?"

"Sweaty, mainly." I let out a small laugh, and Lewis smiles. Some of the tension melts away. "I don't think that's what bravery feels like."

"Maybe it feels different for everyone," I say. "Why did you want to be brave, anyway?"

"Because most days I don't feel anything here," he says. He doesn't look at me and starts placing books back on the shelf. "Maybe it's all the eighties movies I've seen, but I thought your senior year was supposed to be this big thing, you know? Something exciting and meaningful. But every day I come here and remember I'm just a nobody. People may only know you as the girl who snapped, but at least people will remember you at our ten-year reunion," he says. "I'm just the funny fat kid in TV class."

Now it's my turn to not look at Lewis. I just keep shelving books as I ask, "You don't think people will remember you?"

"I don't know how they would. I've been in TV Production since sophomore year, and I've never appeared onscreen. Always just the guy behind the camera."

He seems genuinely upset, and I consider maybe I've misjudged Lewis. I've been viewing every interaction through the lens of my breakdown, but clearly he has his own stuff going on too. "Well, you have a new partner this year, right? Maybe she'll let you be on camera."

Lewis laughs just a little. "What made you want to take TV Production, anyhow?" he asks. "Doesn't really seem like your thing."

I lean back on my hands. "Wasn't my decision. Wexler and Mr. Keith are making me. They said the only way I could stay in the AT program was to drop the tennis team and sign up for some easier electives."

"Wait. The day Cal and I saw you in the studio . . . ?"

"Was the day I met with them, yeah. They had my permanent record out and everything."

"What did it look like?"

"I don't know. A bunch of different papers. I didn't exactly get a good look at it."

"I always thought the idea of a permanent record was kind of a messed-up concept. It's like this thing that gets sent around to all these colleges we apply to, and it's just paper. Some basic facts and plotted data points that don't even begin to scratch the surface of who we really are, you know?"

I do know what Lewis is talking about, but it's not just college admissions officers—it's all of us. I've gone to this school every day with Lewis, and I'm only now beginning to really meet him. Who knows what other people might be dealing with?

Something clicks in my mind.

"Lewis, that's it. That's our TV clip."

"Filming ourselves breaking in and stealing our permanent records?" Lewis says. "I'm in."

"No! What you were saying. How there're so many facets to the students here that can't possibly be captured on a transcript or college application. What if we tried to show some of those angles?"

Lewis blinks. "Okay. How would we do that?"

"By making mini-documentaries." It's such a perfect idea that I jolt upright and start pacing a little. "Five-minute clips that feature a different senior every other week. We take a student who's really known for one thing, then flip the script and show that there's a whole other aspect to their life that hardly anyone knows about."

"You think people would like that?"

"How could they not? It's interesting and meaningful and just the sort of thing Mrs. Hansen wants." And most of all, it shows that I can take a class as frivolous as TV Production and still make something really great out of it.

"Hm, yeah. Maybe." Lewis starts lining the books back up on Mr. Rosco's shelves, and I can almost see the gears turning in his mind, weighing out my idea. I know this will work. I know this can be something good.

For the first time this year, I find I'm actually looking forward to something.

FOURTEEN

LEWIS

S o explain this to me again," Rebecca says, moving her goalie just in time to block Cal's shot.

"I got detention." I sigh.

"For something you didn't do?" she clarifies.

"Yes, I was trying to help a friend."

"A lady friend," Cal says, spinning one of his rows of players force-fully for emphasis. I glance up at him, but his eyes are set firmly on the game. We're in Cal's basement playing foosball. He's so good that he plays against Rebecca and me at the same time and still usually dominates.

"She's my TV Production partner. There were all these people in the hall starting to point and whisper, and it felt really messed up. You know half the school still talks about what happened last year."

"When she snapped," Cal says, shifting one of his rows of players, dancing with the ball for a moment, and then sending it into his goal. "Oh, hell yeah!"

"What do you mean she snapped?" Rebecca asks.

I step in before Cal can respond. "She didn't snap. She just . . . stopped her car for a bit."

"Oh, that girl at the front of your school?" Rebecca says. "I remember that. I saw some of the videos."

"And now she's an alcoholic," Cal adds.

"She's not an alcoholic," I say. "The flask was empty. Look, it was one detention. It wasn't that big of a deal."

"I don't know, man. First you're sharing a locker together, and now you guys are spending hours together alone in a room after school. Sounds like it's getting pretty serious," Cal teases.

"You like this girl?" Rebecca asks.

Across the table Cal is smirking at me. Sometimes he can be a real dick on purpose. "No. I just . . . What was I supposed to do? Walk away and let her take the blame alone?"

"Of course not," Cal says. "Like you said, she's your partner now." He smiles and scores another goal, but then his crotch lines up with one of my rows of players, and I jam the rod hard in his direction, and he collapses to the floor.

I don't really mind if Cal teases me about Hayley in private, but I wish he wouldn't do it in front of Rebecca. Honestly, I think he does it because he's trying to get me to finally make a move. He's been manufacturing these scenarios for Rebecca and me to hook up for years.

After our eighth-grade graduation, Cal had a party in his basement where he convinced everyone to play kissing games. He rigged it so that Rebecca and I ended up in the closet together. We were supposed to spend seven minutes making out and exploring each other's bodies, but the only things we explored were the boxes of Christmas decorations. When Cal screamed "Time's up!" and opened the door, expecting to find us locked in each other's arms, all he found was that we had wrapped ourselves in rainbow lights and tinsel.

"Ta-da!" I had exclaimed as Rebecca hoisted a golden angel over our heads.

"You guys are so weird," Cal said.

Then last year, Rebecca and I went to prom together. As friends. My mom took a bunch of pictures of us by the mantel and on the stairs, and even though we weren't really a couple, I thought we looked pretty great.

At the dance, Cal made all these excuses to leave us alone. He kept waving at no one across the room and saying he was going to talk to someone else, even though he only has, like, three other friends. Rebecca and I had fun dancing, losing our minds when they played "Come On Eileen" since it's the first song on the '80s mix I made. During slow songs, I felt a certain rush of adrenaline as Rebecca stepped in close and rested her head on my shoulder.

But there was no dramatic scene of us looking into each other's eyes and realizing that we were always meant to be together.

After the dance, we all went to a late-night diner where we ate pancakes and drank root beer floats. At the end of the night, Rebecca hugged me and gave me a kiss on the cheek outside her apartment complex. When I got back in the car, Cal asked me what happened.

"Nothing. She said she had a good time, and we said good night."

"Man, when are you guys just going to date?"

"I don't know." I sighed, feeling kind of defeated. "Maybe we won't. If it didn't happen tonight, maybe it's not going to happen."

"Or maybe you just need to stop being so scared and put yourself out there. You've never even asked her on a real date."

I understand Cal's point of view, and I've spent plenty of nights lying awake in bed wondering what would happen if I just asked Rebecca out. I know I run the risk of ruining our friendship if she doesn't feel the same way, but I also know that's an old excuse cowards use to justify not putting themselves out there.

Cal groans from the ground, holding his crotch where I jammed the foosball stick. "Not . . . cool . . . dude."

"Wait," Rebecca says, pointing between me and Cal. "So you guys aren't working together in TV class this year?"

"No. Mrs. Hansen wanted to change things," I say. "Hayley and I are still trying to figure out what sort of clips we want to make. She thinks we should make mini-documentaries about seniors at Groveland."

"What would that even look like?" Cal asks, hoisting himself back up to the table.

"Just little profiles about their life, I guess. We see so many people at school day after day, but how many do you actually know? Just a handful, right? Wouldn't you like to know about the others?"

Rebecca's face lights up. "That could be pretty cool, actually."

"Really?"

"Yeah, I think that could be really interesting, and I'd bet you'd be good at that, Lew. You always have a way of making people comfortable. I bet they'd open up to you. Will you show them to me afterward if you do it?"

"Uh, yeah. Of course." I've shown Rebecca the stuff Cal and I have made for TV Production before, but she's never shown this kind of interest. She usually just laughs and rolls her eyes through our ridiculousness. This is something else. This is genuine intrigue.

And now I really want to make something that will impress her.

FIFTEEN

HAYLEY

After spending a couple classes ironing out the concept, Lewis and I pitch our documentary idea to Mrs. Hansen. Of course she loves it. I knew she would. I might not know anything about TV Production, but after three years in the AT program, you can bet I know how to read a teacher. It's kind of a gift. Show me their syllabus and give me a few days in their class, and I can tell you how they take their coffee by the weekend.

"So I guess the question now is who should be our first subject?" Lewis asks as we recline on the small worn sofa in the studio. "You?"

"Oh, definitely not. I want to do the work, not be the focus. People have seen enough videos of me already," I say. "I think these documentaries could shatter perceptions and preconceived notions. We should profile people known for one thing and then show a whole other side of their personality, part of them no one really knows about."

Lewis picks at the loose stuffing that's breaking through one of the couch seams. "But if we're trying to show hidden aspects of someone's personality, how are *we* supposed to know about those hidden aspects?"

"It will require a little detective work," I say, scrolling through my Instagram feed. "Luckily, I have our first lead." I stop when I land on the picture I was looking for, a cinder-block wall covered in a beautiful spray-painted mural. It's a black crow soaring into flight, her uplifted wings highlighted in strokes of blue and purple. In her wake is a wave of color, yellows and oranges, spreading in swooped lines like fire. I tilt my phone to show Lewis.

"*TwilightTin?* Yeah, everyone follows that account. I mean, it's like our town has its own Banksy, but what does that have to do with this?"

"Do you know who TwilightTin is?"

"No, no one does." Lewis sits up a little straighter. "Wait, are you saying it's someone at Groveland?"

"Yup," I say, savoring the secret a little longer.

"No way! Who?"

I look up and realize just how many students are milling around the studio. I doubt anyone's listening to our conversation, but I don't want to risk it, so I pull Lewis to his feet and out the big studio doors. Once we're down the hall several yards, I whisper, "Do you know Camilla Rodriguez?"

"On the tennis team? Yeah. Isn't she, like, a prodigy or something?"

"Yeah, she has college recruiters lining up to look at her at almost every tournament."

"And you're telling me she does this in her free time?"

"Yeah."

"How do you know?"

"I have my ways." Really, I just put two and two together. One day last year, Camilla gave me a ride home from practice when my car was in the shop. I saw a couple spray-paint cans rattling around in the floorboards of her backseat. I didn't think too much of it, but then she let me pick out some music for the ride, and when she unlocked her phone, I caught a glimpse of her Instagram. She was logged in as TwilightTin. I think she realized her mistake too, because she was incredibly friendly while she took me home. Even offered to spend some extra time with me after practice helping me improve my backswing. "Because we have to look out for each other, right?" she said as she dropped me off. I moved to get out of the car, but she took hold of my arm. "We have to have each other's backs, right, Hayley?" She said it without smiling, and it was so intimidating that I just nodded in agreement. When she actually did help me with my backswing, I figured we were even if I never said anything.

"Okay." Lewis sighs. I can tell he wants to press me for more particulars, but he apparently decides to let it go because the next thing he asks is, "And you think she's ready to go public with this?"

There's the key question. Something I've been mulling over myself. What could convince Camilla to possibly go public after uploading content anonymously for more than a year and racking up thousands of followers? Could this hurt her college options? If a school finds out she's also a part-time vandal—even if the vandalism is really beautiful—they might be hesitant to make her an offer. Convincing her to go along with this is going to be a challenge. "Let's just talk to her after school and see what happens," I tell Lewis. "Bring a camera."

After school, Lewis meets me at Groveland's side entrance with one of the TV Production cameras in hand. All day, I've been trying to think about what I'm going to say to Camilla, but everything I come up with feels like a gambit. Outside, rain is coming down steadily, and students are flipping up hoods and hoisting open umbrellas. Near the edge of the student lot, I catch sight of one of the embroidered green-and-white umbrellas the tennis team got at the end of last season. "Start filming now," I tell Lewis as I open the door.

"Are we, like, ambushing her?" he asks, juggling the camera and trying to get his own umbrella opened.

I ignore his question and keep moving across the quad. "Camilla, hey!" I yell. "Camilla!"

She stops and turns, the curls of her black hair tucked under the slick hood of a yellow raincoat. "Hey, Hayley."

I move in close so that we're both sharing her umbrella, so close that she can probably hear my heart pounding louder than the rain. This is going to be hard, staring her in the face. *Please just say yes, Camilla.* After a moment, Lewis appears, the camera raised in our direction. "I was wondering if you might be interested in helping me with a little project," I say. She eyes Lewis and the camera suspiciously. "This is my friend Lewis. We're in TV Production together this year."

"Okay. What's up?" Camilla asks.

"Uh, Lewis and I are hoping to make some mini-documentaries about some Groveland seniors this year. Obviously, you're a super interesting person, so I was wondering, uh, we were both hoping you'd be interested in being the first subject."

"You want to make a documentary about me? Like, about tennis or something?"

"Sort of. We'd like to talk a bit about tennis for sure. But we'd like the main focus of the documentary to be about your, uh, alter ego?"

Her eyes flash to the camera momentarily and then back to my face. "What?"

"You know, your side project," I prod, working hard to keep my eyes locked with hers.

Camilla scrunches her eyebrows like she doesn't know what I'm talking about. I hold my phone up, displaying TwilightTin's latest post. Her eyes move from my phone to Lewis and the camera and then back to my face. "I think you know what I'm talking about," I say.

Camilla looks unfazed. "I really don't," she says, turning away.

I let her take a few steps while I gather my courage. I was hoping it wouldn't come to this, but if I'm going to be the pond scum this year, it's not going to be pleasant for everyone. "Well, here's the deal, Camilla," I shout over the rain. "We're going to make a documentary on TwilightTin with or without you. A film where we lay all of our evidence on the table and show exactly how it leads to you. Now, you can either be a part of that documentary and help us guide the narrative, or you can wait and see it on the morning announcements like every other student at Groveland."

"Wait, what?" I hear Lewis say.

Camilla stops and moves back toward us. "What evidence?"

"Guess you'll see. Come on, Lewis." I turn to walk away, grabbing Lewis's arm and moving us back toward the school. Nervousness claws at my insides. This is my final gamble, and I'm not exactly proud of playing this hand.

Camilla charges in front of us. "Wait," she says, looking around. "Follow me." She leads us out to her car, walking quickly and not bothering to avoid any puddles. I slide into the passenger seat while Lewis lowers his umbrella and climbs into the back. Camilla turns to me from the driver's seat and finds the lens of Lewis's camera right in her face.

"Can you put that goddamn thing down for one second?" she says. "God, I haven't seen the right side of your face this whole time. It's like some bizarre *Phantom of the Opera* shit."

"Sorry," Lewis mumbles. He points the camera at his feet, but I notice he doesn't stop recording.

"Now. Explain this to me again," Camilla says, taking the time to enunciate each syllable. Her skin is slick with rainwater, and the inside of her car is already humid, the windows half fogged.

"We're starting to make documentaries about Groveland seniors. It's going to be a series. We'd like you to be the subject of the first one. All of you," I say, struggling to keep my voice steady.

"And if I don't want to, you're just going to do it anyway. Is that what I'm hearing? Because that's some manipulative bullshit. What happened to you, Hayley? Some unflattering videos of you got posted online so now you've joined TV Production so you can get some sort of sick revenge by making videos about other people?"

"That's not what this is," I protest. This isn't about revenge. This is about proving I'm still the same Hayley I was before my breakdown. I'm trying to figure out the best way to explain it when Lewis steps in.

"Camilla, what do you know about me?" he asks.

"Huh?" she says, twisting in his direction.

"What do you know about me? Seriously. Anything you know. Do you know my last name?"

"It starts with an *H*, right?"

Lewis nods. "Holbrook. Yeah. What else?" Camilla glances over at me like she's looking for guidance, but even I'm not sure where Lewis is going with this. "Come on," Lewis says. "We've gone to this same school together for three years. You have to know something."

"Uh, you do this TV stuff," she says, motioning vaguely to the camera.

"Okay." Lewis chuckles. "Anything else?"

"Well, we don't exactly run in the same circles." Camilla sighs.

"So, what do you think people know about you?"

"Fuck if I know. Who cares?"

"See, I think you do care," Lewis prods. "I think this art thing is your way of showing people you're more than a good serve."

"What makes you think that?" Camilla says, smirking and folding her arms.

"Because I know you're not just a stupid jock. We had English together last year, remember that? I remember because you didn't sit in the back with Harold Lockner and the rest of the student-athlete crowd. You sat in the second row. You paid attention. You memorized and recited a T. S. Eliot poem for extra credit. You actually care about artistic stuff. That's what I know about you. So, how about you really show that side of yourself to other people?"

Camilla seems stunned. For the first time, she doesn't have a quick defensive response.

Okay. So maybe I should have actually talked to Lewis about my plan instead of just telling him to show up with a camera. This whole time I thought we were going to have to twist Camilla's arm and begrudgingly get her to go along with our documentary, but here comes

Lewis with a speech that might actually make her *want* to say yes. I'm impressed.

We're all silent for a few moments, and then Camilla says, "It's kind of creepy that you were watching me that closely," but there's not much sting in her voice. "I would get final approval on this thing before it aired, right?" she asks.

"Absolutely," Lewis says, catching my eye.

I nod and say, "But we do need to actually film you in the act."

Camilla sighs and pulls her backpack onto her lap. "Fine," she says, digging out a scrap of paper and scribbling down an address. "Meet me on the roof. Wednesday night, eleven p.m." Lewis gives me a wide-eyed look, clearly surprised his prodding actually worked, and for the first time, I think this might be the start of a really good partnership.

SIXTEEN

LEWIS

O n Wednesday evening, my parents are in their room by ten thirty, so I turn off my bedroom light and shut the door before sneaking downstairs and out into the backyard. It's not a very daring escape, I know, but I've never needed to sneak out before, so there's no reason for dramatics. I don't have a life-size dummy rigged with a snoring soundtrack like Ferris Bueller, and I don't have a rose trellis conveniently located outside my window to act as a makeshift ladder. Outside my window is just a two-story drop to the ground. I guess I could've tied some sheets together to use as an escape rope, but any plan that's dependent on my knot-tying skills is probably not a good one. I'm not a Boy Scout.

Hayley is parked at the end of my block, and when I climb into her car, I realize I might be underdressed. She's wearing black jeans and a baseball cap pulled low. All I did was toss a hoodie over the same T-shirt I had on at school.

"Should I have gone more burglar chic?" I ask. Hayley just rolls her eyes and pulls away from the curb. Downtown, we find parking on a side street, and Hayley shuts off the car before slipping the paper from her pocket, checking the address Camilla gave us. We walk along a few empty blocks, and I watch our reflection as we pass storefront windows, trying to determine if we look suspicious or not. "I think this is it,"

Hayley says, stopping in front of a two-story white bakery with a pale pink awning.

"And she wants us to meet her on the roof?" I ask.

"Yeah," Hayley says, moving toward the alley. There's a twist in my gut. Even though we haven't done anything illegal yet, I can already feel sweat gathering in my armpits. How does one look *not suspicious* when darting into an alley? I do my best to move nonchalantly, walking up to where Hayley's already located the ladder. It's rusted, and the bottom third is covered by a locked gate, making it inaccessible. I give the lock a jiggle, and it doesn't move.

"Did Camilla mention a key?" I ask, looking around on the ground as if I'll find a spare stashed away under a doormat or beneath a potted plant.

"No," Hayley says. "She didn't mention this."

"Can we pick it? Do you have a hairpin? That's a thing, right? Picking locks with a hairpin." I've seen that in movies, for sure.

"I don't think that's really a thing," Hayley says.

"Maybe Camilla's bringing the key?"

"Maybe," Hayley says, but her voice is distant, like she's not really listening. "Here, help me move this." She walks to the far side of a dumpster and places her hands against it, clearly wanting to push it closer to the ladder so we can stand on it and bypass the gate. I stand beside her, and she gives a countdown from three, and we begin pushing. The dumpster wheels let out a metal squeal as they start moving, and it echoes throughout the alley. So much for inconspicuous. We both freeze for a moment, waiting for the police to leap from the shadows and point some flashlights in our face. But they don't show. After several moments of silence, we start pushing again, getting the dumpster situated beside the ladder.

Standing on the dumpster, Hayley is able to take hold of the ladder and climb over the gate. She does it with such speed and ease that it makes me wonder if she's broken into places before. My attempt is much clumsier. As a larger person, I'm not exactly known for my agility. I sling the video camera over my shoulder and wiggle my way to the top of the dumpster, the plastic lid buckling a bit under my weight. When I go to climb the ladder, my shoes slip on the grate and fall back against the dumpster with a loud thud.

"Shhh," Hayley hisses, looking down at me from several rungs up.

"Sorry," I say. "I didn't know I was going to have to Cirque du Soleil my way onto a roof tonight."

On my second attempt, I manage to clear the locked gate, and I make a mental note to add some weight lifting to my running regimen. At the top of the ladder, Hayley takes my hand and helps me climb over the ledge and onto the roof. Just ahead of us is a low wall where the bakery roof meets the neighboring building. It's dazzlingly white, the perfect canvas for a spray-paint mural.

"Guess Camilla's not here yet," Hayley says, moving along the edge of the roof.

"Guess not," I say. "Maybe we should stay away from the edges. Just so no one sees us."

"Good point," Hayley says. She takes a seat against a large air conditioner unit, and I lean against the wall across from her. "So . . . we wait?" she says, looking around.

"Seems that way."

SEVENTEEN

HAYLEY

I fully realize this whole thing could be a setup. Maybe Camilla truly has no interest in being a part of this documentary and she just sent Lewis and me to a random downtown rooftop in the middle of the night for fun. Maybe she's lying in her bed, thinking about what idiots we are and laughing at this very moment. Or maybe she's calling the cops, acting like a concerned citizen and reporting that she's spotted some suspicious people lurking around the roof of a bakery. Maybe the police are going to roll up any minute. Every passing car I hear down on the street sends a shiver through my legs. Lewis must be feeling concerned too. He keeps fiddling with the camera. Hard to believe this is the same seemingly fearless guy that was going to take the blame for my flask.

"It's kind of dark up here, huh?" I say, staring at the purple sky. A lot of the stars are washed out by the ambient light of downtown, but there are a handful of brighter ones twinkling through.

Lewis unfolds the side screen on the camera and points it around a bit. "Yeah, but it should still work. We can brighten the footage in post if we need to."

"*In post.*" I laugh. "So professional."

"Whatever," he says, picking up a small pebble and flicking it at me. We both go quiet, but Lewis must be having some of the same concerns as me about Camilla not showing up because after a bit he says, "Is this dumb?"

"Sitting on a random roof downtown at eleven p.m. on a school night, waiting for our classmate to show up so we can film her committing a Class B misdemeanor? No, I think it's perfectly normal."

Lewis laughs and furrows his brow. "Class B?"

"I looked it up," I admit. "I like to know what I'm getting myself into."

"Clearly." He stares out at the taller buildings farther down the street, all of them lit with shades of orange and yellow from the lampposts below. "I'm assuming you had to sneak out tonight."

"Actually, no," I say. "I told my parents I was staying at my friend Lucy's house."

"In the middle of the week?"

"They trust me." I shrug. "Did you sneak out?"

"If you could call it that," he says. "I just waited for my parents to go to bed and walked out the back door." Lewis picks up a couple small loose rocks beside him and skips them across the roof. "I always thought the first time I ever snuck out of the house it would be for something fun and dangerous. Not for homework."

"Homework," I scoff. "We're meeting up with an anonymous graffiti artist. It's not exactly a book report."

"I guess I just always thought I would be sneaking out to a house party or something. This is . . . not that."

"No, it's not," I say, looking out at the high-rises on the next block. I push up the sleeves of my jacket, enjoying the cool night air on my skin, the first sign that fall's coming. "You never snuck out before?"

Lewis shrugs. "Never had a reason to, really." He looks around a bit. "This is probably the riskiest thing I've ever done, actually."

"Oh yeah?"

"Yeah, and honestly, it's pretty terrifying." He fans his arms a bit. "I probably should've put on more deodorant. How are you not freaking out more?"

"Who says I'm not?"

"I don't know. You just seem so calm. Is this just a typical Wednesday night for you or something?"

"Oh definitely, Tuesday is underground rave night, Wednesday night is for roof-hopping downtown, and then on Thursdays, I like to stop my car in the middle of traffic." The words are out before I really think about them, which surprises even me. I've made jokes about my incident with Lucy before, but never with anyone else. Something about the quiet night and Lewis's demeanor weakens my defenses.

"Hmm, I think I might have heard something about that last one," Lewis says.

"Really? I thought I kept it under wraps pretty well," I joke.

"Can I, uh, ask what that was like?" Lewis requests a little uneasily.

I take off my ball cap and lean my head back against the industrial AC unit, the cold of the metal pressing into my scalp. People have asked about my incident before, but even with the girls on the tennis team, it always seemed like they were just trying to get gossipy details. Not Lewis, though. There's a sincerity to his questions that surprises me. "I think the best analogy I can come up with is that it was like being in the ocean. On the beach, you stand in the water and you hear people laughing and yelling, and you get hit by the waves, but when you dive beneath the surface, everything's different. It's quiet. In that moment, everything slowed for me. It was like I wouldn't slow down, so my brain did it for me. Everything went smooth and fluid, and it was all churning together around me. Even with all the honking and stuff, for me it was peaceful. The traffic lights kept changing and changing, and I just . . . didn't move. Couldn't move."

In my pocket, I stab my thumb into the corner of the index cards I have prepared with questions for Camilla. I press into the sharpness until the corner dulls. "Then you know the rest. The cops came and pulled me out. They didn't say anything to me at first. Just opened my door and reached across my lap and put my car in park."

"Were you scared?" Lewis asks.

"No. I don't think so. I was still sort of in this trance. Moving my body was weird, I remember that. Like when you try to move your legs after they've fallen asleep. Eventually I was sitting on the curb on the side of the road and answering all these questions about whether I had been drinking, or if I was on any medication, or if I knew what day it was. Then my mom showed up after I gave the police my phone." This is the first time I've recounted the details of that day in a long time. Dr. Kim has encouraged me to talk about it more, which is part of the reason I think she keeps pushing me to check out the support group on State's campus. She says if I loosen my grip on it, maybe it will loosen its grip on me. Talking about my incident in front of a whole group seems terrifying, but maybe I'm taking a baby step by talking to one person. I try to imagine myself letting go and watching that day drift off into the night sky like a balloon.

"I think my mom would lose it if she ever answered a call from my cell and it was actually the police," Lewis says.

"Same. I think she and my dad still worry a lot, but right after it happened was the worst, obviously. We had to have these long, awkward conversations about school and stress and the pressure I was feeling. It was honestly worse than when they gave me the sex talk. Then Lucy came over and told me about how everyone at school was sending around the videos, and there were all these rumors about how I was probably going to be institutionalized.

"When I went back to Groveland on Monday, things were weird. It wasn't the way things are in the movies. In the morning, the hallway didn't come to a screeching halt as everyone stared at me. It was the opposite. I could sense the distinct lack of people looking at me. Everyone seemed to be making a tremendous effort not to meet my gaze. If Lucy hadn't been with me, I probably would've run out and never looked back."

"I'm sorry you had to go through that," Lewis says.

"Yeah, me too."

We're silent for several moments, and then a green backpack flies over the edge of the roof and lands with a clatter. Seconds later, Camilla's head appears at the top of the ladder, her dark curly hair concealed beneath a red beanie. "You guys ready to have some fun?"

EIGHTEEN

LEWIS

"All right, let's do this thing," Camilla says, her tone making it clear that she's not super thrilled about us being here. She brushes some dust off her gray capris and pushes the sleeves of her dark blue hoodie up to her elbows. She moves toward us with such quick, determined steps that I'm half convinced she's about to throw a punch. I instinctively lift my arm in front of Hayley like a mom protecting her kid in the passenger seat when Camilla stops short. She rolls her eyes. "Really?"

"Sorry," I say, feeling dumb. As I drop my arm, I look back at Hayley, and she gives me a weird little half smile that I decide to interpret as her being touched and also trying very hard not to laugh.

Camilla rolls her eyes. "So how does this work exactly?" she asks.

"We, uh, basically just want to film you doing your thing," Hayley says. "During the process, we'll ask you some questions, and you should just give honest answers. We'll need you to wear this wireless mic."

Camilla takes the mic and places it on her frayed collar.

"And speak in full sentences, too," I add. "That'll help with editing later."

"Cool." Camilla picks up her backpack and places it over by the white wall, then she steps back to take it in, studying her canvas. Hayley and I look at each other and wait. After a moment, Camilla turns back to us. "Ready?"

"Ready when you are," I say, turning on the camera and lifting it into position.

Camilla unzips her bag and reveals half a dozen cans of spray paint. I immediately move in, getting a nice shot of her sorting through the cans, standing them up and shaking a couple to rattle the ball inside. Once she's satisfied, she removes the dark green cap from one and walks over to the wall. I'm expecting her to take a deep breath or maybe make a couple of practice sweeps without actually spraying anything the way I've seen Cal do with his swing on the golf course, but she doesn't. Without hesitation, she lifts the can and applies a long, curved line of green to the wall.

A drop of sweat travels the length of my spine.

There's no going back now. If we're caught, we can't just lie and say we're on the roof to do some amateur stargazing or something. I should've asked Hayley if she looked up the consequences for vandalism, too. Is it a fine? Some kind of community service? Is it different if you're just documenting the vandalism and not actively participating?

Hayley speaks as Camilla makes a second line beneath her first. "So, when did you first start spray-painting?"

"It started a little more than a year ago," Camilla says, not taking her eyes off the wall. "I was looking for something in my garage, and I found a milk crate of old spray cans. Thought it would be fun to mess around with them, but I didn't want to just vandalize random walls. So that weekend I snuck into that big junkyard off Ridge. There was lots of stuff to spray-paint there. Wood pallets, old cars, messed-up furniture. It's kind of addicting, I guess. I've never been interested in painting a canvas or drawing in a sketchbook, but this is different. It's . . . bigger."

Camilla walks back to her bag and retrieves a can of blue paint. She applies it beneath the green in the same sweeping motion. I'm not sure what exactly she's making, but it's fascinating to watch. The way she arches her arm and shuffles along the length of the wall. The way she layers in the colors. I move back toward the edge of the wall to get a wide shot.

"Do you scout out these locations ahead of time?" Hayley asks. I recognize the question from the list she sent me earlier this evening. When I checked my phone after dinner, I had a long string of texts from Hayley with more than a dozen questions she thought might be good to ask Camilla. It was a bit overwhelming but also kind of nice considering I'm used to working with Cal, who is a proud member of Team Wing It. Sometimes our lack of planning would really show in the clips we turned in, and Mrs. Hansen would say she "knew we could do better."

"I usually find them when I'm not looking," Camilla says. She points to a five-story parking structure at the end of the block. "I found this wall when I was parking in that garage over there. Caught sight of it and thought it was perfect. Just big and empty." She sprays the blue paint with abandon, moving the can wildly as if her only goal is to fill up space. Up and down and then left to right, creating a large hatch pattern across half the wall. She moves back to her backpack and pulls out a shade of lighter blue. As she layers it in, what she's creating becomes clear. It's a wave, a large swell of water that's arching forward.

"How do you think people will react when they find out you're TwilightTin?" Hayley asks.

Camilla hesitates, lifting her finger from the nozzle of the spray paint but only for a moment. "I don't know. Maybe they won't care. Or maybe they'll just dismiss it. People aren't always interested in getting to really know people. It's easier if they can put you in a category, you know? I'm a jock. That's what most people think of when they think about me. Could be worse, I guess." Camilla returns to her backpack and grabs a can of yellow paint. She laces streaks into the wave, long strands of glistening sun.

It's really becoming a dynamic piece. I move in, getting a close-up of Camilla's face. Her tongue is pressed against her upper lip as she moves the can to eye level and sprays a few quick shots.

"Do you want people to see you as more than just an athlete?" Hayley asks.

"Maybe. I want people to see me as more than one thing, sure, but I can't spend all my time worrying about how other people see me, you know? If people want to really get to know me, here I am. Talk to me. If not, that's okay too. I don't need to be everyone's friend."

For the next ten minutes, we're silent. I know Hayley has more questions she could be asking, but the only sound is the occasional passing car on the street below and the quiet hiss of the paint cans. When I glance over at Hayley, she has a sort of faraway look in her eyes, and I wonder if she's processing what Camilla has said, or if she's just as hypnotized by Camilla's work as I am. Camilla's fast, moving between the wall and her supplies with the same speed and decisiveness she has on the tennis court. When she finally slows down, I realize it's because she's nearly done.

She grabs her white paint and adds a few more highlights.

I'm amazed. The colors are bold against the wall, and somehow Camilla has managed to capture the motion of the wave. It looks like it could break and crest if I turn away for even a moment. I pan across the wall to get a close-up and then move back to get the whole piece in frame while Camilla pulls her phone from her hoodie pocket and takes several photos. Then she turns to me and Hayley. "Get everything you needed?"

Hayley nods. "Yeah, I think we're good," I say.

But Camilla's not looking at me. She's looking past me, over my shoulder. When I turn, there are red and blue lights bouncing off the building across the street. Camilla creeps to the edge of the roof and peers over. "Shit," she says, running half crouched over to her backpack and zipping up the cans. "It's the cops. We gotta go."

"Go where?" Hayley says, her eyes wide. "There's only one ladder."

"On this roof, yeah," Camilla says. "But we're not staying on this roof."

Down on the street, two car doors slam shut. A wave of panic descends over me. Camilla tosses her bag over her shoulder and moves to the low wall she just spray-painted, placing her hands on top and leaping over in a smooth motion. Once on the other side, she looks back and realizes Hayley and I still haven't moved. "Let's go," she hisses.

Hayley takes hold of my sleeve and moves forward. I tighten the camera strap across my shoulder and follow her.

We're running from the cops now. We're. Running. From. The. Cops. The realization explodes in my mind, pushing out every other thought, and my heart rate triples. I know I was joking earlier about how sneaking out of my house for homework was lame, but it doesn't feel so pathetic anymore. When I said I wanted this year to be more exciting and push me out of my comfort zone, I was hoping to ease into it by maybe trying a new hairstyle or tasting oysters for the first time, not starting with a police pursuit.

Thankfully, all the buildings on this block are connected, so as we run, we're not leaping across alleys like Batman. Instead, we've just become criminal hurdle-jumpers, clearing several waist-high walls before Camilla ducks behind a raised section of the last roof. Hayley and I follow suit. All of us keep our bodies tight against the wall as we try to calm our heaving chests. After a moment, Camilla peeks out from our hiding spot. "There're two of them," she whispers. "They're poking around with flashlights."

"So, what do we do?" I ask, wiping my hand across my damp forehead. "Wait it out here?" I'm quickly realizing that when I thought I was sweating a lot earlier, I was only kidding myself because now I'm pretty sure you could wring out my underwear and fill a small fishbowl.

"No. We go there." Camilla points to the edge of the next roof, which nearly runs up against the edge of the parking garage she motioned to earlier. "Nearly" being the operative word.

"You want to jump off this roof?" Hayley asks, leaning in to grip Camilla's forearms.

"We only have to clear, like, two feet to the parking garage. Jump, grab the railing, and pull ourselves over. It's easy." She says it like it's nothing, but even I can tell it kind of seems like she's trying to convince herself.

"Easy? It's, like, a twenty-five-foot drop to concrete if we don't make it," I hiss through gritted teeth. "And maybe you haven't noticed, but I'm not exactly Jason Bourne."

Hayley nods fervently. "Yeah. We should just stay hidden."

Camilla rolls her eyes. "You guys stay if you want. I'm going for it." Before Hayley or I can say anything else, Camilla flips the hood of her sweatshirt over her head and sprints toward the edge of the roof.

"Oh, come on," I mutter in disbelief. This must be what I get for trying to become a leading man, because this is a classic '80s movie trope—meddling kids on the run from authority figures. But in the movies, it's usually funnier, like the Breakfast Club sliding around the school hallway to avoid the overbearing gaze of Principal Vernon. It's not supposed to be no-nonsense cops with billy clubs and intimidating mustaches. I don't know for sure that they have mustaches, but that's what I'm imagining.

I try to picture how this scene would play out on the big screen. It starts with a shot of the officers' flashlights tracing Camilla's spray-painted wave. They step into frame, two muscular figures moving in to examine the wall. One presses a finger to it, and when he pulls it away, it's dyed blue. Fresh paint. Cut to Hayley and me quivering in our hiding place, the officers visible in the background. She looks at me, wondering what we should do. I look up directly into the camera, my expression one of fierce determination. Then we pan out to a sweeping shot as a Bon Jovi song swells and Hayley and I start running.

In real life, Hayley is shaking me. "Lewis, come on! We have to go. What are you doing?"

"Trying to remember the lyrics to 'Livin' on a Prayer,'" I say. "Something about Gina working at a diner, right?"

"Are you serious? We have to go!"

The chorus pushes through the fog of panic and snaps into my mind. "We'll give it a shot!" Hayley yanks me forward, and I stumble at first, but then we're running. The camera jostles against my back, and I pray the shoulder strap holds. Our footfalls are loud against the roof, and soon flashlight beams cut across our path and the police start yelling for us to freeze. Camilla has already cleared the jump, and she's beckoning us from the parking garage. "Come on! Come on!" she yells. I'm honestly surprised she cared enough to wait for us.

My heart is pulsating, pushing much harder than it has on any of my runs around the neighborhood, and I think I might be yelling Bon Jovi lyrics. "OOOOH! WE'RE HALFWAY THERE! OOOOOH! LIVIN' ON A PRAYER!"

Hayley and I reach the edge of the roof at the same time, both of us placing a foot right on the edge. Then we're jumping, and there's nothing between us and the parking garage except open air.

NINETEEN

HAYLEY

So I was wrong when I assumed TV Production would be boring hours spent sitting in a studio stitching videos together. This is definitely not that. Running from the police. Jumping from rooftops. If only Principal Wexler and Mr. Keith could see me now. Yes, this is much less stressful than tennis. Nothing at all anxiety-inducing about tonight.

Lewis and I hit the wall of the parking garage at the same time, both of us wrapping our arms around the metal railing running along the top. My feet find purchase, and I climb over as Camilla grabs Lewis's arm and helps him across. "Holy hell," Lewis says, his hands on his knees like he might vomit. I peek over the edge, looking at how far we would've fallen had we slipped. The ground is all glistening concrete and scattered broken glass. I might vomit, too. "We could've died." Lewis exhales.

"We still might," Camilla says, motioning back to the cops. One of them continues to move across the roofs toward us, and the other is yelling into the walkie-talkie mounted on his shoulder. "Let's go." Camilla starts to sprint across the garage. Fresh terror blooms in my chest as Lewis and I follow her, but I force myself to push away any thoughts of getting arrested. I can only imagine the field day the kids at school would have with my mug shot. We dart between rows and rows of parked cars, all of them lit orange by the industrial overhead lights. Camilla points toward an enclosed staircase in the corner, and we burst through the door and move down the concrete steps, jumping two and three at a time, grabbing the railing and swinging our bodies around the landings. When we reach the ground level, Camilla cuts down an alley. I have no idea where we're going; I'm just following her without question. When we emerge onto the street, I'm half convinced there will be multiple squad cars there to greet us, muscular police officers ready to snatch us up and haul us away. But the only thing that's there is Camilla's parked car. She points her key, and the doors unlock with a small chirp. "Everybody in," she commands. Lewis and I both jump into the back, and Camilla gets into the driver's seat.

We're all panting, and blood is rushing to my head.

"What are you waiting for? Get us out of here," Lewis barks, his knuckles white against Camilla's seat.

"Wait," Camilla says, her eyes darting around in expectation. "Everyone down."

Without hesitating, Lewis and I both crouch toward the middle, our faces so close I can see the sweat beading on his forehead. Camilla lies across the front seat. Just out the window over Lewis's head, I see the top of a police cruiser glide by, silent but with the red and blue lights rotating. My heartbeat ticks off the seconds in double time. After a moment, Camilla risks a peek out the front window, and then she sits up fully. "Okay. I think we're good," she says, turning back to us and grinning.

Good is not at all how I would describe what I'm currently feeling. I must not look great either, because Lewis touches my arm and says, "Hey, you okay?"

"I will be when my heart stops exploding," I say, happy Lewis is here. I can tell by his reddened cheeks and the way his eyes keep darting around that he's uneasy with this situation too. Camilla, on the other hand, is smiling in a way I've never seen before, clearly getting some insane sense of joy out of this turn of events. "Are *you* okay?" I ask Lewis.

He closes his eyes and leans his head against the back seat. "I think I'm actively peeing in my pants right now."

"Ew, that's nasty," Camilla says, adjusting her rearview mirror so she can look at us. Something about the way she says it cracks me open, and I start laughing. Just a little at first, but soon all three of us get so worked up that I have to wipe tears from my eyes. Once we all calm down, Camilla starts the car, and we drive in silence for several minutes. Lewis keeps turning to look at me and shake his head in disbelief. This is definitely not what I expected from tonight either. "You guys glad you picked me for your documentary or what?" Camilla says.

Editing our footage of Camilla takes longer than I was expecting, and I know it's mainly because I'm slowing down the process. As Lewis uploads the videos, trims the clips, and starts stitching portions together, he moves at half speed so that he can show me each step and allow me to familiarize myself with the software. Even though it's slow work, it's actually kind of fun reviewing our footage and picking out the best shots. I'm particularly impressed with Lewis's camera skills. He was able to get some beautiful shots in conditions that were far from ideal. I'm sure Lucy will appreciate the cinematography.

We spend some time digging through old footage on the TV Production servers, looking for some clips of Camilla we can use as an introduction to our documentary. It doesn't take long for Lewis to pull up some film from a tennis tournament last spring. There's great footage of Camilla acing a few serves, and a couple of clicks later, I appear onscreen. I'm bouncing on the balls of my feet with my racquet at the ready, hair pulled back in a tight ponytail. The camera zooms out as a ball bounces into frame. I spring forward, slicing at it with both hands and grunting a little as I send the ball back over the net.

"This is kind of intimidating to watch," Lewis says. "You guys are like that clan of female warriors that Wonder Woman comes from. All powerful and focused."

I recognize the footage from the last time we played our big cross-town rivals, Lincoln High. "Ha! Yeah, I remember that weekend. We were all pretty worked up, I guess."

"I can't believe they made you give this up," Lewis says.

In the background of the shot, I can see Mallory and several of the other girls cheering me on. A swell of nostalgia starts rising in my chest, so I tap the esc key and close the video window before it crashes over my head. "Yeah, but now I have all this," I say, leaning back and gesturing around to the mostly empty studio, hoping Lewis doesn't notice the quiver in my voice. "You really like this stuff, huh?" I ask, desperate for a subject change.

"Yeah, I do," Lewis says. "My mom's a news anchor, so it kind of runs in the family, I guess. Cal and I just signed up sophomore year when we both had an open elective slot, and now somehow I'm senior producer."

"Maybe it's a sign. Maybe this is something you could do as a career."

"I don't know. I doubt they'll pay me to keep hanging out in this studio after graduation."

"Very funny," I say.

After a week and a half, we finally have twenty-five minutes of raw video trimmed down to a four-minute documentary with narration and music, and when it's perfect, I make us watch it three times in a row because I'm just so proud. It's interesting and insightful and just the type of thing that shows I'm capable of making even TV Production meaningful.

When we call Mrs. Hansen over to the studio, she watches the video with a clipboard in hand, taking notes. She watches it twice, and despite how much I think I know teachers, it's hard to read her expression. Her mouth is a straight line, and her eyebrows are flat, but Lewis doesn't look concerned.

"Very good," she says after the second viewing. She circles something on her clipboard, then lifts the sheet and hands it to us. There's a red 94 at the bottom of the page.

"A ninety-four?" I say. "Not bad for my first clip."

"Not bad at all," Mrs. Hansen confirms. "You guys had a creative idea, and I think you did a nice job executing it. You clearly work well together."

"So, can I add this to the lineup for next week?" Lewis asks. "I think we have a slot available on Wednesday."

Mrs. Hansen's smile falters. "Oh, I'm sorry, but we can't ever air this."

"What?" I ask. "But you just said it was great."

"It is. It's a great mini-documentary that shows a Groveland student engaging in criminal activity. We would all end up in Principal Wexler's office if I let that air."

"But—but . . . ," Lewis stutters, clearly trying to find some justification or form an argument that will change Mrs. Hansen's mind, but Mrs. Hansen shakes her head.

"I'm sorry, y'all," she says. "This really is great work. Keep going. Just, you know, maybe do one that doesn't involve breaking the law."

I watch Mrs. Hansen walk out of the studio, kicking myself for not realizing this before. Of course we would never be allowed to air a clip that basically endorses an illegal activity and focuses on how the subject intends to keep doing it. I should've known better. On the bright side, I guess Camilla doesn't have to worry about her secret identity being revealed.

"Well, that sucks," Lewis says, saving our work and closing the file. "I think this calls for an excursion." He stands and unplugs the camera. "Follow me."

I trail him out of the studio and up to the main office. The same old woman who denied me a drop slip a few weeks ago is behind the desk, looking just as stone-faced. Lewis doesn't hesitate. "Ms. Plaxico," he says, holding his arms out wide.

The woman looks up, and her face brightens considerably. "Lewis," she says, her mouth forming what looks suspiciously like a smile.

"How was your summer?" Lewis asks.

"Well, not great. My cat had to have an eye removed."

"Oh my gosh," Lewis says, clutching a hand to his chest. "Ulysses or Elroy?"

"Elroy." Ms. Plaxico sighs, lifting a framed photo from beneath the desk ledge. She turns it around, and there are two cats and three eyes staring back at us.

"I'm so sorry to hear that," Lewis says, leaning in closer to get a better look at the photo. "But he's tough, right? I'm sure he's taking it like a champ."

"I think he's being stronger than I am," Ms. Plaxico says.

"I'm sure you'll all get through it together," Lewis says. "Well, look, Hayley and I have our first off-campus assignment for TV Production this year." He pulls a slip of paper from his pocket and slides it across the counter. I catch a glimpse of what appears to be Mrs. Hansen's big looping signature at the bottom. "We're probably going to miss second period. Would you be kind enough to notify our teachers?"

Ms. Plaxico examines the sheet for just a moment and then smiles at Lewis. "Of course. You two be safe out there." She smiles at me, and I get the distinct impression she doesn't remember our interaction from a few weeks ago.

Lewis turns and ushers me out to the foyer. "So." He claps his hands together. "Coffee?"

"What was that?" I ask as we move out the front doors and toward the parking lot.

"Well, you see, sometimes TV Production clips do actually require students to leave campus for a bit, and I just happen to know where Mrs. Hansen keeps a stack of pre-signed forms. Hope you didn't have anything important going on in second period."

Fifteen minutes later, we're sitting outside Bad Pun Coffee with iced chais in hand, soaking in the unusually warm October morning.

"Should we be sitting outside like this?" I ask. "I've never cut class before. I'm a little paranoid about getting spotted."

"Would you rather go drink these behind the dumpster over there?"

"I'll just wear my sunglasses," I say, digging them out of my jacket pocket. "Maybe that'll be disguise enough."

"You AT kids are so precious," Lewis mocks. "With your perfect attendance and your . . . graphing calculators or whatever. You've really never skipped before?"

"No."

"You draw the line at bringing a flask to school, huh?"

"Touché," I say, tilting my cup toward him. "How many times have you done this?"

"This is actually my first time," Lewis confesses. "Well, my first time that didn't genuinely involve some real TV Production work. I hope Ms. Plaxico doesn't call my bluff and check in with Mrs. Hansen."

"Ms. Plaxico seems to trust you."

"We have a rapport," Lewis admits.

"I guess we should start thinking about our next clip, huh?" I ask.

"Or we could just sit here and enjoy what is likely one of the last warm days of the year," he says, lifting his feet into an empty chair. He looks out across the parking lot, and a breeze pushes some hair around his forehead. There's a comfort in hanging out with Lewis. He's not like so many of the AT kids, me included, who feel like they have to constantly work and claw their way up to the top, jockeying for some intellectual rank that only exists in our head. I don't feel like I have to lie with him or put on any sort of confidence mask the way I did when I was with Parker. As much as Parker might pretend to be a party-loving guy when the situation calls for it, I know he has compartmentalized his life. Evenings and weekends for socializing, school hours and afternoons for serious academic focus. He would never dare skip class for coffee, even if he knew it would cheer me up after a rough morning. Lewis is different.

I take a drink of my chai, letting the sweetness fill my mouth.

TWENTY

LEWIS

During the second weekend of October, one of the small local theaters is showing the 1988 Tom Hanks movie *Big* for five bucks, so Cal and Rebecca and I make a plan to meet there on Saturday afternoon. As I'm parking, my phone buzzes with a text from Cal.

Wow. Suddenly feeling very sick. Cough, cough. Guess you and Rebecca will have to sit in a dark room for a couple of hours by yourself. The end of the text is punctuated with two eggplant emojis and a big smiley face.

I send him a *Thank you* back since this is the exact plan (minus the suggestive emojis) we worked out last night when I stopped by his house during my evening run. With school and her job and editorial duties on her school's newspaper, I've hardly seen Rebecca over the past month. And when I have seen her, Cal is usually there too. If I'm going to use this year to become more intentional about acting on my feelings for Rebecca, I have to start with getting some genuine alone time with her. And there's no time like the present.

There's a knock on my passenger-side window, and I nearly fumble my phone. Rebecca laughs as I get out of my car. "Oh man, your face," she says, smiling broadly. I move around the back of the car toward her. "Did Cal text you, too?" she asks. "He's bailing."

"Yeah, he did. Hope he starts feeling better," I say, fighting down a grin.

It doesn't take us long to get settled into a couple of seats with our overpriced popcorn and soda cups so large they barely fit in the cup holders. There're only a few other people in the theater, which I guess is to be expected for a noon showing of a movie that came out more than thirty years ago. Rebecca slides low into her seat, propping her feet up onto the back of the chair in front of her and wrapping her flannel shirt a little tighter around her body. "Ugh, why are movie theaters always so cold?" she groans.

"So you don't fall asleep during the movie?" I guess, pointing the bag of popcorn in her direction. She takes a handful and mashes it into her mouth, her hand curving around her face to make sure she gets all the pieces.

"So ladylike," I say. In response, she opens her mouth and shows me a mass of yellow, half-chewed popcorn. "I've really missed hanging out with you," I say dryly. Despite my sarcastic tone, it's actually very true. The first month of school has been an adjustment period. I went from hanging out with Cal and Rebecca nearly every day to rarely seeing Cal outside of our morning car rides and lunch period, and most of my interaction with Rebecca has been over text.

"I've missed you, too," Rebecca says. "Things have been crazy with the newspaper already. Our budget got slashed, so Amaya and Kennedy have been pitching ideas for fundraising."

It's a little weird to hear Rebecca talk about her friends at Lincoln sometimes. I get so convinced that she and Cal and I are like the Three Musketeers that I forget when I'm doing stuff in TV Production or sitting in precalc, she's off living her own life and having her own experiences. That's the thing about wanting to be the leading man of my own life—I can easily forget that all my "side characters" are off being their own leads "off-screen."

"Amaya wants to have a bake sale, and Kennedy said we should set up some kind of kissing booth, which, by the way, how did that ever become a thing? People paying to kiss other people? That's just, like, diet prostitution, right? Like, I'm not crazy thinking that, am I?"

I laugh and pat my stomach. "Personally, I'd prefer the bake sale."

"You sure?" Rebecca asks. "You're looking a little slimmer these days." She gives me a playful poke in my ribs, and a redness blooms on my cheeks.

Last night, after talking to Cal, I ran two and a half miles without stopping for the first time. It was a gross and incredibly graceless experience where I listened to "Eye of the Tiger" on repeat and kept giving myself little pep talks, but I did it. That's almost a 5K, which I now know is just over three miles.

My parents don't own a scale, and I see myself in the mirror every day, so it's hard to tell if my body's changing. I have noticed that some of my button-ups seem a little looser, but that's about it. It's nice having Rebecca see my hard work, but I've stopped reading fitness blogs and browsing exercise Instagram accounts. I keep reminding myself about what Cal said. My weight, no matter what the number, isn't holding me back.

The movie starts up, and we watch as Josh Baskins makes a wish on Zoltar and transforms into an adult overnight and then gets a job and dances on a giant light-up piano. It's a fun movie, one we watched for the first time two summers ago during Cal's "Wish Fulfillment Week." It was a double feature paired with the significantly cheesier 1989 movie *Teen Witch*. Thinking about it now makes me wonder how many '80s movies I've sat through with Rebecca at my side. Dozens, at least. Hours and hours of us side by side, platonic and separate. Maybe today it's time to break the pattern.

I take a drink of soda and make a show of wiping the condensation on Rebecca's pant leg. She shoves me away, and I give her a light push back, letting my arm fall across the armrest. Before I can talk myself out of it, I rest my hand on hers. She looks at me, and I do my best to give her a genuine smile. When she turns back to the movie, she pushes her fingers between mine. Onscreen, Josh gives a glow-in-the-dark compass ring to his confused adult girlfriend.

After the movie ends, Rebecca and I don't talk about the hand-holding. She has to get to her shift at Graze Daze, so outside the theater, she gives me a quick kiss on the cheek and walks off to her car. I'm left standing on the sidewalk, wondering if I should text Cal and tell him our plan may have kind of sort of worked. But I don't really know what to say. *Hey, man, we held hands!* What does that really mean? It's new territory for Rebecca and me, but it's not exactly some big romantic moment. I'm still thinking it through when I catch sight of Hayley walking across the parking lot next to a lanky kid with cropped red hair. "Hayley?"

She looks my way and smiles. "Lewis? Hey, what are you doing here?"

"I just saw a movie with a friend," I say, motioning to the theater behind me. "What are you up to?"

She places her hand on the head of the boy. "This is my brother, Tanner. He's meeting up with some friends for laser tag." She gestures to the building next to the theater. I look up and see a neon sign that reads LAZER LABYRINTH in jagged letters. "Tanner, this is my friend Lewis; we go to school together."

"Hi," Tanner says a bit shyly.

"Laser tag, huh?" I say. "You know, I've never played. Is it fun?"

"Uh, yeah. It's like real-life *Call of Duty*," Tanner says.

For a moment, I consider telling Tanner that real-life *Call of Duty* would be joining the actual army, but I let it go. Another familiar face passes. An Indian kid with wavy black hair and rigid posture. Rohan Bakshi. He's also a senior at Groveland, and I interviewed him for TV Production last year when he won a statewide chess tournament. "Hey, Lewis." He nods.

"Hey, Rohan." He gives Hayley a small wave but doesn't stop. Just keeps moving past us on into Lazer Labyrinth.

"You know that guy?" Tanner asks.

"Yeah, he goes to school with us," Hayley says. "Why?"

"Because he's, like, a laser tag god."

"Rohan?" I ask. Tanner must be mistaken.

"Yeah, dude's always here. Goes by the name Specter. They have tournaments sometimes, and he always finishes in the top three. He's crazy good."

"You're sure it's that guy we just saw?"

"Yeah. He's cold. Comes in, doesn't really talk to anyone. Just gears up in silence, dominates a few games, and leaves. It's intense." A couple of other boys Tanner's age burst out of the building and come jogging up to him. They all start talking fast about laser tag and drag him back toward the door. Just before they disappear inside, Tanner turns back and waves at Hayley to follow. "Come on!"

She rolls her eyes at me. "Guess I've been summoned."

"Yeah, laser tag glory awaits," I say.

"Eh. He just wants me here because I'm paying. See you at school, Lewis."

Hayley heads inside, and I walk back toward my car. The idea that Rohan Bakshi, a guy who probably weighs 150 pounds soaking wet, is some laser tag legend is a lot to process. Chess champion, sure. Debate team captain, yeah. But laser tag *god*? No way.

Before I start my car, I pull up Rohan's Instagram page and scroll back through two years of photos, searching for a single mention of anything even remotely laser tag–related. But there's nothing. There are only pictures of him holding up debate trophies and a photo of him standing outside the Capitol when Model UN traveled to DC last spring. I jump over to Lazer Labyrinth's official site and find a tab labeled *Blog*. I tap it and scroll through several entries until I find a post from July titled "Summer Tournament Results." And there it is. A photo of the winners in the sixteen- to eighteen-age division. Rohan is in the middle, holding an engraved plaque and a gift certificate, his normal goofy grin replaced with a confident smirk.

Holy hell. I think I may have just found the perfect subject for our next documentary.

TWENTY-ONE

HAYLEY

W ell, our first TV Production assignment turned out to be a disaster," I say, blowing on my mug of steaming coffee as Dr. Kim settles into her seat across from me.

"Oh no. What happened?" she says, pushing her glasses up into her hair.

"We got a ninety-four." I shrug.

Dr. Kim squints at me. "A disaster. Truly."

For a moment, I consider telling her that to earn that grade, we had to run from the police and leap across buildings, but I'm not convinced Dr. Kim isn't reporting back to my parents about our sessions despite her promises of confidentiality, so I leave out those little details. "The grade was good, but Mrs. Hansen said we can't air the clip because it's about a girl doing graffiti, and graffiti is illegal. We worked so hard, and now no one's going to get to see it."

Dr. Kim lets out a short laugh. "You know, I remember a certain someone coming in here a month or so ago talking about how stupid TV Production was going to be. Seems like you're quite passionate about it now."

That's because it's currently the only shot I have at changing everyone's perception of me. Yesterday was the six-month anniversary of my car incident. I wasn't tracking it on my calendar or anything, but apparently Harold Lockner was. He posted a video on TikTok spoofing those sad animal adoption commercials, except instead of trying to get people to rescue puppies and kittens, he was telling everyone that they can "help crazy girls get the meds they need for only fifty cents a day," while Sarah McLachlan's "Angel" played over footage of me being pulled from my car by the police. Videos like that popped up a few times a week during the month after my incident, and they used to absolutely ruin my day, but not anymore. If I'm not going to be the Hayley who runs out of parties sulking, then I'm certainly not about to be the Hayley who lets a stupid video bother her. Instead, I'll let it drive me. But what's the point of being driven when no one can see what I've accomplished? How am I supposed to prove to everyone at school that I'm not the girl they think I am when we can't even air our documentary?

"I'm really quite proud of you," Dr. Kim says.

I'm suspicious. "Why?"

"Because you're *actually trying.* You got thrown a pretty nasty curveball at the start of the year, right? You were bitter about it. You could've taken that resentment and curled up into yourself, but you're not doing that. You're actually embracing the challenge. You're diving in. It's nice to see."

May the record show Hayley Mills has never backed down from a challenge. "I guess you're right. I thought it was going to be awful, but it's actually been okay. Lewis really loves this stuff. It's kind of infectious."

"Maybe, since you're trying new things and hanging out with new people, you might want to try something else new. . . ."

Ugh. Here we go again. Dr. Kim never misses an opportunity to remind me about the support group at State, even though I have no interest in sitting in some *kumbaya* circle and discussing my feelings with strangers. "I'm good," I say, and Dr. Kim lets it drop. For now. "I actually haven't even hung out with the other AT kids in weeks. What if I'm sacrificing my whole social life for TV Production and I'm not even that good at it?"

"Did I ever tell you I was in a sorority in college?" Dr. Kim says.

I sit up straighter and put my coffee aside. "No, you definitely didn't."

"Well, I was. Totally invested in the whole sisterhood thing. I loved dressing up and going out to bars and wearing short, sparkly dresses even when it was twenty degrees outside." I try to imagine a younger PhD-less Dr. Kim standing on a street corner shivering in the cold, her bare legs sticking out of a winter coat. It's nearly impossible to conjure the image. "For a while, everything was great. I was living with a bunch of fun girls, I was dating regularly, and I was keeping my grades up. But eventually the scales began to tip. My grades were slipping. I got too focused on my social life. I couldn't find the balance.

"One week my friend Jennifer from back home came to visit. And that week I had a big ecology test, so the night before, I told her I really needed to buckle down and study, and she was totally cool with just hanging out. But then some of my sorority sisters started drinking, and some boys showed up, and I couldn't resist having some fun. Jenn tried to wrangle me in, but I was a total mess. By two in the morning, I was hugging the toilet and crying."

"Wow," I say, working hard to picture the poised and professional Dr. Kim in front of me as a drunken mess.

"That night, Jennifer took care of me. And somehow, I stumbled to ecology class the next morning, but as you can imagine, the test didn't go well. That night, Jennifer and I had a long conversation about what was going on with me. She helped me realize that sorority life was just not healthy for me. So I quit the sorority. I had convinced myself that I was fine, and life was good, but Jenn helped me realize the truth. I was holding on to something that was destroying me. When you first started coming here, you had a death grip on so many aspects of your life, Hayley. You were scared to let even one thing slip. But over these past couple of sessions, it seems like you've been relaxing a little.

"Sometimes it takes someone from the outside pointing out that what you think is really important is actually killing you. Sometimes you have to be willing to let things go." I can't help but think about Mallory storming the shaved ice stand, demanding I stick with tennis no matter what, and the times Parker and I sacrificed sleep or social gatherings for long AT cram sessions. Did I show any warning signs before I succumbed to the pressure and stopped my car outside Groveland that morning? Would they have cared if I did? Could they have talked me back from that ledge? The questions swirl in my mind.

The next morning, there's a knock on the front door of my house at seven. I'm still half asleep, staring down a bowl of cereal, so I don't even consider protesting when Tanner yells, "I'll get it!" Somehow, he's the only morning person in our family. Sometimes when my alarm goes off, I can already hear him out back practicing his free throws. After a moment, he comes jogging into the kitchen and says, "Look who's here!"

When I glance up, Lewis is smiling at me, his face peeking out from a tray stacked with five coffees. "Lewis?" I croak, wrapping my robe tighter around my shoulders and pulling my glasses from the messy bun piled on top of my head.

"Hey, looks like you could use some coffee," he says, dropping the tray down on the counter in front of me. He starts sorting through the cups. "Let's see. You had a chai the other day, right? Here you go. I got a caramel latte here too if you would prefer that."

"Got anything for me?" Tanner asks.

"Ah, let's see." Lewis pulls another cup from the drink holder. "How do you feel about hot chocolate?" Tanner takes the cup and climbs onto the barstool beside Lewis. He flicks the lid off and starts licking at the whipped cream.

My brain is having trouble processing this whole scene. "Lewis, what are you doing here?"

"Getting a head start on our new documentary," he says, sliding his phone across the counter. On the screen is Rohan Bakshi's Instagram account.

"What am I looking at here?" I ask. Tanner leans over the counter to get a glimpse of Lewis's phone. "Rohan Bakshi?"

"Yeah, after I ran into you guys over the weekend, I did a little bit of research. I can't find a single mention of anything related to laser tag on Rohan's socials. But he's all over Lazer Labyrinth's blog. They have photos of him winning multiple tournaments. I wasn't sure I believed he was some laser tag champ when Tanner mentioned it, but it's true."

Tanner swallows a big swig of his hot chocolate. "Yeah, he's the best player in town."

Lewis presses both his elbows onto the counter and rests his chin in his hands, smiling broadly. A moment later, Tanner strikes the same pose, his mouth smeared with chocolate. I look back and forth between them. "How are you two . . . ? I don't like this."

Mom shuffles into the kitchen, cinching the belt on her robe. "Mmm, I smell coffee." She groans, her eyes barely open.

Lewis lifts a cup from the carrier and places it in front of her. "All yours."

She stares at him for a moment. Then, realizing she doesn't recognize him, pivots toward me. "Who is this strange barista boy in our kitchen?"

"Mom, this is Lewis. We're in TV Production together."

Lewis digs into his hoodie pocket and comes out with a handful of sweetener packets. "Cream and sugar?"

Mom takes a couple packs of sugar and two of the small cups of creamer. "I like this strange barista boy," she says.

"So, you want to film Rohan playing laser tag?" I ask, lifting the stopper from my chai and taking a sip.

"Exactly," Lewis says. "It's just the angle we're looking for, right? I'm guessing next to no one at Groveland knows about Rohan's double-oh-seven laser tag alter ego, so it could be really interesting. Plus, at least this time it will all be legal."

Mom stops stirring her coffee. "What does *legal this time* mean?" she asks.

Lewis's eyes widen. "Welp, gotta go," he says, picking up his coffee.

"Lewis," I say sternly.

"More coffee deliveries to make. People need their caffeine, you know?" He's already out of the kitchen and heading for the front door.

"Lewis," I call.

"See you at school, Hayley!" I hear, followed quickly by the sound of the front door slamming.

Mom stares me down across the island counter. "What a fun morning," my brother says.

TWENTY-TWO

LEWIS

The plastic laser tag vests at Lazer Labyrinth are heavier than I imagined. I adjust the weight on my shoulders while Hayley cinches the straps on her own vest, the lights on the shoulders and chest blinking alternating patterns of green and blue. Next to us, Rohan palms his big plastic laser gun while all around the room, other competitors slide on their equipment. A man with a patchy beard and a half-tucked Lazer Labyrinth polo shirt cups his hands around his mouth as he steps to the center of the room. "All right, let's go over the rules."

Hayley moves in closer to me.

Once she forgave me for barging into her house with coffee and getting her in hot water with her mom a couple weeks ago, Hayley agreed that Rohan would make an interesting subject for our second documentary. The problem was, neither of us were really friends with him, and we doubted he would be willing to take part out of the goodness of his heart. Thankfully, an answer came in the form of Hayley's friend Lucy. She overheard us talking about our idea before school one morning and casually mentioned that she thought Rohan had a crush on her.

"Really?" Hayley asked.

"I'm pretty sure," Lucy said. "He always sits next to me in study hall and sometimes asks if I have any weekend plans."

So Hayley recruited Lucy to help us. They flanked Rohan outside chess club one afternoon, both of them wrapping their arms through his elbows. I could practically see him melt from down the hall as Lucy twirled a strand of his hair around one of her fingers. They probably could've asked him to rob a bank with them and he would've volunteered to bring the ski masks. He was clearly disappointed this afternoon when I showed up with Hayley instead of Lucy.

"Most of you have done this before, but I'm going to review the rules for you newbies," the Lazer Labyrinth employee says. "When I open these doors, you will have fifteen minutes in the labyrinth. There should be no physical contact inside the labyrinth. No shoving, punching, or kicking. We spot you doing that shit, and you're gone. As you can see, you all will have blinking targets on your shoulders, chest, and back. Do not attempt to cover any of these targets. If we spot you doing so, you're immediately disqualified. No questions asked."

Hayley and I were pretty pumped after Rohan agreed to work with us, but what we failed to consider is that Lazer Labyrinth might not be too keen on allowing two noncompetitors to film inside their arena. We called them one afternoon and pleaded our case to the manager, but he stonewalled us and said, "You can't enter the arena unless you are actively involved in the tournament." Hayley looked pretty disappointed about that, but I had an idea.

"What is your policy on GoPro cameras?" I asked, arching an eyebrow at Hayley. She must have realized where I was going with this because she started frantically waving her arms and shaking her head.

The manager sighed heavily into the phone and said, "They're allowed as long as your hands are free." I smiled broadly at Hayley and nodded vigorously while she gave me a couple very enthusiastic thumbs down.

"Great, then we would like to sign up for the upcoming tournament," I said. Hayley dropped to the floor and pretended to die.

That's how we ended up here in this room with GoPro cameras strapped to our heads.

"It's going to get kind of crazy in there, you know?" Rohan says. He's speaking out of the side of his mouth, already trying to distance himself from us and definitely questioning his decision to participate in this documentary. I move my head at various angles while he checks his equipment, hopefully getting some usable footage. Hayley swivels her head around the room, getting a sweeping shot of the other competitors. There's a big guy in camo pants and a skinny kid with dreads and a girl in a tank top with intimidatingly toned arms. There's a guy wearing a hat with a set of crosshairs embroidered on it and another guy in all black and at least a dozen other random participants tightening their vests and fiddling with the guns. "I know you guys want to get interesting footage, but I need you to stay out of my way. Got it? I'm going to be moving quickly, and I don't need the two of you becoming an obstacle."

"Got it," Hayley says. "We'll keep our distance."

"All right," the employee says, clapping his hands. "When the doors open, there will be a twenty-second countdown before the game officially starts. Everyone ready?" There's a scattering of "yeah"s while Hayley locks eyes with me and shakes her head ever so slightly, a very subtle "no." I try to give her what I hope is a reassuring smile, but I'm nervous too. The employee pushes a button on the wall, and the arena door slides open. Everyone starts pushing forward and flooding into the labyrinth.

Hayley moves in close to me and whispers, "We're in over our heads!"

"Come on, your little brother does this all the time, right? How hard could it be?"

Inside the labyrinth, everything is black. The walls, the floor, the ceiling. Everything. There's a low-hanging cloud of fog around our feet, and multicolored laser lights shoot across the arena. Beams of green, yellow, and blue cut through the darkness. Rohan hesitates for only a moment, watching as his fellow contestants stream in all directions. They curl around walls and disappear down corridors. Then Rohan starts moving with purpose, and Hayley and I have to jog to keep up.

He runs along the outer wall and then cuts up a narrow ramp, moving to an upper level that's situated probably seven feet above the main floor. He darts past pillars and a staircase that leads back to the first floor and even a fireman's pole. I try to take it all in, but we're moving fast. On the second level, the wall is low, making it more like an extensive balcony. Below us, there are flashing vests swarming around, and I pause for a moment to try to get a good shot. When the overhead countdown drops below ten, I head back toward Hayley and spot Rohan crouching behind a bunker. Hayley is nearby, sidled up against a column.

"I hope I'm actually getting something good," she says, motioning to the camera mounted to her forehead.

I lift my arms to rigid angles, doing a robotic shuffle dance to the beat of the loudspeaker countdown. "Oh, you're definitely getting something good."

Hayley smiles, pulls her laser gun from its holster, and blasts me right in the chest.

"That's cold," I say.

"Three . . . two . . . one," the countdown announces. Then a horn blast echoes through the arena.

When the alarm sounds, Rohan stands up and fires off a couple quick shots before ducking back to the bunker. I move to the opposite wall so that I'm getting the action at a different angle. Just when I think I've found a good position with a nice line of sight on Rohan, my chest vibrates, and I notice two guys crouched near the stairs. One of them must have tagged me. Since I'm only here to get footage of Rohan in action, my gun isn't even out of its holster. When the guys hit me two more times in quick succession, Rohan looks up.

"Dude, if you keep letting them tag you, you're gonna skew the scores," he barks.

I fumble for my gun, hoping some return fire might make my attackers retreat, but the pistol is big and awkward. Rohan moves over to me, and I think he's going to help, but when he posts up behind me, I suddenly realize I've just become a human shield. The two guys by the stairs peek again, and Rohan fires off some shots that send them scuttling back to the main floor before I can even get my gun aimed. Rohan rolls his eyes at me, then moves back down the ramp. Across the way, Hayley gives me a thumbs-up, letting me know she got that whole humiliating exchange on camera.

We follow Rohan around the lower floor of the arena for several minutes, trying to keep close without getting in his way. It's tough. He rarely stays in one place for too long. Instead, he constantly moves from pillar to window to corner, tagging individuals once or twice before moving on, often hitting them in the back or shoulder. Before they realize what has happened, Rohan is already gone. That must be why he goes by Specter here. He moves like a ghost. The evidence of his presence is all around, but he's nearly impossible to spot. This footage is going to be a pain to edit. It's going to be all dark and jumbled, like *The Blair Witch Project* but with lasers.

The overhead horn lets out a quick blast followed by a robotic voice announcing, "One minute remains."

Even though I think he's already moving at top speed, somehow Rohan picks up the pace. He darts down a hall that looks like a dead end, but then another space opens up to our left. This place really is a labyrinth, all narrow alleys and dark walls, but it's clear Rohan has every corner memorized. He could probably do this blindfolded. He picks off a couple more competitors, and then I recognize the flight of stairs from earlier. Rohan takes them two at a time, and Hayley and I are right behind.

When we get to the top, all hell breaks loose. There are at least ten competitors packed into the second level trying to get off good shots and avoid being hit, but the space is too tight. There's no maneuvering room, so people are right next to one another. Guns are pressed right against vests like a laser tag mugging. Rohan twists to head back the way we came, and I try to follow, but someone else moves toward the ramp, a big guy making the most of his weight. Others start shoving back, and the siren overhead starts beeping, counting off what I'm guessing are the final seconds of the match. Everyone's in a frenzy, swarming like jostled hornets. I get pinned against the wall, and just over my shoulder, I see it. Hayley loses her balance, stumbling back against the fireman's pole and failing to take hold. Her arms windmill, looking for any sort of grip, but there's nothing. Someone screams. She falls out of sight, and I hear her hit the ground with a sickening thud.

TWENTY-THREE

HAYLEY

There's a half-naked girl in laser tag gear staring down at me. She's topless, with only the black plastic vest covering her essentials, and on the bottom she's wearing frayed jean shorts and heels so tall I imagine she's going to have a difficult time maneuvering off the hood of the hot rod she's sitting on. Her platinum-blonde hair is pulled into a high, tight ponytail, and she's kissing the end of her plastic laser gun.

"Yeah, I, uh, was told I wasn't allowed to take that down. Sorry."

I roll onto my side, the cracked leather of the old couch sticking to my arms a bit. Lewis is sitting in a small green office chair. He's looking up at the poster too, a disapproving frown etched into his face. Behind him sits a cluttered desk topped with a boxy computer that seems to be at least a decade old. There's a brown filing cabinet in the corner, and next to it is a tall cardboard box overflowing with discarded laser tag gear. Another poster hangs on the door. Two bikini-clad brunettes pretend to shoot each other with laser guns while an unseen hose sprays water over the entire scene. My vision starts to blur, and I suddenly have a new respect for the decor in Dr. Kim's office.

Lewis leans forward. "How are you feeling?"

My back is throbbing, and my brain feels constricted, likes it's been squeezed into a skull that's two sizes too small. "Not great," I say, blinking a few times. I go to sit up, and a fresh jolt of pain shoots across my shoulders. I let out a low grunt, and Lewis lunges forward.

"Whoa, take it easy. You had a pretty nasty fall."

"What happened?" I ask, inching my feet onto the floor. I try to work back in my memory, but it's foggy. "Did someone tackle me?"

"Something like that," Lewis says. "You fell off the second level. A couple of employees helped me get you onto the couch in here."

"Mmm. Well, that was nice of them."

"Not too nice. They were all very quick to remind me that you signed a waiver releasing Lazer Labyrinth of all liability, so. They did find some Advil, though. Here." He leans over and hands me two small pills and a paper cup of water. I wash the capsules down and rest my head against the back of the couch.

"Why don't you lie back down for a minute?" Lewis says. He stands and gently hoists my feet up while I let my head fall toward the armrest. That's when I realize the stupid GoPro is still strapped to my head. I try to lift it off, but the strap gets caught in my hair.

"Here. Let me help." Lewis frees the headset and places it on the side table. "I'm very much looking forward to watching that footage," he says.

Despite the migraine, I can't keep the smile from creeping onto my face. "Great. Another embarrassing video of me to add to my growing YouTube collection."

Lewis reaches over and brushes a few strands of hair from my face, then starts gently massaging the top of my head. I melt into the couch just a little. This is something I certainly never pictured for my time in TV Production. Lying on a crusty couch in a disturbingly decorated laser tag office being cared for by someone I barely knew two months ago. I crack my eyes open, and Lewis smiles at me.

"Is this weird?" he asks.

"A little," I say. "But keep going."

"Then Lewis insisted on driving me home," I say. "I thought it was a little overly cautious, but it was a nice gesture. He called his friend Cal to come pick up his car so he could drive mine."

"Wow," Lucy says. "That sounds intense." She's bent over a small mirror on the counter, applying gray makeup to her face. Halloween is always the final night at the shaved ice stand before we close for the season, so Lucy and I tack up orange string lights and plastic skeletons, and Mrs. Cambridge tells us to sell everything at half price. Word has gotten around, so parents usually swing by with their kids after an evening of trick-or-treating. "You sure you're okay?"

"Yeah. My back was sore for a couple days, but I'm feeling better now." Lucy pushes up the sleeves of her shiny silver jacket and leans in to add some black circles around her eyes. "So, you're a zombie astronaut?" I ask.

"Hell yeah," she says without looking up.

I pick up her camera and snap a couple of pictures of her. "Could you just not choose between the two?"

"Well, I wanted the fun of being a zombie, but I also liked the statement of being a female astronaut. Dismantle the patriarchy, you know?"

"Wasn't Mallory Scott an astronaut last year?" I ask.

"Hardly. She was a sexy astronaut, remember? All she did was write NASA on a crop top and wear a pair of fake glasses."

"Oh yeah. And Tyler Nash was supposed to be an alien, but he just painted his chest green and wore some antennae."

"Yeah. It looked like they were about to shoot a space-themed porno."

It feels good to laugh with Lucy. "I've missed you," I say. "I've been so focused on TV Production lately that it feels like we've hardly seen each other."

"I know. You're too busy off living your life of adventure. Almost getting arrested and nearly getting a concussion."

I reach back and touch the base of my skull. I guess there are some things I haven't told Lucy about. "Lewis massaged my head," I say.

Lucy puts her sponge down and pivots toward me. "He massaged you?"

"Not in a gross way. It was really sweet, actually. After I fell and he got me the Advil, he sat there and rubbed my head until the migraine dulled."

Lucy's eyebrows shoot up, and she purses her lips. "How did you conveniently leave out that little detail? So there's, like, something going on with you two now?"

"No. Maybe. I don't know," I say. It's something I haven't spent a lot of time thinking about, honestly. Maybe there's something there, but it's hard to tell. I do look forward to spending time with Lewis. He's funny and genuine, and when we're working on our documentaries together, I don't really miss tennis too much.

Lucy just smiles and shakes her head. "Well, when you figure out what's going on, let me know," she says, uncapping a tube of black lipstick.

Once the sun disappears beneath the horizon, trick-or-treaters begin arriving, and Lucy becomes fully committed to her zombie astronaut. "Cool makeup," a little girl in a princess dress says. "Do you eat brains?"

"Yes," Lucy replies. "Brains are important. Not only do I eat them, but I also have a large brain myself. I have a PhD is astrophysics. You don't want to have to rely on Prince Charming, do you?" The little girl gives her mom a confused look, and the whole thing is pretty hilarious. Lucy really puts my Ninja Turtle costume (which consists of a shell design painted on a green shirt, a red eye mask, and some red sweatbands) to shame.

By ten thirty, all of the kids and their parents have dispersed, so we switch off the orange lights and put up the CLOSED FOR SEASON sign. Lucy fills two cups with ice, and we flavor them with syrup.

"To another successful season," she says, tapping her cup against mine. "Our final season."

Sometimes it feels like senior year is just a series of extended good-byes, and this is the first one. I know this job is just one facet of my and Lucy's friendship, but I'm still sad to let it go. I'm going to miss our hours squeezed into this little shack. "Maybe it doesn't have to end," I say. "Who really needs college when we already have such a lucrative career?"

"Too true," Lucy says. "I don't see anything wrong with just earning minimum wage at a business that's only open six months of the year."

"Well, this could just be the start. We'll need to find some investors to build our shaved ice empire. I mean, Starbucks started with only one location, right?"

"Oh God, how do we not have pumpkin spice syrup? That alone could keep us in business another two months of the year."

"See?" I laugh. "You're already revolutionizing the shaved ice industry."

"I bet if we slap up a 'gluten-free' sign, profits would go through the roof!"

I know we're joking, but part of me really does wish we could figure out a way to make this last a little longer. The daily arrival of new college material in my mailbox reminds me that the future is coming whether I want it or not. Catalogs and pamphlets have piled up on my desk, and occasionally I sift through them and try to imagine myself living in a new place. There are universities in northern towns where I envision myself in a heavy wool coat walking through snowdrifts to get to class. There are schools in big cities where I think of myself spending time at little pastry shops and navigating public transportation. There are schools on the coast where I think of myself wading into the tide and sitting around bonfires on the beach. After a while, it starts to get overwhelming, and I just leave all the pamphlets in a pile.

I've spent my whole time in high school working toward getting into a great college, but now that it's almost here, I'm hesitating. Every time I envision myself in one of those scenarios, it doesn't seem right.

When I was little, I had a felt board in my room with heads that you could put on different bodies. There was the head of a little girl, and you could make her a cowgirl by putting her on the body with a vest and a lasso, or you could make her a ballerina by giving her the body with the pink tutu. That's what envisioning myself at college feels like these days, like I'm just taking my head and trying to plop it on a different body. It didn't use to be this way. Before my incident, Lucy and I used to dream about college all the time. She would talk about heading off to California, and I would imagine myself studying in a comfortable coffee shop before going out to dinner with some brilliant guy who may or may not have had a British accent.

But not anymore. Now I'm not even sure I can handle college. Despite my commitment to *being the pond scum* and showing everyone at Groveland that I'm still as smart and accomplished as I've always been, there's still a nagging voice in the back of my mind reminding me of my failures, whispering that the pressure of any collegiate premed program could crush me.

Lucy tosses her empty cup into the trash, then bends down and switches off our little space heater. Tomorrow, we'll come back and take down the Halloween decorations, but we'll only stick around long enough to throw them into a box under the counter. As we lock up, I feel like one of us should say something, that we should share some kind of moment that recognizes the finality of tonight, but there's nothing. Lucy gets into her car, and I get into mine, and we both leave the small, dim hut in our rear view.

TWENTY-FOUR

LEWIS

When Cal gets into my car, I hand him a sausage bagel and latte that I picked up from the Bad Pun drive-through on the way to his house. He accepts them with hesitation. "It's not my birthday," he says, removing the stopper from the coffee and giving it a sniff.

"Are you checking to see if I poisoned it?" I ask. "Do you need me to take a drink of it first to prove I didn't mess with it?" Admittedly he's right to be a little suspicious. There have been times I've messed with his food at Graze Daze. But what can I say? It's pretty funny to watch someone take a sip of their drink after you've secretly stuck an open ketchup packet at the end of their straw.

He gives me one last suspicious glance, then takes the smallest of sips. After a second, he risks a larger swig and seems satisfied, so I start driving us toward school. "Seriously, what's the occasion?" Cal asks.

"No occasion. I just wanted coffee this morning and thought I would pick something up for you, too."

"Well, thank you," he says, unwrapping his bagel and taking a large bite.

"Also, Hayley's going to be your coanchor on the announcements this morning," I say, quickly adding, "Man, what a beautiful day, huh?"

"Oh, come on!" Cal says, his mouth full of half-chewed breakfast. "I knew this was a trap."

"It's going to be fine. Apparently, she was interested in introducing our documentary clip, and Mrs. Hansen signed off on it. I may be senior producer, but I can't go above Mrs. Hansen's head."

Cal shakes his head in disbelief. "Damn Mrs. Hansen for always seeing the good in everyone."

When we get into the studio, Hayley is already sitting at the anchor desk reviewing her script. She has on a navy blazer, and her hair is curled. With her glasses, she looks particularly professional, especially compared to Cal, who's wearing a polo shirt that now has a noticeable coffee stain next to the pocket. She straightens her papers and smiles at us as Cal takes his place beside her.

"Things are pretty straightforward this morning," I tell them. "Nothing complicated production-wise, and as you can tell from the script, it's a pretty short show. The only clip we have is the Rohan piece at the end. Hayley, you'll set that up, and when we're done, we'll come back to both of you for a little reaction banter to close us out, so be ready."

"I'll try to stay awake," Cal says. "I can't believe you all did a clip about Rohan Bakshi. What did he even do, give his opinion on local politics?"

"You'll see." Hayley smirks.

At eight thirty, I give the cue and we go live. Hayley is incredibly poised. I don't know how early she got to the studio, but she somehow has several portions of the script memorized. She stares down the camera with the confidence of someone who's been doing this for years. Cal has a natural charisma onscreen, but Hayley nearly matches it. As much as I was working to reassure Cal in the car, I'll admit I was a little nervous. Some people crack when the red light above the camera comes on and they realize they're suddenly being broadcast live to all of their peers. Not Hayley, though.

"And now we have a piece on Groveland senior Rohan Bakshi," Cal says, pivoting toward Hayley. "I understand you helped produce this piece, is that right, Hayley?"

"That's right, Cal. Rohan is the captain of Groveland's debate team, and he's been active in Model UN since he was a freshman. But there is more to him than meets the eye. My colleague Lewis Holbrook and I recently had a chance to spend some time with Rohan while he engaged in one of his favorite hobbies. Let's take a look."

I can't help but smile. Not long ago, she was mocking me for using words like "post," and now Hayley's behind the anchor desk referring to me as her colleague. I give the cue for the sound booth to play the clip.

Our documentary about Rohan begins with two guys onscreen, a couple of seniors we caught just outside Groveland's theater. One of them is in a green Groveland High hoodie, and the other has a beanie that sits toward the back of his head, his long black bangs sticking out of the front. From off-screen, Hayley asks, "What do you know about Rohan Bakshi?"

The two guys exchange a look, each wondering who might speak first. We didn't tell them exactly what we would be asking before we started filming. Eventually the guy in the hoodie says, "Rohan? He's pretty quiet."

"Yeah," the guy in the beanie confirms. "I think he was in my English class last year. No, wait. I might be thinking of somebody else. Do you have a picture of him?"

The image cuts to two girls in front of a brick wall. "Rohan?" one of them says. "He's, like, really smart."

"Oh yeah, really smart," the other confirms. "Like, future million-aire smart. He's on the debate team, right?"

Hayley's voice-over starts up as the video cuts to Rohan walking along Groveland's front hall, his hands clasping the straps of his back-pack. "Rohan Bakshi is probably not the first person you'd notice in the halls of Groveland High. He's not flashy or loud. On the surface, he's quiet and reserved. Like Clark Kent. And, like Clark Kent, he's hiding an alter ego."

The video cuts to Rohan putting on his laser tag gear. Footage I recorded with my GoPro, slowed down and brightened in post. He lifts the vest over his head and adjusts the shoulder pads. "Rohan Bakshi is a laser tag champion," Hayley announces.

The footage cuts to some quick interviews we conducted at Lazer Labyrinth before the match.

"Rohan? That guy's amazing," an employee says.

"He's a legend around here," Hayley's brother adds.

"They call him Specter," a girl with half of her head shaved says. "You'll play a match with him, and you won't see him the whole time, but somehow he tags you, like, a dozen times."

The music picks up in tempo, and the image transitions to the footage we captured before Hayley took her fall. A montage of Rohan sprinting through the fog of the arena. Rohan lifting his gun and firing off several shots. Rohan ducking and dodging, moving with a grace he's never demonstrated in the halls of Groveland. After several seconds, the clip switches to an interview we conducted with Rohan outside Lazer Labyrinth.

"Most people don't know anything about this side of you, Rohan," Hayley says from off-screen. "They only know the version of you they see at school. Is there a reason you keep this part of your life secret?"

Rohan is silent for a moment, squinting off in the direction of the sun. Then he shrugs. "Eh. I wouldn't call it a secret necessarily; I just don't broadcast it. Who I am at school, that's me. Who I am here, that's me too. One isn't more genuine than the other. I can be more than one thing, you know?"

As the clip winds to an end, I cue the tech room to cut back to the live feed of the anchor desk. Cal is sitting there with his mouth hanging open, and Hayley is smiling confidently. I have to stifle a laugh.

The clip turned out perfect. Hayley and I spent several long afternoons in the studio splicing the footage together and finding the perfect music. I admit that I was hesitant about this whole senior documentary idea when Hayley first pitched it to me, but now I'm sold. Watching the reaction from Cal and the other students in the tech booth as the video aired was priceless. They were surprised and fascinated, and it filled me with a sense of triumph. I can't wait to show Rebecca.

I know there's a fair amount of students who just scroll through their phones and completely ignore the announcements altogether, but maybe we can make them take notice. Maybe Hayley and I can make something really good.

I wave my arms at Cal and gesture to the red light over the camera, letting him know he's on the air. He snaps upright. "Well, that was . . . unexpected," he says, turning toward Hayley.

"Thank you, Cal. That is the first in a series of documentaries we will be producing this year, spotlighting certain members of our senior class." She pivots toward camera B as we shift to her close-up. "If you're a senior and interested in being a subject in one of these upcoming documentaries, there will be a sign-up sheet posted outside the TV studio. Simply write down your name, your email address, and a talent or skill you have that not many people know about, and we'll be in touch."

Two days after our documentary about Rohan aired, the sign-up sheet we posted outside the TV studio was full. We added a second sheet, and by the end of the week, it was full too. People started tacking up Post-it notes with their info. On Friday afternoon, Hayley and I collect everything and spread it out between us on a table at Bad Pun Coffee. As we work through the names, I'm surprised to find that only a handful of them are clearly fake. Betty Humpter. Phil MaCrackin. You can guess what kind of things they wrote for their hidden talent.

Looking at all the notes is overwhelming. I don't know how to sort them, and before I can think of the best way to proceed, Hayley slaps her hands down on the table so hard it jostles the sugar packets. "Okay. So first I say we get rid of the ones that are clearly boring or creepy," she suggests.

At first I think she might be joking, but then she uncaps a red

Sharpie and starts making her way down the first page. "Poker champion? I'm not interested in filming someone sitting at a card table for hours. Sorry, Chuck Billows." She makes a long red slash across the paper with a flourish. It's fun to watch her get so excited about this stuff.

She offers the pen to me, and I scan the list until I come to another bad one. "Amateur taxidermist? Definitely not, Sean Rutherford." I draw a red line, and Hayley laughs a little. Maybe this isn't such a bad method of sorting after all. When we're done with the first pass, a quarter of the list is gone.

Next, Hayley rips a piece of paper from a spiral notebook and slides it across the table. "Okay. Now you go through and write down the top ten that seem the most interesting to you. I'll do the same, and then we'll compare lists." I know this maybe isn't the fairest way to judge our possible subjects, picking them on a whim of whatever strikes our fancy, but I can't think of a better process, so I take another pass at the list. After fifteen minutes, we both push our lists to the center of the table for comparison.

"Really? The girl who said she's learning to unicycle is in your top ten?" I say.

"That could be really interesting!"

"Watching someone fall off their unicycle a bunch of times is not interesting. We're looking for people who already have well-developed talents. Not people who are trying to get them."

"Fair, but what about you?" Hayley asks. "You put Nick Paulson on your list."

"Yeah, he says he's a stand-up comedian. I thought that could be really funny."

Hayley places her hand on top of mine. "Oh, sweetie, no. Nick is on the boys' tennis team, and one time he sat next to me on the bus during the drive to a tournament. He's not funny. There were a lot of fart jokes that I'm pretty sure would've even made my little brother roll his eyes."

I concede. "Well, how could I have known that?"

"Let's just focus on the ones we both like," Hayley suggests.

I scan our lists. There are four matches.

TWENTY-FIVE

HAYLEY

As winter settles in, November becomes a blur with Lewis and I working hard to crank out new documentaries on a weekly basis. Class time is spent arranging filming schedules and editing, and our afternoons and weekends are dedicated to recording.

First, we film Angus Li, a local cup-stacking champion, as he competes in a statewide tournament. I didn't even know competitive cup-stacking was a thing until Lewis showed me some YouTube videos, and even then, I was still pretty confused. The atmosphere is tense in the community college gymnasium as competitors gather around their tables and stretch. Once the competition starts, Lewis and I record as their hands fly, building up towers of cups at an unnatural speed and breaking them down even faster. I try to remind Lewis that we're sup- posed to be unbiased journalists, but he can't hold back his cheers when Angus takes second place overall. He accepts his trophy with very little enthusiasm, just a curt smile and a small nod to the crowd. As we're interviewing Angus afterward, Lewis asks him if he's going to drink some celebratory sparkling grape juice from his cups, and Angus doesn't even crack a smile. He just motions to his cups and says, "No, these cups are strictly for stacking."

Next, we film Rachael Matthews, who is a total goth, but she also makes handcrafted kites in her garage. This time, Lewis was the skeptical one. When he heard "kites," I think he was picturing basic diamonds of cloth stretched across two sticks, but Rachael creates true works of art. When we step into her garage, I audibly gasp. There are kites that look like pirate ships, with multiple sails; kites that look like dragons, twisting and winding; and kites that look like birds, frozen midflight. They're all beautifully intricate, and it's fascinating to watch her work as she sheds her long black coat, wraps a bandanna over her purple hair, and dives in. The only bad part, is the weekend we film her is noticeably not windy. We convince her to let us take some of her work to a local park, but she knows they won't fly, so she refuses to even try. We end up with a lot of unusable footage of Lewis running through a field, dragging around a stunning kite while a small group of middle schoolers on bikes laugh at him from the parking lot.

After that, we film Isaac Iverson, who's been consistently playing lead roles in all the school musicals since freshman year, as he does wood carving. I don't mean little two-by-fours hammered together to make a nice birdhouse wood carving. I mean taking an honest-to-God chain saw to large branches and pieces of downed tree trunks to make sculptures of eagles and foxes and even, oddly enough, a handful of Pokémon. When we're in his workshop, I ask him what the biggest thing he's ever made is, and he gestures to an item in the corner covered by a tarp. Pulling off the covering, he reveals a small canoe with seating for one. "There's a creek that runs through the woods back there, so I made this over the summer." Lewis's eyes light up, and we all trudge down to the half-frozen creek to get some shots of Isaac pushing his vessel into the water. He doesn't travel very far, but it doesn't matter because the winter sun is setting, casting long orange streaks across the whole scene as it cuts through the trees, and it's just beautiful.

In order to keep producing one documentary a week, Lewis and I are spending more time together than ever. Our afternoons become a quick after-school run through the Bad Pun drive-through and then back to the Groveland studio for at least a couple hours of editing. Usually by the time I leave school, the sky is already a deep purple. One evening, I find Parker leaning against my car in the parking lot.

"Hey, what are you doing here?" I ask.

He motions back toward the school. "We had a student council meeting that ran long, and when I came out, I saw your car was still here, so I thought I'd wait for a few minutes to see if you showed up."

"Here I am," I say, extending my arms. A tinge of guilt stabs at my stomach. I know several unreturned texts from Parker have stacked up on my phone. I've been so busy with school, it's easy to let them go unanswered.

"Here you are," he says, giving me a quick hug. "What are you still doing here?"

"Editing. Trying to put the finishing touches on another mini-documentary."

"You guys have really been cranking those things out, huh? Feels like they've sort of taken over your life a little. I've hardly talked to you at all this semester."

I can understand why Parker would be surprised by my sudden devotion to TV Production. If our roles were flipped, I would certainly be confused too. But the roles aren't flipped. While Parker continues to get complimented for his charm, his smarts, and his leadership skills, right now, these documentaries are all I have. People have stopped me in the hall and at lunch to tell me they enjoy them, and teachers have talked to me about how their class perks up a little on Friday mornings when we introduce a new clip. For the first time in months, I'm not immediately filled with anxiety when I see someone has tagged me in a post online because these days, it's just someone sharing the YouTube links to my and Lewis's work. Still, I'm not going to try to explain all this to Parker right now. "I know. I'm sorry. Guess I've been pretty preoccupied."

"Well, I wanted to see what colleges you ended up applying to," he says.

"What?"

"What colleges did you apply to? I know a lot of the ones you were considering had their early decision deadline last week."

He's right. I think of all the deadlines I have flagged and highlighted in the brochures beside my bed. I've tried to apply to some places, but the process is exhausting. This concrete vision I used to have for college feels increasingly fuzzy, and I can't seem to conjure the image with any clarity these days. How am I supposed to convince an admissions officer that I deserve a spot at their school when I know there's a fault line running through my brain that might shift at any moment? Besides, it's just early decision, I tell myself. I still have time to figure things out. I don't need to panic. *I am not panicking.* "Yeah. I, uh, I actually haven't applied anywhere yet."

"Really? Not even UNC?"

I shrug my backpack from my shoulders and open my back seat. "Nope. Still mulling things over," I say, tossing my bag into the car.

"I thought for sure you'd at least have a couple applications in."

I really don't want to talk about this right now, and I especially don't want to talk about it with Parker. He's probably already got multiple colleges locked in a scholarship bidding war to get him to commit. "Just want to think about it a little more, I guess," I say. I lift my hand to look at the wristwatch I'm not wearing. "I better get home. My mom wants to have a family dinner tonight."

"Oh, okay. Hey, let's grab a coffee or something soon," Parker says.

"For sure." I nod, already climbing into the driver's seat and turning the ignition. I pull away, giving Parker a quick wave without really looking back.

TWENTY-SIX

LEWIS

By late November, people are starting to talk a lot about college. Rebecca is looking for a school with a good journalism program, and Cal is just hoping to head anywhere that will afford him more opportunities to golf. I keep scrolling through various college websites, thinking I might find something that catches my eye, but a lot of them look the same. *Oh look, another group of racially diverse students sitting in the grass in front of an old stone building.* I guess I don't really know what I'm looking for because I have no idea what I want to study. Dad keeps saying I should major in "something practical," but when I google "practical college majors," most of the articles point to computer science and engineering, neither of which seem particularly interesting.

Mom got me a book from the library that promises to be "the ultimate resource for choosing the right college." I find it sitting on my bed one evening, and I flip through it for about thirty seconds before melting into a puddle of apathy. The thing is a brick. Just page after page of tiny print with information about student body sizes and admission standards. I take a selfie with the thing and send it off to Rebecca.

I think my mom is trying to tell me something.

A moment later she replies. *Looks like you've got some reading to do. Let me know if you need any help with the bigger words.*

Some evenings I toss on a hoodie and go out running to give myself time and space to think. Winter running is not my favorite, when it's as dark as midnight at six p.m. and the freezing winds scratch at my cheeks and knuckles, but there's something rejuvenating about feeling the cold air fill my lungs as I jog through the neighborhood. I know I should be working on coming up with a plan for after graduation. How can I truly be dedicated to becoming more intentional about how I'm living when I can't even decide what to study or where to study it? Shouldn't a leading man know what he's interested in? Shouldn't he have some kind of inner compass to help guide him?

Unfortunately, things aren't going much better with my plans for pursuing Rebecca, either. On the first evening of Thanksgiving break, I'm sitting in a corner booth at Graze Daze nursing a milkshake and pretending to read through my college guidebook while Rebecca works the register at the front counter. Occasionally, she circles the dining room, wiping down tables and stopping for a bit to talk to me between customers. It's good to see her in person, but we haven't had any real alone time together since our movie outing more than a month ago. Our schedules just never seem to line up. When I'm free, she's working, and when she's available, I'm buckled down in the TV studio. I have been sending her links to my and Hayley's documentaries since I remember how excited she was when I first told her about the idea. She always seems to enjoy them, but I would love to actually sit beside her while she watches, talking to her about the process and sharing some of what went on behind the scenes. We can't really do that—or much of anything else—when I'm just hanging out at her job. What am I going to do, ask her if our hand-holding meant anything to her while she fulfills drive-through orders?

When I look up, Rebecca is smiling at me as she walks along behind the Graze Daze counter, slowly lowering her body so that it looks like she's descending an unseen flight of stairs. I smile and get up to go talk to her, but then a couple of families with a disturbing number of children plow through the doors, and Rebecca turns her attention to them. On the table, my phone vibrates with a text from Hayley.

Hey, where are you?

Just hanging out. What's up?

I'm at the football game. You should come check it out. 😉

The text is punctuated with a winky face emoji. Hayley has sent me emojis before, like thumbs-up or the occasional crying-laughing face when I make a joke, but winking seems flirtatious. People aren't out there shooting off winky faces all fast and loose, are they? Something unexpected lights up within me at the thought that Hayley might be interested in me. Or maybe I'm just reading too much into a simple text. Either way, hanging out at the game with Hayley sounds a lot better than trying to pick some colleges. I close the book, give Rebecca a parting wave, and head out the door.

There's always a flag football game on the Wednesday before Thanksgiving. The coaching staff and a few other brave teachers take on the football seniors as a fundraiser, and the crowd turnout is usually pretty high. Once I purchase my ticket and get into the stadium, Hayley waves me down from up in the bleachers. She's standing next to several other girls whom I recognize as members of the girls' tennis team.

"Hey, Leeeeewis," Hayley says. She wraps her arms around my neck and pulls me close. We've never really hugged before, so the move catches me off guard, and I stumble a bit, unsure of where my hands should land. I place them on her waist and, after a moment, ease back so I can look her in the face. Her cheeks are flushed, and her smile is big.

"I didn't know you were a football fan," I say.

"Lucy and I are hanging out after. She's taking pictures for yearbook." She motions down to the edge of the field, where Lucy has her camera poised and ready. "These are some of my friends from tennis. Do you know Mallory?" Hayley gestures to the girl beside her. She has brunette hair and is sporting an expensive-looking down coat.

"Not really," I say, giving a little wave. "Nice to meet you."

Hayley sends her voice into a mock British accent. "Lewis Holbrook, Mallory Scott. Lady Scott, allow me to introduce you to Sir Holbrook." She covers her mouth in a useless attempt to conceal the giggle that comes spilling out.

Mallory's mouth twists into a wicked grin as she watches Hayley's face shift to a brighter shade of red. "Charmed," she says, extending her hand daintily toward me and also speaking with a British accent, though not nearly as pronounced as Hayley's.

"The pleasure's all mine," I say, taking her hand gently. "Do I kiss this now or . . . ?"

Hayley's laughter rises an octave, and she slaps Mallory on the arm. "See? I told you he was funny."

Mallory tilts her head at me. "Yes, you did."

We all take a seat, and it doesn't take long for the chill of the metal bleachers to press in through my jeans. I look around and notice a lot of other people have blankets or cushions they're using as padding. I don't even have gloves, so I stuff my hands into my coat pockets. On the field, the coaching staff is celebrating a touchdown, high-fiving and jumping around as the seniors wave them off. Lucy raises the large lens of her camera to get a shot or two.

Mallory hands a bottle of Sprite to Hayley, who takes a long swig. She wipes her mouth with the back of her hand and smiles at me, pushing the bottle against my side. "You should have some of this," she says, arching her eyebrows mysteriously. I unscrew the top and bring the bottle to my lips, but the smell hits me first.

"This isn't Sprite," I whisper, like this might be new information for Hayley.

"I know," she says with a snicker, looking back at Mallory. Mallory and a couple of the other girls smile at me expectantly. I notice Camilla is not among them.

I turn my attention back to Hayley. "This bottle's half empty," I say. Again, probably not new information.

"Or half full, depending on how you look at it," she says.

"Was it completely full at some point?" I'm thinking I already know the answer. Hayley places a finger on the side of her nose and slides it toward me, confirming my suspicion. The buzzing inside me that had been growing ever since I got Hayley's winky face text slides from excitement to concern.

"Okay," I say, placing the cap back on the Sprite bottle. "Well, I think we've had enough for today."

"Nooo," Hayley whines, placing her hands on top of mine. "I wanted to share this with you!"

I lower my voice to a whisper, hoping Mallory won't overhear. "That's very nice, but maybe this isn't the time." I look around, paranoid that Mr. Rosco or another administrator might pop up and apprehend us. After the flask incident, there would surely be no leniency this time, not with Hayley clearly already well on her way to drunk.

"I'm being the pond scum," she says.

"The what?"

"The pond scum. You remember." She holds her hands together, as if she's holding an invisible ball. Slowly, she expands them, mimicking an explosion. "Pssssssssh!" I literally have no idea what she's talking about.

"Yeah, we should get you home," I say.

"The game's not over, Lewis," Mallory says, staring me down and placing a hand on Hayley's knee. Her glare is intimidating, and I internally kick myself for being unnerved by a girl with cat-eye makeup. Still, I get the feeling something bad is happening here. Mallory's sober intensity makes it clear she hasn't been drinking nearly as much "Sprite" as Hayley.

"Yeah, we're watching the game!" Hayley insists, suddenly standing. "Go, Groveland!" It's not really clear who she's cheering for since technically everyone on the field is from Groveland. Some of the other spectators around us turn to look at her, and sweat begins dampening my armpits. The construction crew in my mind is scrambling. I can't just take the bottle and throw it in the trash or convince Hayley to leave without making a scene.

One idea works its way to the center of my mind: don't do anything. It seems so dumb, but the more I consider it, the more it makes sense. So what if Hayley gets a little loud? This is a football game. Most people here are loud. As long as she doesn't get sloppy or start vomiting, we should be fine. It's not like someone's going around inspecting beverages for secret alcohol, right? Once the game's over, I can recruit Lucy to help.

Despite feeling marginally okay about the plan, sitting through the last half of the game is torture, especially as the girls continue to pass along the bottle and I watch all of them take gingerly sips while encouraging Hayley to take big gulps. What's happening here? I thought these girls were Hayley's friends. I keep worrying Hayley's going to slip off the bleachers or start slurring, but it turns out I was right. People don't really care if you're loud and passionate during a football game. In fact, people around us keep high-fiving Hayley and cheering with her, even adults. At one point Hayley makes up a little dance to cheer on our Groveland Wasps. It involves putting a finger on her butt and shaking it like it's a stinger. When Mallory whips out her phone to start recording Hayley, I know I should intervene, but all I can think to do is stand and dance too. I unzip my coat and lift my whole shirt up so that it covers my face as I shake my stomach. It's extremely embarrassing (not to mention cold), but I figure anyone who may see that video will be too distracted by the chubby kid gyrating to even notice Hayley.

When the final whistle blows, I'm so relieved that it's time to leave, I don't even know who won. As we begin to make our way down the bleachers, it becomes very clear that Hayley is not doing well with walking on her own. I do my best to prop her up in a way that appears totally natural, but keeping her upright is kind of like holding a bundle of Slinkys. Mallory and the other girls do little to help.

Once we get to solid ground, Lucy spots us, and I frantically wave her over.

"I gotta catch my ride," Mallory suddenly says. "You got her, right?"

"Uh, yeah, I guess, but—"

"Great! See you later, Hay!" She turns and disappears along with all the other tennis girls into the crowd of fans streaming toward the parking lot.

"Lucy!" Hayley exclaims, wrapping her friend in a headlock.

"What the hell?" Lucy says to me, her neck trapped in Hayley's grasp.

"Yeah. We have an issue," I say, happy that backup has arrived.

"Do you want some *not Sprite?*" Hayley snickers.

"What did you do to her?" Lucy asks.

"Oh no, no, no. I had nothing to do with this. She was like this before I even showed up. It was Mallory and some other girls from the tennis team."

"Mallory?" Lucy asks, and the way she says it, I can tell there's some history there that I'm not aware of.

Hayley puts her face very close to Lucy's. "I'm being the pond scum, remember?"

"Oh God," Lucy moans.

"She keeps saying that. What does it mean?" I ask.

"It's just some nonsense she came up with. We have to get her off school grounds now."

"Yeah, did you drive?"

"She was my ride." Lucy sighs.

"Well, she's obviously in no condition to drive."

"Yeah, I might cause another incident!" Hayley exclaims, teetering a bit from Lucy's grip and then righting herself.

"I'll get her keys," Lucy says. "Help me get her to the car."

TWENTY-SEVEN

HAYLEY

Okay, my friends smell good. Lewis and Lucy are on either side of me, and we have our arms around one another, so we're real close. I lean toward Lucy. She is surprisingly warm and smells like a mix of vanilla and the ocean. Lewis smells like a man, like he lives in a tree house and bathes in fresh rainwater and uses a pine cone as a hairbrush. He looks over at me, and I wink at him. I wonder if he can smell my lavender shampoo. The woman in the commercial bewitches a cute barista with just a flip of her hair. Maybe I should try that. I lower my head and whip it back seductively.

"God, she's squirrelly," Lewis says.

Oh yes, it's definitely working.

The November air is cool on my face. I love the fall. "Oh, Lucy, let's jump in a pile of leaves!"

"Maybe when we get home, Hay," Lucy says. She and Lewis are moving me through the parking lot fast, and when I look over, I see why. Harold Lockner is leaning up against his stupid car with half the soccer team and their girlfriends, standing around like he's holding butthole court. God, he has such a punchable face.

I can't do this. I can't keep letting everyone be intimidated by Harold and his merry band of douche canoes, so I dig my heels in and shift in his direction. "There he is! Harold COCKner!" I yell. *Ha! Nice one, Hay.*

Lucy grips my arm tighter and tries to keep me moving, but I'm not having it. I ratchet my arms and escape her grasp, marching closer to Harold. The sudden movement makes me feel a little shaky, but I steady myself and point a finger at him. "That's you! Harold COCKner. 'Cause you're a dick."

"Oooh!" Harold's friends are all smirking.

"Damn, man," Tyler says. "You gonna let her talk to you like that?"

"She's just messing around," Lewis says, appearing beside me. "She's been doing it to everybody. Totally burned me earlier with some sick Yo' Mama jokes. All right, Hayley, time to go." He takes my shoulders and tries to pivot me away, but I stand firm.

"No, I need to say this." My tongue feels big in my mouth, but I'm determined to get the words out. "Harold, you are dumb. And your car is not adequate compensation for your shitty personality."

Harold's mouth twists into a grin. "Is she drunk?"

Am I drunk? If this is drunk, I don't hate it. My blood feels like it's buzzing through me, electrifying my muscles and nerve endings. I'll have to thank Mallory later. I thought I was going to have to sit by myself at the game, just waiting for Lucy, but then Mallory insisted I sit with the team. It was so nice to see everyone finally putting their anger about my decision to quit tennis in the past. They were even super generous with that special Sprite, which was nice because Sober Hayley would never confront Harold like this. "I'm serious," I say. "Your car is sad. I mean, compensating much?!"

Harold's boys "Ohhh," and now I realize some of them have their phones out. A sizable crowd has gathered. Good. Maybe I can show everyone that we don't have to just accept Harold's bullying. Maybe if people see someone finally putting him in his place, they'll follow suit. I start to lay out a list of all the things Harold needs to change in order to be an actual decent human being, but I only make it about halfway through before Lewis and Lucy start pulling me away again. This time I let them since I think I've made my point. When we start making our way through the crowd, there's a sudden jerk on my left, and I turn to see Parker pulling Lewis around.

"What the hell is going on here?" he asks, staring down Lucy and then Lewis.

"You mad, bro?" I say, laughing before I even finish getting the words out. God, I really am funny tonight.

"We're just trying to get out of here," Lewis says.

"Is she drunk? What did you do?" Parker asks, the anger rising in his voice.

"Why do people keep thinking this is my fault?" Lewis says.

"Well, she never even touched alcohol when I was dating her, so I know she didn't do this on her own."

"I'm fiiine," I say, starting to feel irritated. Parker isn't my boyfriend anymore. I don't need him taking care of me. I already confronted Harold, so I might as well set the record straight with Parker, too. "I did do this on my own. I've been fine without you this year, Parker. I don't need you defending me against Harold or reminding me about college. It's exhausting, dude." Parker reaches out to touch my shoulder, but I lurch away. "Go be perfect elsewhere!"

"Ouch, *dude*," Harold says, mimicking me.

"Oh, shut up, Harold," I say. "I'm not even sure you know how to read."

Some people in the crowd laugh, and it feels good. Lucy and Lewis go to move me, but Parker grabs hold of Lewis's arm.

"Seriously, man? Is this really the time?" Lewis sighs.

Cal appears, putting one hand on Lewis's shoulder and the other on Parker's. "It's really not. Because we're on school grounds and there are still parents around, and in about thirty seconds, the administration is going to be here and we're all going to be in big trouble."

"Yeah, we need to get out of here now," Lucy says. "You boys can have this dick-measuring contest later."

"Are y'all really fighting over that bitch?" Harold yells. "I mean, I heard crazy chicks are great in bed, but damn."

"What did you say?" Parker hisses, turning back toward Harold. Harold stands up straight, readying himself for a fight, but then, just as Cal predicted, the administration shows up. Mr. Keith speeds through the parking lot in a little golf cart with Wexler in the passenger seat yelling through a bullhorn that we all need to disperse. It's honestly not a very intimidating sight, especially since they've strapped what appears to be a novelty police light to the top of the cart, but people start running in every direction. Lucy and Lewis whirl me around, and the electric current of my blood rushes to my head. Lewis tosses his keys to Cal and asks him to drive his car home.

When Lucy unlocks my car, I crawl into the back seat and lie down. She and Lewis climb into the front and start shouting about directions or something. Then the car starts moving. Quickly. Lewis and Lucy keep bickering, but I can't make out what they're saying exactly. Their voices fill the car like a white-noise machine. During the drive home, I look up out the window, watching as telephone poles and trees blur by. It's very soothing.

TWENTY-EIGHT

LEWIS

This should be fun," Lucy says, pulling into Hayley's garage. She hits the button on the remote attached to the car visor, bringing the garage door down behind us.

"Are we going to have to *Weekend at Bernie's* her inside?" I ask.

"Weekend at what?"

"*Weekend at Bernie's*. It's a movie where some friends have to pretend their boss isn't dead, so they put sunglasses on him and walk him around like he's still alive."

"That sounds like nonsense."

"Well, it was the eighties." I look back at Hayley. She's lying across the seat, the side of her face smooshed against the leather. "Do you think her parents are home?"

Lucy steps out and I follow suit. "Their car is gone," she says, making her way to the side door and opening it quietly. She peeks into the kitchen for a moment, then makes her way back to the car. "I think the coast is clear. We should hurry."

We open the back door of the car, and Lucy reaches in to shake Hayley. "Hay, time to wake up. We're home, okay? You need to do some walking now." Hayley groans but doesn't even lift her head. Lucy pulls at her coat until she's sitting upright. "Come on, we need to get you to bed." Hayley begins to fall back across the seat, and Lucy tries to catch her, but it's pointless.

"I don't think she's going to be able to do this on her own," I say.

"Okay." Lucy sighs. "Let's just carry her in."

Moving her isn't easy. Lucy gets her legs rotated, and I run to the other side of the car and crawl inside so I can lift Hayley's upper body while Lucy pulls. It's a clumsy, tiring effort, but after several moments, we have Hayley out of the back seat. Lucy has her legs, and I have my arms under Hayley's so that her back is resting against my chest.

We move slowly, stopping every few feet to readjust the weight. Eventually, we make it to the side door, and Lucy kicks it open. When we step inside, Hayley's little brother, Tanner, is sitting at the kitchen counter drinking a Capri Sun and staring at us. We all freeze, none of us really knowing how to proceed.

"Uhhh," Tanner says after a moment of silence just long enough to allow a nervous sweat to sprout on my forehead.

"Hi, Tanner," Lucy says too cheerfully.

"Hi, Lucy," Tanner says. "What's up?"

I look down at Hayley's body. Her eyes are closed, and her head is slouched. I thought having to deal with Harold and Parker was going to be the worst part of my evening, but apparently not.

"Well, as you can see," Lucy starts, "Hayley's not feeling very well. She got a little sick at school, so I thought we would help get her up to bed and tuck her in."

"She looks half dead," Tanner says.

"Well, u-uh," Lucy stutters.

"That's kind of my fault," I chime in. "Hayley told me she wasn't feeling well, and I gave her some medicine. But I accidentally gave her the nighttime version, so it kind of knocked her out on the ride home."

"Uh-huh," Tanner says slowly, squinting at me. I suddenly feel like a suspect staring down the detective in a police procedural. Who knew middle schoolers could be so intimidating? More than anything, I'm worried that if Tanner's home, it could easily mean Hayley's parents are here too.

Lucy looks back at me. "Well, I don't know about you, Lewis, but this is getting kind of heavy for me," she says, hoisting Hayley's legs a little. "Why don't we get her upstairs?"

"Lead the way," I say. Tanner's eyes follow us as we move out of the kitchen and through the living room. "Good to see you again, Tanner," I call out as we reach the stairs. It's not easy to make our way up, but we manage. Once we get to the second floor, Lucy shoulders open Hayley's door and drops her legs onto the bed while I maneuver her head to the pillow.

Lucy and I stare at her for a moment. Her breathing is loud and deep.

"I thought you said the coast was clear," I hiss.

Lucy moves to shut Hayley's door. "It was when I looked, but then it took us some time to get her out of the car. I guess her brother came home and we didn't hear him."

"God, I knew we should have *Weekend at Bernie*ed this."

"It's fine," Lucy says. "Tanner will be fine. I've never had any issues with him."

"Have you ever shown up holding his unconscious sister in your arms before?"

"Relax. I'll talk to him." Lucy sits back down on the bed and starts taking off Hayley's shoes.

Hayley's room is messier than I envisioned. There's a long desk under her window covered in so many university catalogs that some have started to spill onto the floor. Looks like she's about as decisive as I am when it comes to college. On the wall, there's a framed photo of her and Lucy jumping on a trampoline. They're both midair, looking at each other and holding hands. They look young.

"You guys have been friends a long time, huh?" I say.

"Me and Hayley? Yeah. We met in fifth grade when my parents moved here. That picture was taken the summer before freshman year. We spent hours on that trampoline. Once, I almost broke my wrists because we were having a contest to see who could bounce the other person the highest, and Hayley sent me flying off the thing." She strokes Hayley's hair. "Even then she was competitive."

I look over at the dresser in the corner of the room. The top is covered in trophies of various sizes, the tallest of which could probably double as battering rams. Over the dresser hangs a corkboard covered in even more awards. "Seems like she wins a lot," I say.

"Yeah, winning kind of means a lot to her. It really drives her. I think that's why her car incident has shaken her so much. She's achieved a lot at Groveland, and now all people see her as is the girl who had a breakdown."

I've spent so much time with Hayley over the past few months that I hardly even think about her breakdown. When I think about Hayley, I think about coffee runs and darting across rooftops and lounging in weird laser tag back offices and long editing sessions in the studio, but I suppose not everyone has had those kinds of experiences. "You really think that's all people remember?" I ask.

"Sort of," Lucy says. "That's why she's so dedicated to the documentaries you guys make. Sure, she wants to show that people are more than their surface perceptions, but mainly I think she likes that she's the one pointing that out. She's getting the pats on the back she's always craved while possibly getting people to reevaluate their perceptions of her."

For the first time, I'm realizing just how personal our TV Production work is for Hayley. It's not just about getting a good grade; it's about rebuilding her reputation. "You think she's going to be okay?"

Lucy sighs, placing her hand on Hayley's forehead. "Tonight? Yeah, I'll stay with her. Maybe this will be some kind of wake-up call."

"What do you mean?"

"I just don't really see why she's so worried about all this stuff. People are gonna think what they're gonna think. Why try to change that? It's just high school."

I get what Lucy is saying, but as easy as it might be to try to dismiss stuff as just high school, what people say tends to stick with us, no matter how much time passes. I have vivid memories of people making fun of my weight—jokey comments and stupid nicknames that actually stung—and those weren't recorded and saved to the internet for mass consumption, so I can only imagine what Hayley's been through. "I don't know. Wouldn't you try to change peoples' misconceptions about you if you could?"

Lucy deadpans, "Lewis, I'm one of, like, a dozen Black people at our school. Our mascot is a wasp, for God's sake. You think people don't have misconceptions about me?"

"Touché." Maybe Lucy's right. I've been fine with Hayley and me knocking out these documentaries on a weekly basis because I think they're fun and interesting, but maybe this pace isn't so great for Hayley's mental health. Maybe we should slow things down. "So what now?" I ask.

"Now I guess I settle in for the night. Probably go talk to Tanner. Thanks for helping me get her here."

"No problem. Will you text me with updates?" It's hard to leave, but I'm not sure there's anything else I can do. I'm so out of my element here, and I have a feeling when Hayley wakes up, she'll be happier to find Lucy hanging out in her room rather than me. Plus, Lucy seems more equipped to handle this, so we exchange numbers and she promises to keep me posted.

I descend the stairs as quietly as possible, slowly easing my feet into the carpet to muffle my steps. When I make it to the first floor, I hear the TV going in the living room, so I rush out the front door and don't look back.

TWENTY-NINE

HAYLEY

I wake up in bed sweating. It takes a moment for me to realize it's my own room because at first everything seems kind of foreign, but it comes together in pieces. My bookshelf. The trophies on my dresser. The collage of glossy photos tacked up next to my closet. The green numbers on my bedside clock glow 4:37. I rub my eyes and realize I'm wearing jeans and a sweater. No wonder I'm so hot. *How did I get here?*

Somewhere in the back of my throat, there's a burning, a warning that whatever's bubbling in my stomach won't be contained much longer. I swing my legs off the bed and discover Lucy curled up in a sleeping bag on my floor. Standing too quickly, I nearly collapse backward. I don't have much time to right myself because I need to get to the bathroom. Urgently. I'm a weaving, stumbling mess as I move down the hall. Once I'm in the bathroom, I shut the door and run to the toilet, where I promptly vomit.

It's a clear, burning bile that comes in several heaving waves. When I spit out what I hope is the last of it, I look up to find Lucy leaning in the door wiping the sleep from her eyes. "Welcome to your first hangover," she says groggily.

I drop my knees onto the dark blue floor mat and rest my head on the rim of the toilet. All I can do is groan. Lucy steps into the bathroom and shuts the door behind her. She grabs a small cup from the counter, fills it with water, and hands it to me. "Thanks," I manage.

Lucy sits down beside me and rests her back against the tub. I sip the water gingerly. The coolness is nice against my raw throat, but I'm hesitant to add anything else to my turbulent stomach. Lucy rubs my back and says, "You had quite the adventure."

"Oh God," I say, closing my eyes. "What happened?"

"You tell me."

"Apparently I got drunk."

"Great detective work, Sherlock."

I open my mouth to tell Lucy I don't appreciate her sarcasm, but another wave of nausea sweeps over me. I stick my head into the toilet but only end up dry heaving a few times. It's nice to have Lucy here to help me, but I'm not thrilled about her seeing me in such a crippled state. Once the impending urge to vomit passes, I strip off my sweater and lie on my back. The coolness of the bathroom tiles feels nice against my bare skin, and my head rests in Lucy's lap. She runs her fingers through my hair and says, "I would say you better not throw up on me, but I took these pajama pants out of your drawer, so I guess it's okay."

I laugh, and it sends a jolt of irritation through my gut. "Ugh. Don't make me laugh."

"Okay," she says. "Your parents are out of town?"

"Yeah, they went to pick up my grandparents for Thanksgiving. They'll be back in the morning."

"Well, that's good, I guess. I kept trying to think of what I was possibly going to say to them to explain why I was here and you were passed out in bed. Then your brother told me they were gone."

"Oh God. Tanner. What did he see?"

"Not much. Just Lewis and me carrying your lifeless body up the stairs."

My eyes shoot open. "Lewis was here?"

Lucy looks down at me. "You think I was able to get you into bed by myself?"

A wave of embarrassment hits me, making the waves of nausea seem more like ripples. "I was kind of hoping I made it there on my own."

"Definitely not. What exactly do you remember?"

I close my eyes and try to retrace my memory. There are only brief glimpses of recognition, tableaus of my evening. I see myself at the football game with Lewis and . . . Mallory? She hands me a bottle and laughs. I see myself in the Groveland parking lot talking to Parker. Are we fighting? I see trees passing by overhead as I lie in the back seat of a car. "Not much," I admit.

Lucy fills in the details. She tells me about Lewis waving her down at the game, about the confrontation in the parking lot with both Harold and Parker, and about how she and Lewis carried me to my room. It's a lot to take in. Hearing that I basically turned myself into a huge burden for my friends is incredibly humiliating. Shame settles in, dulled only by the fact that I can see on the clock that it's just after five in the morning and I can barely keep my eyes open. Lucy helps me back to my room, where I sleep off and on for the next several hours. Around eight thirty, we get up, and Lucy graciously makes coffee. She asks if I want anything for breakfast, but even the thought of food sends my stomach lurching. I massage my head while we sit at the kitchen table.

"I'm assuming this is not what you were envisioning when you decided to 'be the pond scum,'" Lucy says, stirring some sugar into her coffee.

"Yeah, not exactly what I had in mind."

"Why were you even hanging out with Mallory Scott?"

"I don't know. I thought maybe we could be friends again. And there were other girls there from the tennis team. I miss them."

Lucy reaches across the table and places her hand on top of mine. "I know, but you have to be careful. I mean, they got you drunk and then abandoned you, Hay. Thankfully, Lewis and I were there to pick up the pieces this time."

I know Lucy's right. I wanted to show people that I'm still fun, that I'm not just another high-strung AT kid, but I still have to be smart. Clearly I owe Lucy one. And Lewis. And from what Lucy told me about last night, it sounds like I might owe some other people an apology. "Tell me about the parking lot again," I say.

"Which part?" Lucy asks, blowing the steam off her coffee. "When you called Harold Lockner 'Harold Cockner' or when you told Parker to 'go be perfect elsewhere'?"

Ugh. I'm certainly not about to waste time feeling sorry for Harold, but Parker surely didn't deserve to be berated. This whole year, he's only tried to be a friend to me, and I've been distant and dismissive. I make a mental note to reach out and apologize to him.

A minute later, Tanner walks into the kitchen. He goes to the freezer, pulls out a box of Eggos, and pops two in the toaster. "You feeling better?" he asks, looking at us from across the island counter.

Lucy gives me a look. "Uh, yeah, a little," I say.

"That's good. You were really out of it last night."

"Yeah, about that." I stand and cross to the counter. It takes a little extra effort because the pounding in my head has me feeling unsteady. "We should keep that between us, okay? I wouldn't want Mom and Dad to worry."

Tanner looks at me for a moment. He takes a seat at the counter, leans forward, and laces his fingers in front of him. A wicked smile forms on his face. "Okay. I think a new video game would keep me too busy to tell them anything."

"Are you serious?" I say.

"Otherwise, who knows what might slip out at Thanksgiving dinner today with Grandma and Grandpa here."

I stare him down, wanting to call his bluff, but he doesn't back down or break eye contact. "Fine," I say begrudgingly. "I'll take you to the store later."

Tanner's smile widens. The toaster dings, and he hops off the stool to grab his food. "Pleasure doing business with you," he says on his way out of the kitchen, twirling the syrup bottle on his finger.

"Damn," Lucy says. "That kid's cold." I go back to the table and bury my head in my arms. The idea of facing Thanksgiving hungover kind of makes me want to start drinking again.

THIRTY

LEWIS

On Monday morning, Hayley meets me at our locker with a folded piece of paper. On the front, she's drawn two stick figures, one with red hair saying, "I'm sorry!" to the one who's flexing some bulging stick-figure muscles.

"That's us," she says. "You can tell that's you because that stick figure is so strong, and a little birdie recently told me you had to carry me to bed."

"Yeah, I think I have some vague memory of that," I say, opening the card. On the inside, it's the same two stick figures, only this time they're both holding giant cupcakes.

"That's us after you've forgiven me," Hayley says. "Look how happy we are!"

It's a pretty good card. "So are you telling me we're going to go get cupcakes?"

Hayley smiles and pulls two wrapped cupcakes from behind her back.

"Are you serious?" I ask. "You just one-upped my card apology. Do you have to do everything better than everyone else?"

Hayley shrugs. "Do you want the cupcake or not?"

"You know I want that cupcake," I say, tacking her card up on our locker door next to the one I drew back at the start of the semester.

We walk to TV Production eating our treats. If it's wrong to eat cupcakes at eight in the morning, I don't want to be right. "Seriously, though, sorry about what happened at the game," Hayley says. "I may have seen a video of you outdancing me on Mallory's Instagram."

Oh no. With everything that happened with Hayley after the football game, I kind of forgot about what went down during the game. How could I ever forget the sound of half the girls' tennis team laughing at me while my shirt was pulled over my head? "Wonderful. So glad that's getting shared."

Hayley pauses for a moment, turning toward me and placing a hand on my arm. "Well, I could tell what you were doing, and I want you to know that I really appreciate it. And I'm sure Lucy was glad you were there too."

"She's a good friend," I say.

"Yeah. She is," Hayley agrees.

I spent the weekend thinking about everything Lucy told me in Hayley's bedroom. I don't want to keep pushing us to produce our documentaries at such a fast pace if it's not good for Hayley, if it's only feeding her anxiety around how she's perceived. "Hey, what do you think about slowing things down with the documentaries?" I ask. "We've already done five this semester, which means we only need to turn in one more segment to fulfill our class requirement, and I don't know about you, but I could use a little more time to focus on my other classes now that we're about to get into finals."

"I guess that's a good point," Hayley says. She chews a bite of cupcake and considers my proposition. "Okay. One more. One final amazing documentary this semester."

"And you remember who's next on our list, right?"

Hayley smiles. "How could I forget?"

Brie "B. B." Baker is five foot one and has unequivocally the bubbliest personality of the entire Groveland student body. With her thousand-watt smile and a walk that borders on skipping, she's basically a Disney princess. Seriously, she kind of constantly seems like she might burst into song at any moment, and I wouldn't be surprised if birds flew into her room to help dress her each morning. Her radiant positivity practically makes Mr. Keith look like Eeyore. That's why it's so weird to be following her through a local cemetery just after midnight on Friday night.

"So, B. B., how long have you been a ghost hunter?" Hayley asks, her cold breath coming out like a cloud that dissipates instantly.

"Well, first off, I don't really like the term 'ghost hunter,'" B. B. says, pausing and pivoting toward Hayley. I shift the camera to zoom in on her face. "Hunters go out to kill and destroy. I'm a paranormal investigator. I want to see a ghost, maybe get one on film if I'm lucky, but it's not *hunting* really. It's more like being a bird-watcher. Except I'm looking for spirits." She pauses and points her phone and flashlight toward the mausoleum several yards away. Brie records all of her exploits to post on her own personal YouTube channel. Hayley and I watched some of her videos earlier this week, and it was fascinating. She goes to these dark and creepy places, inviting the spirits to show themselves, but her voice is so light and sweet that it's kind of like listening to Mary Poppins narrate a horror film.

We move through the rows of headstones in silence, the only sound our shoes pressing into the frozen grass and the occasional crack of a tree branch. With the lingering fog and the all-encompassing darkness pierced only by the beams from our flashlights, I have to admit this place is pretty spooky. I have a new respect for B. B. considering she usually investigates places like this solo.

"And have you ever seen a ghost?" Hayley continues with her questions.

"Depends on who you ask," B. B. says. "Most people would probably say no because I've never caught any on camera before. But I've definitely felt the presence of something. I've got footage of things moving unexpectedly and unexplainable shadows. One time, I even heard the voice of a little girl singing."

Oh, hell no. Of all the ghosts I definitely don't want to encounter tonight, child ghost is at the top of the list. Followed closely by old-timey soldier ghost and then dog ghost. Unless the dog ghost is like the ghost of that dog that plays sports in all those movies. That might be kind of cool.

B. B. pulls out a small device that she says can record the voices of ghosts. She asks questions into a microphone and watches the blinking lights on the device's screen as they bounce around from green to yellow and red. For half an hour, we follow her around while she asks, "Are there any spirits here this evening?" and "Do you want us to leave?" As the moments pass and nothing really happens, my terror level drops, replaced by rising concern that hypothermia may be setting in as I begin to lose feeling in my fingers, and it gets harder to operate the camera. After a while, B. B. asks us to give her some space because she thinks it might help her commune with the spirit world a little better. So she drifts off to an open part of the cemetery while Hayley and I take a seat beneath a large oak tree.

"Why did we wait until December to do this one? I'm freezing," I say, zooming in to get a shot of B. B. as she extends her hands to the sky.

"Oh, hold on, I've got something that might help," Hayley says. I watch her flashlight beam bounce as she runs off to her car, and when she comes back, she sits down and tosses an unzipped sleeping bag over our shoulders. "I keep this in my car for when I spend the night at Lucy's."

"Nice," I say, pulling the fabric closer. I put the camera down and breathe into my hands.

"Here," Hayley says. She pulls off her gloves and takes my hands in hers and starts rubbing them together, building heat. "Better?"

Her face is so close to mine that I can make out the ridges of her lips. "Yeah. Thanks."

We both turn and watch B. B. as she moves slowly around the field, stepping with delicate precision. We're quiet for a moment, and then Hayley says, "This documentary's going to be bad, isn't it?"

It's so precisely what I'm thinking at that exact moment that a bark of a laugh escapes me, splitting the silence of the cemetery, and I quickly use my hand to cover my mouth. "Yeah, I think it is."

"Should we . . . I don't know. How can we make this better?"

"Short of getting an actual ghost to show up, I'm not sure there's much we can do."

Hayley's phone vibrates in her pocket. At first, she ignores it, but her leg is pressed against mine, so I feel it when it vibrates three more times in rapid succession. She pulls it out and her expression falters. "Oh no."

"What is it? Is everything okay?"

Hayley taps on one of the notifications, and a video loads on her screen. Initially, I just see her standing in a parking lot, but then I realize Lucy and I are there too. The Hayley onscreen stumbles forward and slurs, "Yeah, get a shot of this, Harold COCKner!" Several more notifications pop up at the top of Hayley's screen.

"Harold posted this?" I ask.

"Of course he did," Hayley says, watching Lucy and me struggle to redirect the intoxicated version of her.

"What an asshole. Don't even give him the satisfaction of watching this."

"I should've known Harold always gets the last laugh," Hayley says quietly. Her gaze lingers on the screen a few seconds longer, but then she says, "You're right. I don't need to watch this." She mutes her notifications and slides her phone back into her pocket.

I know the lingering embarrassment that clouds my thoughts after most of my interactions with Harold, so I'm no stranger to what Hayley's feeling now. Still, I don't even know how to comfort myself after my run-ins with that guy, so I definitely don't know how to make Hayley feel better. I wish I could figure out how to put the right words in the right order, but nothing seems to click. It's pushing one in the morning, and the construction crew in my mind called it a night long ago. As I'm still trying to think through a response, a vague glowing light appears across the field near B. B.

"No way," I mutter.

Hayley looks up. "That's not . . . I mean, it—it couldn't be . . . ," she stutters.

I turn the camera back on while Hayley stands and tosses off our sleeping bag. We move across the field as the light builds in intensity, lighting up a huge patch of fog. B. B. is frozen, her phone aimed right at it. I do my best to keep the camera steady, praying a herd of ghost adolescents are not about to descend on us like the scary choir boys in the "Total Eclipse of the Heart" music video that Rebecca, Cal, and I have laughed at on YouTube so many times.

Then the fog splits, and the light is blinding. We all shield our eyes as a darkened figure moves in close. As the beam drops and the details of the figure become clear, he speaks. "What are you kids doing here?"

A flashlight. Dark pants held up by a utility belt. A patch for a badge sown above the breast pocket. It's a security guard.

"We're filming a documentary," Hayley says.

"Yeah, you can't be doing that," the not ghost says. "You kids gotta go."

As Hayley and I load the camera and her sleeping bag into the back of her car, I realize I'm going to miss this. It will probably be six weeks until we pick back up with filming more mini-documentaries next semester. And even though this particular one probably won't turn out as well as we hoped, I still had a lot of fun tonight.

Before I drive away, I watch Hayley for a moment. She sits behind the wheel of her car and stares at her phone. She swipes on it a few times, then tosses it to the passenger seat, clearly frustrated. I wonder if she was watching that video Harold posted again. Somebody should really give that guy a taste of his own medicine.

Suddenly, I realize maybe I do know a way to make Hayley feel better. And maybe just because we're not filming any more documentaries doesn't mean our little adventures have to stop.

THIRTY-ONE

HAYLEY

On Saturday evening, I find Lucy and Lewis standing on my front porch. Lewis has a dark beanie pulled down close to his eyebrows, and Lucy is wearing a black hoodie zipped to her throat.

"Are you two, like, hanging out now?" I ask.

"When circumstances call for it," Lucy says. "We need you to come with us. Put on something black."

"Am I being inducted into a secret society or something?"

"Better." Lewis smiles.

I rush upstairs and slip on my black fleece sweatpants and a dark green Groveland Tennis sweatshirt, my heart rate ticking up a couple notches. I don't know what Lewis and Lucy have in store, but I'm excited. After a day of notifications regarding my recorded drunken antics, I could use a night out with friends. As I grab my coat, I tell my parents I'm heading out for a while. Mom is reading at the dining room table while Dad brews some decaf coffee. In the living room, my brother is fully engrossed in some shooting video game that set me back sixty bucks just so he would keep his mouth shut at Thanksgiving. Mom tells me to check in if I'm going to be late, and then I'm out the door. In the back seat of Lewis's car, I nudge up against several plastic bags full of toilet paper, Saran Wrap, and a couple cans of Silly String. Lucy gets into the back seat on the other side and smiles at me.

"So what exactly are we doing?" I ask.

Lewis starts backing out of my driveway. "Well, we kind of figured it was time for someone to redecorate that nice car of Harold's," he says.

"Are you serious?"

"Why not?" Lucy says. "After he posted that video of you—not to mention the general jackassery he displays at school every day—don't you think he deserves it?"

"But what if we get caught?" I ask.

"Yeah, but what if we don't?" Lewis responds, smiling at me in the rearview mirror. I'm thankful that it's dark in the car because I might be blushing. I think back to when Lewis and I were on that rooftop the night of the police chase. He was frozen with fear and I had to practically drag him away, but now he's arranging late-night illicit activities and he doesn't even seem to be nervous. When did that change happen?

My reluctance starts to melt away. "Okay. But why are we sitting in the back like you're our Uber driver?"

"We have one more stop to make."

Moments later, we park in front of a brick house with dark green shutters, and Lewis shoots off a text. After a couple of minutes, one of the second-story windows opens, and a skinny boy dressed in dark colors climbs out. He shimmies along the edge of the roof and clumsily eases down the rain gutter. As he moves toward us, running half crouched, the front door opens and light spills across the front lawn. The boy freezes as a middle-aged woman with blond hair steps onto the porch.

"Cal, honey, I really wish you wouldn't leave that way. You're going to mess up the gutters," the woman calls.

The boy stands up straight. "The gutters are fine, Mom."

"Well, you need to be careful. I don't want you getting hurt."

Lewis is laughing hysterically, his forehead pressed against the steering wheel.

"Are you going to be out late? Do you have your phone?" the woman says.

"Yes, I have my phone. We're going on a secret mission, Mom. I can't tell you any more than that."

"Oh, hi, Lewis!" the woman calls, waving.

"Hi, Mrs. Raglin!" Lewis yells back, wiping tears from his eyes.

"Okay. You boys have fun on your *secret mission*. Be safe!"

"We will!" Lewis says. When the passenger door opens, I catch a glimpse of Cal's face in the overhead light. He's clearly embarrassed.

We pull away from the curb, Lewis working hard to stifle more laughter. He keeps glancing over at Cal, as if he's anticipating something. "What?" Cal eventually spits.

"You look like a cartoon thief," Lewis says. Cal is wearing black sneakers, black jeans, and a dark gray hoodie, and he even has a light that wraps around his head. "You're just missing a big sack with a dollar sign on it."

"Hey, you guys are dressed in black. Plus, you said this was a serious mission."

"I never said the word 'mission.'"

"I'm one hundred percent sure you called this a mission."

"Why would I have called this a mission?"

"You tell me."

"I wouldn't."

"Except you did, so."

I clear my throat, and Cal shifts toward the back seat. "So you have a grudge to settle with Harold too?" I ask.

"God, who doesn't? That guy's been mooning people since the eighth grade. Pulling his pants down in the bleachers at football games, drive-by moonings in the school parking lot. I've even seen him get props involved. One time, he had a little Groveland pennant on a stick tucked between his butt cheeks."

It only takes about fifteen minutes of driving through the suburbs to spot Harold's blue Mustang parked on the street among a long line of cars. "Looks like someone's having a party," Cal says. Lewis slows down as we cruise past the house, loud music spilling out into the street. We circle the block, making sure the coast is clear, then park on a side road around the corner. We all get out of the car without speaking and ease the doors closed, as if the sound of a car door shutting would raise suspicion. Lucy and I walk calmly down the sidewalk with the bags of supplies while Cal makes a big show of darting from bush to tree to mailbox. He motions for all of us to join him behind a shrub only a few yards from Harold's car.

"All right, we need a plan of attack. Has anyone ever TP'ed a car before?" he asks. Lucy and I exchange glances and shake our heads. Lewis shakes his, too. "Okay," Cal continues, pointing to Lucy and me, "you guys hit the windows with the Silly String first while Lew and I work on the toilet paper. We'll finish up with the Saran Wrap. We should try to keep talking to a minimum. If I whistle once, that means duck. If I whistle twice—"

Lewis interrupts. "It's TP'ing a car, Cal. Not a Green Beret operation."

"I just think we should have a plan," Cal says.

"We do. The plan is TP the car," Lewis says.

"Well, maybe we could get a little more specific."

"Okay. How many squares of the toilet paper should we use on the roof?"

"Now you're just being purposely condescending."

I can't sit and listen to Cal and Lewis bicker any longer. My nerves are electrified. No one is on the street or lawn, so I pull Lucy to her feet and we charge toward Harold's car.

We make quick work of covering the windshields, painting them with blue and pink Silly String. Lewis stands on the driver's side of the car and tosses Cal a roll of toilet paper while holding on to the tail. Cal catches it and rolls it under the car back to Lewis. This goes on for several moments—over and under, over and under—while Lucy and I start circling the Mustang with another roll. There's a nervousness humming through my whole body. I've never done anything like this before, and I keep looking up and down the street, convinced the police might roll up at any minute. Lucy and I move from the hood to the trunk, stifling laughter while ducking Lewis's and Cal's passes. We drape the paper on the fenders and wrap the side mirrors. I don't know how long we're at it. The street remains quiet except for the dull thump of bass coming from the party.

When the toilet paper rolls are empty, we move on to the Saran Wrap, wrapping the car just like Lewis and Cal. As Lucy feeds the tube over to me and I roll it under to her, my hands shake, but I know it's not just from the cold. I do my best to take long, even breaths like I used to during intense tennis matches, tamping down my skittishness and fighting the urge to flee. We keep working, trapping the toilet paper a little tighter with each layer. Lewis fishes Lucy's camera from her bag and takes several photos of our handiwork while Cal empties the dregs of the Silly String over everything.

The music volume rises, and Lewis looks up toward the house. I follow his eyes. Tyler Nash is hanging out of a second-story window. "Hey!" he yells. "What are you guys doing?" Lucy and Cal freeze, and my already pounding heart rate ratchets up to an even faster pace.

Nat Sampson appears beside Tyler. "Shit, man. Isn't that Lockner's car?" They disappear back into the house, and I know they're coming for us. Despite the December chill, sweat blooms on my forehead.

"Everybody, scatter!" Cal shouts, starting to run into the neighbor's yard.

"No, just head for the car!" Lewis shouts.

Now I give in to my urge to flee, releasing the reins and letting it take over. Lucy grabs her bag, and we all race down the middle of the street, our footsteps quick and heavy against the pavement. Lewis and Cal reach the car first and open all the doors. Lucy and I have barely jumped into the back seat when Cal starts screaming, "Go! Go!"

"Is everyone in?" Lewis shouts, and we all yell "yes" simultaneously. He pulls away from the curb and crests a hill before coming to an abrupt stop. "Shit."

"What?" Lucy asks. I look out the front window and immediately understand why Lewis is upset. It's a dead end. We must have missed the signs when we parked.

"We have to go back," Lewis says. A rising tide of panic sloshes in my chest.

"Are you serious?" Lucy asks.

"Do you see any other options?"

"Oh God," Cal moans.

"Everybody, hold on," Lewis says, tightening his grip on the wheel. There's something steady and reassuring about his voice. Lewis has never sounded more in control, and it calms me just a little. He presses hard on the gas and squeals through a U-turn. We speed back toward Harold's car, and when we're only a block away, Lewis lowers his window and takes off his seat belt.

"What are you doing, man?" Cal asks.

"Just take the wheel," Lewis says. There's a giddiness in his expression as he eases his feet up on the driver's seat. Cal looks frightened, but he follows Lewis's command. We're right outside the party now. Harold and Tyler and Nat are all out looking at Harold's car, examining our handiwork.

"Hey, Harold," Lewis yells, "take a look at this!" Suddenly his bare ass is hanging out of the window, and he's smacking one of his cheeks. I can't see his face because the whole top half of his body is out of the window, but I'm pretty sure he's yelping. Harold is fuming, lips pressed together and fists clenched at his side. Tyler looks disgusted, and Nat shields his eyes. Lucy leans over me and snaps a photo of the three of them, the flash lighting all of their expressions brilliantly.

"Lewis, get back in here; we're losing speed," Cal says, tugging on Lewis's pant legs.

Lewis pulls his pants up and awkwardly shuffles back down into his seat, pressing hard on the gas. His face is red, and his eyes are wild. Lucy and I are laughing to the point of tears. Cal's mouth is hanging open. Once we get out of the neighborhood and onto a main street, Lewis turns to everyone. "So, what now?"

THIRTY-TWO

LEWIS

I feel light-headed, which is probably not good because I'm operating a motor vehicle. I try to calm myself by focusing on all the things I know I should be doing, like checking my mirrors and signaling when I change lanes, but it's hard to concentrate. What just happened was insane. My heart is pounding way harder than it has on even my most intense evening run. Also, I think my butt might be chapped.

When I texted Lucy and told her I thought we needed to get a little revenge on Harold, this is not what I expected. I thought we might blow off a little steam TP'ing his car, but I never imagined we'd get to relish his expression when he saw what we did, and I certainly never thought I'd give him a drive-by show. There's so much excitement buzzing through my body that I have to beat on the steering wheel just to release some energy. "Whooo!"

"I know where we can go," Hayley says from the back seat. She leans forward and places a hand on my shoulder. "Take a left here, and I'll direct you."

Moments later, I'm parking next to a small white hut. We all get out and Lucy unlocks the door, waving Cal and me inside. We step up and move all the way forward to the counter as Hayley flips on the light. The room is so small that there's hardly room for all four of us inside, and the place smells like concentrated sugar.

"This is where you work?" I ask, looking over the shelf of syrups.

"Technically, where we used to work," Hayley says.

"I've always wondered about this place," Cal says. "I drive by it all the time, but I've never stopped here."

"You're missing out." Lucy shrugs.

"And you guys just have a key?" I ask.

"Well, we're currently the only two employees, so yeah," Lucy says. "The owner's my neighbor." She reaches under the counter and turns on a small space heater, the coils glowing orange.

Hayley claps her hands together. "So, you guys want to try some or what?"

She and Lucy fire up the big silver machine on the counter and start feeding it large blocks of ice. The rumble practically shakes the whole hut. They grab cups and catch the ice shavings as the machine spits them out. The whole process is a ballet that they clearly know by heart. I half expect them to start flipping the syrup bottles like flashy bartenders.

"How does Hawaiian Delight sound?" Hayley asks, pouring neon blue syrup onto one of the cups.

"Weirdly sexual?" I say. When they're done, everyone is holding a different flavor.

"Okay, I propose a toast," Hayley says, lifting her cup. We all pivot toward the center of the room. "To finally giving Harold a taste of his own medicine."

"To a spectacular display of teamwork," I add.

"To completing the *mission*," Cal says.

"And to hopefully never seeing Lewis's pale white ass ever again." Lucy smiles.

We all crack up and tap our cups together.

As the space heats up, we strip off our coats and settle in. There's only one chair, so we mainly scrunch up together on the counter, shoulder to shoulder, where we trade spoonfuls of shaved ice so we can all test the other flavors. Lucy brings out her camera and passes it around, so we all get a good look at the shot she got of Harold and the boys as we drove by. We laugh and take some selfies and reminisce about something that just happened.

At one point, Cal demands a demonstration of the ice machine, and Lucy relents, even though she tells him she doubts he has the skills to woo Bertha. Hayley and I grab our coats and drift out to a small wooden bench in front of the stand.

"Thanks for making me come out tonight," she says, looking up at the sky over the grocery store across the street. "I think I needed this."

"Yeah, I had great time."

She turns to me. "I just keep thinking how funny it would have been if your car broke down right as your butt was dangling out the window."

"Oh my gosh. Don't even joke about that."

"Come on, it would've been funny!"

"No, it wouldn't have! Have you ever seen someone pee their pants while their pants are already down?"

"Ew, that's gross," she says, slapping my chest.

I shrug. "Then be happy it didn't happen."

We're quiet for several moments as the traffic lights on the street blink through a couple cycles. A lone car passes. Hayley lays her head on my shoulder, and the sky goes Technicolor.

"I wish this feeling would last," Hayley says.

"What do you mean?"

"I mean this feeling of . . . satisfaction. This feeling of freedom and unexpectedness, like you don't know what's going to happen next, but you know it's going to be great. You know what I mean?"

"Yeah." I do know. I feel it too, and I think it's one of the reasons I didn't want to have to wait until next semester to have another adventure with Hayley.

"But it's so fleeting." She groans. "Tomorrow, when I wake up, I'm still going to be Messed-Up Mills."

"Not true," I scoff.

"Lewis, come on." Hayley sighs. "I know what people think. I've seen enough of the comments online."

"I don't think that. Lucy doesn't think that. Hell, after tonight, I know Cal doesn't think that."

"But that's because you guys know me. You have real memories with me. Most people at Groveland don't. All they know is that dumb video of me stopping my car in front of school. Oh, and now the video of me drunkenly confronting Harold. Not exactly my finest moments."

This is the same sort of thing Lucy told me back in Hayley's room a few weeks ago, and maybe they're right. Maybe most people have formed an opinion about Hayley based off of only those two videos, a caricature that's nothing like who she really is. An idea plants itself in my mind, a seed that's already starting to grow. I think I have the power to fix this.

THIRTY-THREE

HAYLEY

Our documentary about B. B. is not our best. In fact, it might be our worst. While the interview footage we have of B. B. is pretty good, and it's interesting to see the juxtaposition between her usually cheerful personality and the serious persona she takes on when she's hunting ghosts—excuse me, *investigating the paranormal*—the footage from the cemetery is barely usable. I was hoping the fog that night would give the footage a spooky vibe, but the low-hanging clouds mixed with the even lower temperatures means the camera lens kept fogging up, so half the time, B. B. looks like a blurry ghost herself. Every few minutes, Lewis's hand comes into frame to wipe down the lens with the sleeve of his coat, so we have to edit around that.

Plus, there's just not much of a story. We went to a cemetery, followed B. B. around for a while, and then got kicked out by a security guard. Lewis and I do our best to stitch it together in some sort of interesting way, trying to build something resembling a narrative arc, but in the end, it looks a lot like a cheap found-footage horror movie. At one point, Lewis even tried using the night-vision mode on the camera to brighten the footage, but it really just succeeded in turning everything green and giving everyone glowing eyes.

"That's our angle, right there," Lewis says. "We really zoom in on the eyes and say B. B. became possessed."

"Lewis, no."

"We can even mess with the sound." He pulls up the audio bars of the footage and drags them all down, dropping the pitch of B. B.'s voice so she really does sound like a demon. It's funny in a this-is-terrible-and-I'm-not-sure-we-can-fix-it sort of way.

If we had more time, I would suggest trying to get additional footage or maybe scrapping this one altogether and starting over, but we can't. Winter break is less than a week away, and we both have other finals we need to focus on. So we scrape together what we can, and when Mrs. Hansen gives us a low B, I try not to take it too hard. I know with all the other great clips we've turned in that it's not really going to put a dent in our overall grade, but I was really hoping to end the semester on a high note, to show the kids at Groveland that the documentaries are only getting bigger and better and give them something that would make everyone forget all about the video Harold posted.

Lewis waves our grade sheet in front of my face. "This calls for a celebration."

"You want to celebrate our lowest grade ever?"

"No, I want to celebrate the fact that we did it. One semester of documentaries in the books."

It seems like kind of a silly thing to celebrate, but Lewis is relentless. He smiles wide and shakes the paper aggressively in my face until I crack a smile. Maybe he's right. Dr. Kim always reminds me not to focus on the negative, so I guess it couldn't hurt to lighten up and relish the fact that we've created so much good content this year. "Okay, but I can't skip second period, if that's what you're thinking."

"All right, well, how do you feel about cheap breakfast food?"

As Lewis and I settle into a booth at Waffle House later that evening, our waitress flips over a pair of mugs on the table. She's an older woman with a waddle for a walk and a genuine smile. "Y'all want coffee?" she asks.

Lewis smiles and points at me across the table. "Hot chocolate?"

"Hot chocolate actually does sound good."

"Two hot chocolates," the waitress confirms, heading back behind the counter.

There're only a few other customers in the whole restaurant, a man nursing a cup of coffee at the counter and a couple of college students studying in the corner. Lewis grabs my hand and pulls me toward the jukebox in the middle of the restaurant. It looks like a relic from the early '90s with large yellowed buttons used to flip physical pages behind the big glass display window.

"I'm guessing you've got some eighties hits in mind?" I ask as Lewis flips through several pages of songs.

"Normally, yes. But Waffle House is a little different. When you're here, you have to play Waffle House songs. Though, to be fair, I'm pretty sure most of these are actually from the eighties." Lewis hits the buttons a few more times before he finds what he's looking for. "Here we go."

I've been to Waffle House plenty of times, but I've never bothered with the jukebox, which is why I'm surprised to be staring down at a page of songs literally about the restaurant. "'I'm Going Back to the Waffle House' is pretty great if you're looking for something upbeat," Lewis says. "But if you want something a little more soulful, I suggest 'Special Lady,' which is basically a love song from a trucker to a Waffle House waitress."

"Oh my God," I mutter. "Well, how can I choose?"

"Oh, I know," Lewis says, perking up even more. He drops two quarters into the jukebox and presses a few numbers. I look for the corresponding listing and learn Lewis has just selected a song called "Last Night I Saw Elvis at the Waffle House." As the first notes emerge from the crackling speakers overhead, I realize Lewis is right. This song probably is from the '80s. A gruff gentleman starts crooning about literally seeing Elvis at Waffle House while a jazz saxophone blasts in the background. I don't even know how to react to this restaurant-themed genre of music. It's so terrible in the best way. Lewis saunters back toward our booth seeming satisfied, and I notice our waitress is shaking her head like she's definitely heard this song a thousand times too many.

After we order our food, Lewis lifts his mug of hot chocolate into the air. "To a successful semester of filmmaking."

I tap my mug against his, and he takes a sip. When he places his cup back on the table, there's a clump of whipped cream dangling from his nose. I can't help but laugh. "What? Is there something on my face?" He takes a napkin and wipes everywhere around his mouth, purposefully avoiding the whipped cream. "Did I get it? Surely I got it."

"Yeah, you got it," I say, lifting my phone and taking a photo.

Our waffles arrive and we dive in.

"All right," Lewis says, pointing a forkful of waffle at me. "Favorite documentary we've made so far. Go."

"Hmmm . . . Well, I almost got a brain hemorrhage at one so probably not that one," I scoff.

"Yeah, but we almost fell off a roof while being pursued by police at the first one," Lewis counters.

"I'll take *almost* falling off a roof over *definitely* falling off a laser tag course any day."

"Good point," he relents.

"So what was your favorite?" I ask.

Lewis's expression turns serious, and he motions to our water cups. In a flat tone he says, "We really shouldn't be drinking out of these. These cups are purely for stacking."

I almost choke on a bite of waffle from laughing. "Cup-stacking was your favorite?"

"How could it not be? I'm gonna say it; I love Angus Li. His passion for stacking those cups was so pure."

"Uh-oh. Should I warn Cal? Sounds like you might be trying to get a new best friend."

"Well, I could do a lot worse than Angus, that's for sure. Though he's probably too popular for me now. Since that documentary aired, I think he has more friends than ever. I've definitely seen some people asking him to do cup-stacking in the cafeteria. They record him and everything. I think he might have even started a YouTube channel."

"Good for Angus," I say. It's nice to know people can still learn new things about each other. "I'm honestly kind of jealous of the people we make these documentaries about. They get to share their full selves with everyone at Groveland. They're embracing who they really are, and people seem to respond to that."

Lewis chews some waffle and stares off toward the parking lot. I can tell he's thinking about something, but then he just holds out his arms and says, "Hey, you can share your full self with me. And if we hang out here long enough, maybe Elvis, too."

THIRTY-FOUR

LEWIS

When Rebecca climbs into the back seat of my car, she hands me a party hat decorated with sparkly fireworks and then gives another to Cal. "Happy New Year, boys," she says, reaching forward and using the rearview mirror to straighten her own hat.

"Oh boy, props," Cal says, snapping the elastic band under his chin.

"It's so we don't lose each other in the crowd," Rebecca says.

"Yeah, I'm sure no one else will be wearing hats," I say, positioning my hat over the beanie I'm already wearing so that the tip scrapes the roof of my car. We're heading downtown to watch the star drop, which is our town's answer to New York City's ball drop. It's not nearly as spectacular as Times Square because it's just a large glowing star that glides down a lit-up pole mounted to the top of the parking garage that Hayley and I nearly died falling off of several months ago, but there's live music and food vendors, so it's fun. I drive around a bit and circle several blocks before I'm able to find a place to park. Then we get out and start following the throngs of people making their way to the heart of downtown.

We stop at the first drink vendor we spot and fork over too much money for small cups of coffee. The sound of music bounces off the buildings, growing louder as we walk, and then we turn the corner and spot the blue and pink spotlights of a raised stage. "This looks like it could be a very elaborate gender reveal party," Rebecca jokes. As the crowd grows denser, we stick to the outskirts so that we have some room to breathe. The band is actually pretty good. We particularly like it when they play a cover of Whitney Houston's '80s hit "I Wanna Dance with Somebody." Cal pulls his party hat from his head and starts using it as a lip sync microphone while Rebecca and I lock arms and twirl each other out in the closed street. As we dance, I realize how much I've missed her, an ache building in my chest. This year, I've spent so much time working on documentaries while still trying to find time to go running and figure out college stuff that it feels like my relationship with Rebecca has almost slipped through the cracks. At the start of the school year, I had this plan to start living with more intention, and the whole purpose was to move to a place where Rebecca and I could be together. What happened? Somehow, all of that got lost.

After a few more songs, the band quiets and everyone counts down in unison as we watch the star drop to its base. There's an eruption of cheers, and dual confetti cans blast out from the stage over all of us. As the colorful paper swirls around, I pull Rebecca close and give her a lingering kiss on the cheek, a promise that I haven't forgotten about her and still care. She smiles at me, and I feel the same spark of exhilaration that I've always gotten.

The joyous atmosphere of the crowd dissipates pretty quickly. By twelve thirty, we've already seen two guys almost get in a fistfight and spotted one poor girl puking with an incredible amount of velocity onto the curb, so we decide to head home. I drop Cal at his place first and then start making the drive to Rebecca's apartment complex. The streets are surprisingly empty, and Rebecca is weirdly quiet, picking at the tip of her party hat now in her lap. "Everything all right?" I ask.

"Hmm? Oh, yeah. It's, uh, just the holidays. Always kind of a weird time with my folks. But we survived another year, I guess." She gives her hat an unenthusiastic shake. Rebecca doesn't talk about her parents' divorce much, and when she does, I never really know how to respond.

I want to say something supportive and not just repeat some hollow platitudes she's heard a million times, but mainly I just stay quiet and listen. She shifts in her seat toward me. "Remember that time you came over to my house for Thanksgiving?"

"Oh yeah. When was that, like seventh grade?"

"Yeah." She smiles. "Another lifetime, right?"

"Seems that way sometimes. I remember your dad was singing that song while he mashed the potatoes. God, what did he call it?"

"The Tater Mash."

"Yeah. The Tater Mash," I say, hitting the steering wheel. "He changed the words to 'Monster Mash,' right?"

"It's the Tater Mash! It was a Thanksgiving smash!" Rebecca sings. "He had a dumb song for everything. When I was younger, he changed the words to 'Kung Fu Fighting' to make it about brushing my teeth."

"And your mom had on that hat shaped like a turkey."

"Yeah, I don't even know where she got that thing. I think she was just trying to get me excited about all the American holidays we didn't have in New Zealand."

"That was a fun day."

"Yeah, they were really happy then. I don't understand how they couldn't see that was something worth fighting for."

I put my hand on top of Rebecca's as we drive on a bit longer in silence. When I pull into a spot close to her apartment, she doesn't move to get out. Instead, she unbuckles and turns toward me. "I had fun tonight. It was just what I needed. I always have fun with you, Lewis."

"Yeah, I had fun too. A good start to the new year."

Rebecca sits there in silence, as if she might be mulling something over in her mind or anticipating something. After a minute, she opens her door to get out, and I'm reminded of the moment we shared in that dressing room back at the end of summer. How many more moments like this have to come before I have the courage to make a move? As she goes to hop out, I say "wait" and pull her back to me, pressing my lips against hers.

I can tell she's surprised, and she hesitates for a moment, so I do too, but then her hand is on the back of my head pulling me closer to her. Any spark I felt from the kiss on the cheek I gave her less than an hour ago is engulfed by a new, stronger flame. This is a moment I've dreamt about for so long, but I never imagined these details—the scent of her hair and the taste of her lips, still sweet from the mocha she drank earlier. I pray that whatever force is cradling this moment together keeps holding and stretches on for hours or days. I'm suddenly so awake I feel like the sun could rise and set again, and I could stay here, content to remain in this car, kissing Rebecca. Eventually, she breaks away and leans her forehead against mine.

"Thanks for always being willing to talk to me," she says, her breath warm against my lips. "And thanks for, uh, *that*."

"Anytime," I manage to say in a whisper so soft I'm not even sure she can hear.

Then she eases away, hops out of the car, and makes her way inside.

For a moment, I sit there staring at her door, dumbfounded. Part of me wants to crank up some music and start break-dancing here in the parking lot. Another part of me wants to roll down my windows and drive through the night cheering. Another part of me even considers calling Cal and shouting the news at him through the phone. But I don't really do any of that stuff. Instead, I put my car in reverse, pull away, and drive home from Rebecca's place like I've done so many times before. I stare out at the road, gliding through pools of gold cast by the streetlights overhead. This really is going to be a good year.

THIRTY-FIVE

HAYLEY

I'm tired of just explaining all of the documentaries to Dr. Kim, so during our first session of the new year, I decide to actually show her a couple. I pull up the one we did of Camilla on my phone, figuring if we can't show it on the morning announcements, at least someone should get to see it, and then we move on to the one about Rachael and her kite-making. Dr. Kim sits back and watches them as I sip on my coffee. She still has her holiday decorations up. There's garland draped over her bookshelves and a pine-scented candle burning on her desk.

"These are very good, Hayley," Dr. Kim says, handing my phone back to me. "I can see why you enjoy making them so much."

"Yeah, TV Production has certainly had the most interesting homework of any class I've ever taken. I've already been texting Lewis about some new ideas I have for this semester."

"Seems like you two make a good team."

"Yeah, I think we do." For a brief moment, I wonder how different my life might be if Lewis or I had selected a different seat that first day of class. I can't imagine spending this year making clips with anyone else.

"You're smiling, Hayley," Dr. Kim says.

"So?"

"So it's nice is all." She gives me a lingering look and then lets it drop. "Any plans for your last few days of winter break?"

I think about all the half-finished college applications saved on my computer. I should definitely devote some time to finishing those. I have no excuses left, and the clock is ticking. "You remember when you told me about how you quit your sorority?"

"Of course."

"Did you ever consider just dropping out of college altogether?"

"Hmm. Well, I'm sure the thought crossed my mind, but I don't think I dwelled on it too long. Why do you ask?"

Because I don't know if I can go. I don't know if I can handle the stress of leaving my family and friends and basically starting over somewhere new. "I guess I'm kind of having a hard time envisioning what next year might be like. How do you decide where you want to spend four years just by reading some websites?"

Dr. Kim uncrosses her legs and then crosses them the other way. "Well, for one thing, I think it's important to remember that you're not stuck with your decision if you get there and you're unhappy. No matter where you choose to go, you can also choose to leave if it's not the right fit. But you're a smart young woman, Hayley. You should trust your instincts."

That sounds like such a simple solution, but trusting my instincts is the exact thing I've been fighting against this year. Instead, I've questioned all of my decisions, examining and reexamining them from every possible angle, working hard to take only measured steps that will allow me to be seen in the most flattering light.

"Maybe I can just not go to college." I sigh, sinking lower into my chair. "How do I become one of those girls on Instagram whose whole job seems to be looking pretty in exotic locations?"

Dr. Kim chuckles. "If I knew that, do you think I'd be here with you right now?"

"Wow."

"I'm kidding."

"Maybe I'm not so worried about college being a different place. Maybe I'm worried that no matter where I go, there I'll be."

Dr. Kim looks a bit perplexed. "Unpack that for me."

"Well, no matter what college I choose, when I get there, I'm still going to be the same Hayley I am here. And the Hayley I am here had a mental breakdown."

"You know, I think you're right," Dr. Kim says, leaning forward. "Who you are here is who you'll be at college. But I think that's a good thing. The Hayley sitting in front of me is smart and accomplished and driven. Any college would be lucky to have you."

I want to believe Dr. Kim. At one time, I did feel that way. But now I can't help but wonder, if I couldn't even handle the stress of junior year, how am I possibly going to handle the stress of college? Dr. Kim must recognize I'm still worried because she says, "One moment does not define you, Hayley. You're complex and nuanced. Everyone is. I mean, isn't that the whole point of all these documentaries you've been telling me about?"

She does have a point.

"Plus, let's go back to my own college experience," she says. "After I spent too much time drinking and nearly failed half of my classes during one semester, you think I wasn't shaken? You think I wasn't embarrassed? I can assure you I was. But I kept moving forward. Just like you've done and will continue to do."

Somehow, even when think I just want to sulk in my own self-doubt, Dr. Kim finds a way to make me feel a little better. "So you're saying I shouldn't become an Instagram model?"

"I'm saying I think you would *rather* go to college."

I know Dr. Kim's right. Even if I pick the wrong school and decide to transfer, I would be even more disappointed in myself if I never even tried. When I look up, Dr. Kim is smiling at me. "What?"

"Well, I was just going to say, if you're feeling nervous about college, I do know of a support group that meets at State that you might want to check out."

She's clearly never going to drop this support group thing. "I guess I walked right into that one, didn't I?"

"You really did."

THIRTY-SIX

LEWIS

On the first day of the spring semester, I'm up before my alarm, so I decide to sneak in a quick run. The cold morning air wakes me up, and I find I'm feeling weirdly excited about the second half of senior year. For once, I actually feel like a leading man, not just the leading man of the fantasy in my head. I'm becoming more disciplined than ever, things with Rebecca are moving in a great direction, and now it's time to start diving back into the documentaries with Hayley. What could be better? Plus, after what Hayley's been saying lately, I think I may have the best idea for how to start this semester of documentaries with a real bang.

After a brisk couple of miles, I take a shower and then head to the kitchen. I've just finished scrambling some eggs when Mom and Dad enter.

"Good morning, you two," I say, shutting off the stove burner and grabbing a couple of glasses from the cabinet. "Can I interest either of you in a glass of orange juice?" They take a seat at the counter as I display the juice carton like a waiter showcasing a pricey bottle of wine.

"Uh, yes, please," Mom says, confused. Dad just scratches his head, but I pour him a glass anyway. "What's happening here?" Mom asks.

I lift the skillet from the stove and divide the eggs between two plates, then lift a paper towel from the dish already on the counter, revealing several pieces of crispy bacon.

"Well, it's the first day of my final semester of high school, and I just thought it might be nice to make you both some breakfast," I say, pushing the eggs in front of them. I grab my backpack from one of the kitchen chairs and load up the last of my books.

"Aren't you going to eat?" Mom asks.

I grab a slice of bacon and chomp one end. "I'd love to stay. I really would. But I have a project at school that I need to get to work on."

"On the first day?" Dad asks.

"That's life in the TV business. Right, Mom?" I nudge her with my elbow. "Tell him."

"Uh, yeah. Right," she says.

"Dad, I'd like to grab a little treat for my TV Production class. Do you think I could borrow twenty bucks to pick up some doughnuts on the way to school?"

"I suppose that's fine." Dad retrieves the money from his wallet and hands it to me. I thank him, give Mom a kiss on the cheek, and head for the door.

I make it to Groveland in time to get the studio to myself for half an hour. I munch on a chocolate crème–filled doughnut as I work my way through all of the footage of Hayley from last semester. There's a lot of good material ripe for editing, and I want to make sure I pick the best clips.

At the first bell, I walk into TV Production class with the other twenty-three doughnuts in hand. It's common knowledge that there's no better way to become popular in high school than to offer up some free food. Once he gets his hands on a maple bacon glazed, Cal is even willing to forgive me for the fact that he had to get a ride to school from his mom this morning.

"Someone's feeling generous," Mrs. Hansen says, taking a plain glazed.

"Well, as senior producer, these kids really look up to me. I think there's a real chance they're going to give me the *Dead Poets Society* 'O Captain! My Captain!' salute by the end of the year."

"Yeah, I wouldn't hold my breath," Mrs. Hansen says.

Hayley and I post a new blank sheet outside the studio and invite a new round of seniors to sign up. After freezing our butts off in the cemetery last month, we agree to stick to indoor documentaries until spring blooms.

After school, Cal and I meet up with Rebecca at Bad Pun for some coffee before her evening shift at Graze Daze. As Rebecca and I wait at the end of the counter for our drinks, her hand brushes mine, and she slowly tucks her pinky finger around mine. We still need to have a conversation about what New Year's meant, but this tells me that what happened was not an accident. What we did, we did on purpose. Cal emerges from the bathroom, wiping his damp hands on his jeans. Rebecca drops her hand, and we both stare at him. "What? Did I miss something?" he asks.

I spend the next couple days sneaking extra hours in the TV studio, slowly stitching the best clips together and getting the narrative just right. The work is time consuming, especially without Hayley's guidance. She has great storytelling instincts and a knack for figuring out the best order for the clips, but it's not like I'm a newbie. I know how to tell a great story too, and I can't get her help this time. Not with this one.

By Thursday, everything's ready. It's not a classroom day, but I'm still in the studio as a producer. Cal takes his normal spot at the anchor desk, and excitement builds in my bones. He looks over his script, pausing when he gets to the clip portion. "Wow. Really?" he asks, pointing.

"Yeah," I nod.

At eight thirty, we go live.

THIRTY-SEVEN

HAYLEY

Cal's a good anchor for the morning announcements, even though it's clear he doesn't take the gig too seriously. He often makes little unscripted jokey comments between segments or speeds through the more boring portions, but there's something undeniably engaging about his screen presence. I'm in my AP English class watching him, making mental notes about how I might improve my own performance the next time I have coanchor duty, when he says, "Now get ready, everyone, because we have our first senior documentary of the semester." I perk up a little. We do? Lewis and I haven't filmed anything yet. "And this is a very special edition. For this one, our own Hayley Mills steps out from behind the camera and into the spotlight. Let's watch."

What?

Several classmates turn toward me, and I try my best to smile like I definitely know what's happening. Footage of me playing tennis appears onscreen, and I immediately recognize it as the same clips that Lewis and I found when we were looking for video of Camilla. Lewis's voice comes in to provide narration. "What do you think of when you think of Hayley Mills? Maybe you think of her as the tennis star who helped lead Groveland in an amazing season last year." The image shifts to a still frame of me at the anchor desk studying my script for the announcements. "Or maybe you think of her as a leader, someone who's known for her passion and tenacity. Or maybe you think of this." The photo warps to grainy footage that I recognize immediately. I've watched it on YouTube over and over. A police officer is leading me out of my car while a long line of vehicles waits for the intersection to clear. I've suddenly forgotten how to breathe. I do my best to force the air out in a steady stream, but it's ragged. "This is what most people associate with Hayley Mills. An overachiever who became overburdened and lost control. This particular video has racked up more than three hundred thousand views on YouTube. There are many others posted across multiple social media platforms. Still, despite how many people know about this event, very few have taken the time to really get to know Hayley herself."

The image shifts to me sitting near a low white wall. I'm wearing dark clothes and a baseball cap, and it takes a moment before the recognition snaps into place. It's the night we filmed Camilla spray-painting. I talked about my incident that night. Lewis had the camera. *He secretly filmed me.* A deep rage swishes in my gut, and I curl my toes and push my feet into the floor to keep from exploding out of my desk.

"My mom and dad still worry a lot," TV Hayley says. "We have these long, awkward conversations about school and stress and the pressure." I dig my nails into the edge of my desk, fighting the urge to rush up and pull the whole TV from its mount. This can't be happening. Lewis would never do this. He would never take the private, intimate details of my life and broadcast them for mass consumption. Lewis is my friend.

A sinister thought worms its way to the center of my mind. *Was this his plan all along?* Has this been some sort of long con of shared coffees and late-night exploits just to get me to open up so he can have some sort of inside scoop on Groveland's most tragic head case?

The documentary shifts to one of my and Lewis's go-to techniques, asking other students what they think of the subject before we subvert their expectations. Faces of my classmates appear onscreen in rapid succession.

"Hayley Mills? Oh yeah, she's definitely crazy," one guy says.

"I honestly just feel sorry for her," says a girl I don't recognize.

"Oh, if that happened to me, I would definitely change schools," a guy says.

His friend laughs and agrees. "Definitely."

The image shifts to new footage, a montage of clips Lewis captured during our outings. Me holding a camera and dancing to an unheard song. Me laughing as I attempt cup-stacking for the first time. Me fumbling a laser tag gun as I try to spin the trigger around my finger. "But Hayley Mills isn't what most people think," Lewis announces.

I can't sit through any more of this. It feels like my skin is on fire. I stand and march out of class without saying a word. Mrs. Colpher calls after me, but I keep moving. I know that if I even open my mouth, a scream will come ripping out. Down the hall, past the library, and into the TV studio. Lewis is giving the cue to wrap up the broadcast when I arrive, and I'm in his face as soon as he slips off his headset.

"What the hell was that?" I ask.

He falters. His eyes move around my face, studying my expression. "Did you . . . You didn't like it?"

"Of course I didn't like it."

He motions around the studio. "Everyone here thought it was great."

"Yeah, I'm sure everyone loved getting an inside look at the tragic, broken girl."

"No, the whole point was to show that you're *not* broken. You saw the whole thing, right?"

Cal leans over the anchor desk. "Lewis, did Hayley not—"

"Shut up, Cal. Lewis, that was some trauma tourism bullshit. You didn't have the right to air that!"

Lewis glances over at the control room, and I follow his gaze. Half of the studio is staring at us, and the other half is pretending to be deeply involved in some work while actually listening to every word of our conversation. I take hold of Lewis's forearm and pull him out past the heavy studio doors and into a secluded part of the hallway.

"Hey, look," Lewis says. He reaches for my shoulders, but I lurch away, so he slowly lowers his hands like I might be a wild animal that's going to charge him. He might not be far off.

"You didn't have my permission to do this," I spit. "I didn't even know you were filming me!"

"I—I know," Lewis stammers. "I thought it would be a nice surprise."

Nice surprise? It's the most insane justification I can imagine. Hearing Lewis say that throws me off so much that I can't even form a cohesive response. My hands grip the sides of my head like the extra support might stabilize my thoughts. "No . . . That's not . . . Why would Mrs. Hansen even sign off on airing that?"

Lewis's gaze drops to his shoes. "I told her you were on board with it."

A tear threatens to spill over, but I wipe it away, pretending I'm just adjusting my glasses. "Of course you did."

Lewis rakes his hands through his hair and swallows hard. "Clearly I made a mistake," he says.

"Clearly." I wait for Lewis to make the logical follow-up when someone realizes they've made a mistake—an actual apology. I wait, but he doesn't say sorry. He just stares off down the hall with a stunned look on his face, and I erupt in frustration. "How could you possibly be this dumb, Lewis? Did you even consider my feelings? I've been working very hard to build a future that has meaning and purpose, but I can't do that if people are just going to keep reminding me of my failures. Look, I know you're fine with being this laid-back C student who's just cruising through life with no real ambition, but some of us have actual goals, okay?"

Lewis shifts his attention back to my face, and his expression crumples from stunned to hurt. It's devastating to watch, and I suddenly realize I've stepped out-of-bounds. "I know. From the very beginning, this has been all about you," he says.

"What?"

His expression is hardened now. His defenses are up. "Let's be honest here, Hayley. It's not like we were super concerned about our subjects' feelings in the beginning. You were fine with blackmailing Camilla into participating, and then you and Lucy just flirted with Rohan until he said yes. It's not like they jumped on board willingly. But it didn't matter because you got what you wanted. You got to make a documentary and have Mrs. Hansen give you another gold star to add to your collection. Another A-plus for Hayley Mills."

"That's totally different," I say. I am not going to let Lewis turn this whole thing around like I somehow brought this on myself. "Sometimes I push a little, but that's because I'm willing to make an effort and do the work. Why do you think Mrs. Hansen paired us up, Lewis? Because she needed you to teach me how to work a camera? Does that really make sense? Maybe it was because she knew you needed a safety net, because she couldn't risk having her senior producer just cruising through the year."

I know it's mean, and I realize that half the reason Lewis and I are partners is only because he happened to sit next to me on the first day, but it still feels good to spit the words out. Part of me wants to hurt him just as much as he hurt me.

"Maybe." He shrugs.

And the casual way he rolls his shoulders pushes me over the edge. I can't even look at him anymore, let alone try to rationally explain my feelings. I walk away, and he doesn't even try to follow. I spend the rest of first period hiding out in the back of the stacks in the library. When the bell rings, I venture out to find Lucy. She'll know how to make this better. She'll know what to do.

But the hall is so loud. Kids are yelling at one another and jumping around. I swear people are looking at me too. Pointing and whispering. Every cell phone seems to be aimed in my direction. I stare down the lenses, daring them to snap a photo. Suddenly, Harold appears in front of me, flanked by his soccer bros, Tyler and Nat. "Hayley, great documentary this morning," he says, his voice dripping with sarcasm. "You really outdid yourself."

"Not the time, Harold," Lewis spits, coming up from behind me. Great, now I'm trapped.

"What? I just wanted to tell you how moved I was by your clip. I mean, it's not every day that we get an inside look into someone's clearly messed-up head."

"Back off, Harold," Lewis barks.

Tyler pretends to shiver in fear. "Yeah, back off, Harold," he says, flashing his big, braces-straight teeth. "You should be more sensitive. Can't you see she's in a very fragile place right now?"

Fragile. The word has been buried in my mind for months, and now it finally finds fertile ground, blooming immediately. The worry I've been carrying around all year suddenly confirmed. This is how people see me, how they'll always see me. I can't change that, no matter what. It doesn't matter how many interesting documentaries I make or what college I get accepted to or how fun-loving I try to be. I will always be fragile.

"You need to move on, Harold," Lewis says, stepping in front of me.

"Or what, Cheese Fries? Your girlfriend's gonna go psycho on me? The thing about you two—"

Before Harold can finish his sentence, Lewis charges. This boy, who stroked my head when I got hurt at laser tag and who covered his nose in whipped cream just to make me smile, catches Harold under his arm and tackles him into a locker bank. Then they're on the floor wrestling, and everyone starts to crowd in to get a better look. Lewis's whole face is red as he punches at Harold.

Students start nudging me out of the way, and I'm filled with an overwhelming urge to run. There's a panic expanding in my chest, pushing in on my lungs and my heart, and I don't know what's going to happen if I stay in this crowd. I turn to make my way out, and suddenly, Lucy is there beside me, shoving people out of the way and slapping down phones as we go. She leads me up the stairs and into the nearest restroom. I stand by the door as Lucy checks under each of the stalls to make sure we're alone. "I'm so sorry, Hayley," she says as she makes her way back to me. "I mean, what the hell happened this morning?"

Everything crashes over me at once. The documentary, Lewis's words, Harold and his boys. It's all too much, and suddenly everything Dr. Kim has ever told me about controlling my anxiety seems like complete nonsense. I lurch forward and smack at the metal paper towel dispenser, and it clatters against the wall, clearly loose. Another good smack sends it bouncing from the nails and onto the floor. I pick it up with both hands and smash it against the thick ceramic sink. The impact sends vibrations shooting up my arms, but it feels good. It brings the same sort of release I used to get from acing serves on the tennis court. I bring the dented dispenser down again, and my vision starts to blur as hot tears stream down my face.

Lucy's screaming. A deep guttural yell that settles in my ears like a muffled hum. No, wait, it's me. I'm the one screaming. And I can't stop. My voice claws its way up my throat and past my lips. With a third whack, the dispenser bursts open, and folded brown paper towels scatter across the bathroom. I lose momentum and drop to my knees, gripping the edge of the sink and crying at the U-pipe until Lucy kneels down behind me. She wraps her arms around my chest and sits me back against the wall.

"Hey, it's okay. It's okay," she says, rocking me.

That's when Mrs. Hansen walks in.

THIRTY-EIGHT

LEWIS

Principal Wexler leans back in his chair and rests his interlocked fingers on his stomach. He releases a long sigh and glances up at Mr. Keith, who's standing beside him like some sort of bodyguard. A ridiculous image, considering Wexler easily has sixty pounds on Mr. Keith, and today the T-shirt under Mr. Keith's blazer has a shooting star zooming across the chest holding a book and proclaiming, "Reading is out of this world!" Mrs. Hansen shuts the conference-room door and takes a seat at the table next to Hayley, who's holding some crumpled tissue like it's the rosary. Seeing her puffy eyes and blotchy skin makes me feel terrible. The guilt settles in heavy around my ribs. Beside her, Lucy is sitting with her arms folded, and across the table, Tyler has an ice pack pressed to the side of his face while Harold has a bloody tissue shoved up one of his nostrils. Next to me, Cal chews on the tip of his thumbnail, his leg bouncing fast. The collar of his shirt is torn, and there are a couple of fresh red scratch wounds etched into his forehead.

"So this morning there was a little incident, and I understand you're all wrapped up in this together," Wexler says, scanning our faces. No one replies. I would say something, but I'm pretty sure sitting perfectly still is the only thing keeping me from vomiting on this table. So much of my body aches, it's hard to figure out exactly what's injured. Is this what internal bleeding feels like? Am I going to start peeing blood?

This was my first fight, and it turns out I was very unprepared.

Lots of '80s movies have fighting in them. Half of the action films made in that decade have a sweaty and shirtless Schwarzenegger or Stallone on the poster. However, most of the time, they're also holding a comically large gun. So even though I've seen most of those movies, any information I may have learned about fighting wasn't pertinent to my brawl with Harold since we were both weaponless. There are '80s movies with hand-to-hand combat. *Bloodsport*. *Road House*. All three *Karate Kids*. But they weren't incredibly helpful either because it turns out there's rarely enough prep time to accurately execute a roundhouse kick to someone's face during an unchoreographed spar.

After I tackled Harold, we went down to the ground and became intertwined chaos, both of us swinging our arms and neither of us landing any dramatic punches. Just short jabs to the ribs and back—but that didn't make them any less painful. When Tyler jumped in, so did Cal. I think he may have hit Tyler with his history textbook. All of my pent-up anger toward Harold boiled over—my rage about the hurtful nicknames and my annoyance about his general attitude toward anyone who's not in his little soccer gang. All I could think about was hurting him as the construction crew in my mind cheered me on, burly men of grease and steel exhilarated and clapping. Eventually some teachers charged in and broke the whole thing up, and we all got dragged to the office.

"Now, I want to get to the bottom of this," Wexler continues. "Based on what I've heard from Mr. Lockner, it seems this whole thing started when you four vandalized his car."

"No. Definitely not," Lucy interjects, lurching forward in her chair. "This whole thing started back at the beginning of the year when he made some rude comments in front of a bunch of people at a party."

"Oh yeah, that makes sense," Harold scoffs, pulling the reddened tissue from his nose. "I made a joke at a party four months ago and

Cheese Fries suddenly decides to punch me today?" I push my fingers hard into the underside of the table, aching to flip it so I can get another shot at Harold.

"It goes back even earlier than that," Cal says. "You've been a jerk since eighth grade, Harold. You've mistaken playing soccer and being mean to people for an actual personality."

"Exactly, thank you, Cal," Lucy says, crossing her arms and sitting back in her chair.

"Why are you even here?" Tyler asks her.

"I could ask you the same thing, *sidekick*," Lucy retorts. I bite my busted lip to keep from snickering.

"Okay. Okay," Mr. Keith says, waving his lanky arms over his head. "We're not going to turn this conference room into an episode of *Jerry Springer*. We're here to gather the facts."

"So you all are saying you didn't vandalize Mr. Lockner's car?" Wexler asks with a tone that suggests he already knows the answer. Harold smiles.

"No, we did," I say, my voice coming out low but even. "But it's not like we did permanent damage. We just wrapped it in toilet paper."

"Ah, and that makes it okay?" Mr. Wexler stares me down over the rim of his glasses.

"Nothing about this is okay," Lucy mumbles.

"Excuse me, Ms. Campbell?" Wexler says.

Lucy sits up straight and pivots toward him. "I said this is not okay," she repeats, over-enunciating each word. "Groveland clearly has a bullying problem, but you have us all sitting here like we're all to blame. My friend was just humiliated out there, and now what? You want her to make nice with her abuser?"

Holy hell. I was feeling kind of good about myself for throwing a couple of punches at Harold, but apparently Lucy has balls the size of this table. She's debating Wexler and not flinching. I think I even catch a smirk on Hayley's face, but when I blink, it's gone.

"Excuse me, I am not some *abuser*," Harold interjects, lifting his fingers as air quotes.

"You definitely are," I say.

"One hundred percent," Cal agrees.

"You know what's abusive?" Harold says. "Tackling someone into a locker bank."

Wexler brings his hand down on the table. Hard. "Stop it." Everyone goes silent. "This is not how we behave here at Groveland. I thought, as seniors, you all might be able to sit down and talk this thing through rationally, but clearly I was wrong. So what's going to happen now is you're all going to go sit out in the waiting area while Mr. Keith and I call your parents. I want at least one empty seat between each of you, and do not even think about talking to one another. Is that understood?" We all nod, and Mr. Keith opens the door to let us out.

Lucy's dad is the first to show up, a large intimidating man wearing dirty jeans and a baseball cap. Apparently, he runs his own home renovation business and left in the middle of a job to come pick up his daughter. I know this because he is even louder and more passionate than Lucy, and we can all hear him yelling at Wexler from down the hall. Cal keeps pretending to cough, but he's really just laughing into his hand. When Lucy's dad stomps out of the office, muttering insults that I can't really make out other than "incompetent" and "waste of time," Lucy follows behind, smiling and satisfied. Things don't go that way for me. When Mom shows up and we meet with Wexler together, she doesn't defend me or raise her voice. She basically just agrees with everything he says. *Yes, this kind of behavior is unacceptable. Yes, I'm very concerned too.* Any attempt by me to justify my actions is met with scornful glares, so eventually I just shut up. I think even Ms. Plaxico and the photo of her one-eyed cat glare at me on the way out.

Once we get past the entryway and out into the parking lot, Mom grabs my arm and turns me to face her. "What in God's name is going on, Lewis?"

Great. Time for lecture round two. "Can't we talk about this at home?"

"Oh, we're definitely going to talk about this at home. Especially with your father. You can bet we're going to talk about this for quite a while. But right now I think I deserve a little explanation."

I stare out into the parking lot, not really wanting to look at her. "It was a bad day, all right?"

"No. Not all right. None of this is all right. When they called me at the TV station to tell me my son was in trouble for fighting, I didn't believe them. My son would never do such a thing. I made them repeat your name three times. I made them describe what you were wearing. I blindly defended you, and now I look like an idiot."

It's impossible to stifle my annoyance. "I'm sorry you looked like an idiot in front of some school secretaries you'll probably never see again."

"Don't you dare. Don't you dare get smart with me right now. You do not get to act like you're above it all after behaving so childishly." She starts digging around for her car keys in her purse. "I hope it was worth it, because you are not going to be enjoying freedom for a long time."

I'm tempted to tell her that of course it wasn't worth it. This day has been one horrible misjudgment after another, starting with me airing that stupid clip about Hayley. I made her relive the worst moment of her life in front of the whole school, and now she hates me. She didn't even look my way once during the whole time we were all in the front office.

"Get in your car. We're going home," Mom says.

During the short drive home, Mom tails me in her car, and I send a text to Rebecca, letting her know I'm probably not going to be seeing her for a while. Once we get to the house, Mom follows me into my room and quickly starts reverse Marie Kondo–ing my life, snatching up anything that might bring me joy. I sit on my bed while she grabs my phone and computer and even an old Game Boy I'm pretty sure I haven't touched in years. "I have to get back to work, but you are to stay in this room for the rest of the day unless you're using the bathroom—is that understood?"

"Yes," I say.

"No TV. No video games. No communication with the outside world."

"Got it."

"Lewis, this is so disappointing," she says, shaking her head as she gives me one last look. Then she exits and I lie back on my bed, contemplating how it took less than half a day at Groveland to completely shatter what I thought was going to be a great year.

THIRTY-NINE

HAYLEY

My parents don't make me go to school on Friday, and after a tense weekend, they don't make me go on Monday either. They don't even try. It's mildly disorienting when I open my eyes and find my room filled with bright midmorning light and the green numbers on my bedside clock displaying 10:23. I lift my phone from the nightstand, and a wall of notifications stares back at me. I start swiping them away one at a time without reading them, but when one disappears, another loads in its place. Soon, I grow frustrated and just turn my phone off altogether, dropping it in the nightstand drawer with a clunk. I stay in my room for a long time, staring at the ceiling and counting off the hours by watching the light from my window move around the walls.

I try desperately not to think about school, but even when I press my fists into my closed eyes, I keep seeing that fuzzy footage of me on the TV in Mrs. Colpher's class. A toxic mix of sadness and anger and bitterness churns in my head. Last night, I ventured to the bathroom to get some water after I thought everyone had already gone to bed, but I could see the light was still on in my parents' room, so I leaned close to the closed door to hear them talking. Dad seemed to be at a loss, torn between forcing me to go back to school and giving me time to process, while Mom kept referencing some parenting message board she's been going to for advice. It's so reassuring that strangers on the internet are helping to guide my future.

By the early afternoon, my growling stomach forces me from bed. In the kitchen, I only have enough motivation to pour myself some cereal. I wander around the house as I eat, dragging my socked feet over the carpet, feeling the static building in my toes. Occasionally, I stop to stare out the front window. The street is empty, and there are long stretches of time where a single car doesn't drive by the house. During those moments, it's easy to think there's been some kind of disaster and now I'm the last person alive on Earth. If the rapture means I get to be alone in my house eating sugary cereal and not wearing a bra, I say bring on the rapture.

Later, Lucy shows up unannounced when I'm not exactly looking my best. I know this because Lucy says, "You're not exactly looking your best," as she shoves a coffee from Bad Pun into my hands before heading upstairs.

When she opens the door to my room, I see the place with fresh eyes. The sheets on my bed are a crumpled mess, and several of my dresser drawers look like they're actively regurgitating articles of clothing. Lucy pushes a scattering of notebooks and college mail to the back of my bureau and leans against the cleared surface. "I'm not even going to ask about your recent showering schedule," she says.

My hand flutters to the greasy knot of hair piled atop my head. "That's probably for the best."

"This isn't, like, the start of you becoming a hoarder, is it?"

"I am not becoming a hoarder," I say, flattening out my sheets a little and sitting on the edge of my bed.

"You say that now, but if this trend continues, we're only a few years away from a hazard team coming in here and finding the bones of that cat you thought ran away."

"I don't even own a cat."

"Look at this room, girl. You're real close to having a whole mess of cats."

I laugh despite myself. It feels good. Watching Lucy smile and take a long drag of her coffee makes me realize how much I've missed her over the past several days, even though I've been actively ignoring her many attempts to reach me. Sadness is this weirdly seductive thing. You can sink into it so easily, disappearing into the belief that no one cares about you or understands what you're dealing with. But that's not true.

"So what's the plan?" Lucy asks. "I gave you a few days on your own, but now I'm about to be very much up in your business."

I shrug because I don't really have much of a plan. "Well, I'm pretty sure I'll be back in school tomorrow. If I know my parents, they might be empathetic enough to give me a couple days, but I don't think they'll let this go on. I'm definitely not going back to TV Production, though, that's for sure."

Lucy sighs and puts her coffee down on my desk. "Look, I know what Lewis did was messed up. It was the worst. But I think you should consider forgiving him."

The idea of even trying to talk to Lewis at all seems insufferable. Lucy might as well ask me to be her Sherpa on an expedition to the top of Mount Everest. I'm just as likely to do that as I am to forgive Lewis. "Forgive him? You saw what he did. It was humiliating."

Lucy walks over, sits down beside me on my bed, and places a hand on my knee. "Yeah. It was shitty. And I know I don't know Lewis as well as you do, but he seems like a genuinely nice guy, Hay. He helped me carry you up here when you were drunk. He punched Harold Lockner. You got to give him credit for that. And look at this." She pulls out her phone and brings up her text log with Lewis. She drags her finger along the screen and releases it. The string of texts scrolls for a long time. "This started the night you drank too much. I thought he was just worried about you choking on your own vomit or something, and I'm sure he probably was, but he *kept* texting me even after he knew you were fine. Very little of this is me and Lewis bonding, by the way. A lot of it is him checking up on you or just wanting to know more about you." I knew Lewis and Lucy had started to become friends, but I didn't realize

he was so interested in me. "And some of it's just annoying," Lucy protests. "I mean, he texted me at six thirty in the morning last week to ask
me what your favorite doughnut is. Who does that?"

I think back to the first day of TV Production this semester when
Lewis walked in with two boxes of doughnuts and I was so happy to see
that there were three strawberry glazed when he cracked them open. I
almost smile at the memory. Almost. "I don't think he meant to hurt
you," Lucy says.

I collapse back on my bed, dropping one of my arms so that it drapes
across my face and covers my eyes. I know what Lucy's saying is probably
true, but it doesn't make me feel any better. "It doesn't matter what he
meant to do. He did hurt me."

"I know he did. And it's okay to be sad and upset and angry, but
at the very least, you should talk to him about it. Try to clear the air a
little. Don't just run away from this."

"It's not worth it, Lucy. It's my last semester of high school. I don't
need TV Production, and I don't need Lewis."

"Fine." Lucy sighs, and I can hear the irritation in her voice.

I peek out from under my arm. "Why are you so invested in this?"

"I'm just tired, Hayley. I've been trying so hard to be supportive,
especially this year. I've stood by you through all of your decisions, even
the ones I've disagreed with."

"And I appreciate you being such a good friend," I say, shooting
her a big smile and placing a hand on her back. She stands and shakes
me off.

"Your friend? Is that what I am? Because I'm starting to feel like your
emotional crutch. I mean, my God, Hayley, you stopped your car at the
front of school for a few minutes. It wasn't some gravity-shifting event,
and yet you've let it guide every single decision you've made this year."

I sit up, irritation sparking in my chest. "Are you serious right now?
It was on the news!"

"For, like, two minutes. You've let this thing consume you, Hayley.

And now you're asking me to support yet another stupid decision based off something you've blown up in your mind to a ridiculous proportion."

"I'm sorry my life is so pathetic," I spit, feeling the anger consuming my insides. "I didn't realize I was being such a downer by expressing my feelings. That must be a real mood-killer. I'll be sure to stuff them deep down inside from now on. I'm sure that's healthy."

"Well, you've been making plenty of unhealthy decisions for the past six months; why stop now?"

Rage pulsates against my ribs. "This is great," I say. "I'm so glad I have you to help guide my decisions. Remind me, where did you get your degree in psychology?"

"Ha! I wish." She laughs. "At least your therapist gets paid to listen to you whine about your problems. I have to put up with this shit for free."

That stings. "Sorry to bug you with my friendship!"

"Friendship is a two-way street, Hayley. When is the last time you ever asked me about my life? When is the last time we had an extended discussion about anything that didn't eventually circle back to you and 'the incident'?" She holds up her fingers to make air quotes around "the incident," sending her voice into a mock quiver.

My mind can't focus on any rational line of thought. Any piece of advice Dr. Kim has ever given me about maintaining control is thrown out the window. All I can see is Lucy, who has fought alongside me for the past six months, suddenly switching sides. "Get out," I manage to choke out, heat consuming my face.

"Enjoy your coffee," she says, shutting the door to my room. I hear her steps descend the stairs, and I fall, smothering my face into my pillow and willing the tears not to come.

When I flip over and turn toward my dresser topped with awards and accolades, my rage boils over. I grab a cardboard box out of my closet and with one swift movement sweep the trophies off my dresser like I'm brushing crumbs from the kitchen counter. They make a hollow clunking sound as the flimsy fake gold pieces knock together. The weight of all of them in the box is heavy. As I go to toss them into my closet, one of the trophies snags my sweater, the arm of one of the tennis figures gripping the fabric. I try to shake it off, but it won't come. Frustrated, I sit the entire box on my bed and use both hands to pull the trophy from my shirt. Once it's free, I place one hand at the base and wrap my other over the slender figure. With a quick twist, it snaps in half. I drop both pieces into the box and hurl the whole collection into the back of my closet. The corkboard crowded with ribbons and certificates slips off its hooks easily, and I slide it behind my dresser where I don't have to see it.

FORTY

LEWIS

Cal plops down into my passenger seat and pulls his phone from his pocket. "Ta-da!" he exclaims, holding it like he's a presenter on a game show. I nod and lift my phone from the center console. "Hey! Phone bros!" he says, tapping his against mine.

Cal and I both ended up with a week of in-school suspension for fighting. Same for Tyler and Harold. ISS is basically the high school equivalent of prison, just with less bartering for loose cigarettes. We all had to sit in a windowless room together and do our schoolwork while being monitored by the girls' volleyball coach and a student aide. We weren't allowed to talk at all, even when they brought us lunch. Then after school, I got to go to my house and experience ISS Home Edition (now with more chores!). Mom would leave me a list of tasks every day that she expected me to have done by the time she got home from work, and she would call on the landline at random times to make sure I wasn't hanging out with friends when I was supposed to be vacuuming.

Things at home have been tense. We've shared more than one silent dinner. But this morning, at breakfast, Mom and Dad silently slid my phone across the counter. I didn't touch it until Dad said, "This is a sign that you are beginning to regain our trust. Don't abuse it."

Once I got it charged, I saw that all of my social media timelines were overflowing with shaky videos and blurry photos of my fight with

Harold. I deleted the ones I could and untagged myself from the others without bothering to read the comments. I scrolled through my texts and then restarted my phone and checked them again. There were some funny messages from Rebecca, but any joy they brought was overshadowed by the fact that there was nothing from Hayley. I started to send her a message, but after scrapping several terrible drafts, I gave up on the idea altogether.

Cal must be reading my mood because he says, "C'mon, man. You got your phone back. No more ISS. No more having to look at Harold's and Tyler's stupid faces every day. Shouldn't you be excited?"

There are some things I'm excited about. I'm excited that I don't have to dust furniture and wash dishes every day. I'm excited I can go grab a burger at Graze Daze after school. But I'm worried, too. I haven't talked to Hayley since I aired that documentary more than a week ago, and now I'm about to go sit next to her in TV Production. How does someone apologize for something like that? Not to mention all the other stuff I said about her being selfish when we fought. I shouldn't have become so defensive. How do I even begin to convey how sorry I am?

"Come on, I know what will cheer you up," Cal says. He reaches forward and skips to track ten on my '80s mix. "Here we go. You ready?" He twists up the volume dial, the distinct snare rhythm at the beginning of R.E.M.'s "It's the End of the World as We Know It (And I Feel Fine)" blasting from the speakers. Cal is grinning manically. When we were bored one day last summer, we took the time to look up the lyrics and memorize them. It's one of those perfect summer projects that's really only accomplishable when you have no school or job or any other demands for your time. It took us several hours, considering the pure sheer amount of lyrics crammed into four minutes and the insane rate that they're sung. We were constantly pausing the track and going back to listen to certain stretches over and over. Michael Stipe starts in with "That's great, it starts with an earthquake," and Cal is singing along, grabbing me by the shoulder and shaking me as we move down the street. I shake my head as he yells through the first verse, matching the song word for word in a way that would surely blow the collective mind of any casual karaoke bar.

I'm really trying not to give Cal the satisfaction of caving, but despite my sour mood, his enthusiasm is infectious, and despite the fact that it's been months since our day of studying the lyrics, surprisingly, the words are all still there. Just like I'll always know the mitochondria is the powerhouse of the cell, I guess I'll always know that Lenny Bruce is not afraid. So after the first chorus ends as we sit at a red light, I give in, allowing myself to melt into Cal's excitement. I turn to him, shouting, "Six o'clock, TV hour!" at the top of the second verse, and he shouts back all the louder. At one point, he rolls down his window, letting the frigid late-January air pour in as he keeps time by pounding his hand against the outer side of his door.

By the time we get to school, I actually am feeling better. Maybe this could be a good day after all.

That feeling melts away when I round the corner and find Parker standing at my locker with Hayley. He has a hand on her shoulder while she loads books into her backpack. All of them. When she's done, she puts her bag on the ground, then pulls her collapsible shelf from the locker and folds it up. She tries to shove it into her backpack, but the thing's already so stuffed with her notebooks and supplies that she can't get it to fit. After a few unsuccessful attempts, she heaves her whole backpack against the locker bank in frustration. Parker kneels down and places a hand under her chin, and they talk for a minute before standing up. He hoists her backpack onto his shoulder, and Hayley goes to shut the locker door but hesitates. She looks at the two cards hanging there—two stick-figure apologies—and puts her hand on the corner like she might take those, too. But she changes her mind and shuts the door. Parker wraps his arm around her as they move down the hall, and I shuffle into the corner like an idiot so that they won't see me as they pass.

Once they round the corner, I go to the locker and open it. All of my stuff is there, but not a trace of Hayley remains. All week in ISS, this is what I was worried about. I had long, unbroken hours of quiet to sit with my thoughts and wonder how Hayley might be feeling. I don't have to wonder anymore. I slam the locker door, and it bounces on its hinges, the clatter of metal on metal echoing down the hall.

In TV Production, while everyone is still talking and settling into their seats, I set a produce bag containing four apples on Mrs. Hansen's desk. She looks at them and then up at me, silently awaiting an explanation.

"Giving an apple to a teacher is, like, a sign of respect, right?" I ask.

She smirks. "Something like that."

"I know it's an old tradition from when teachers taught in wooden schoolhouses and every child in the village would run to school pushing a hoop with a stick or something, so maybe this is stupid or whatever, but I didn't know what else you might like. Do you eat apples? Don't answer that. It's too late for me to take them back. One apple seemed kind of cheap, so I bought you four apples. The good kind too. Those are Honeycrisp."

"You're giving me four Honeycrisp apples?"

"Right. I know I messed up last week by lying about having Hayley's permission to show that clip of her, so I wanted to apologize and bring in these apples as a peace offering. To show you that I'm sorry and I'm serious about doing better. I'd like to still be your senior producer, if that's okay."

She pushes the top of the bag open and takes a better look at the fruit. "Well, thank you, Lewis. I accept your apples, and I look forward to a productive semester. Senior producer."

"I'm guessing Hayley and I aren't going to be partners anymore," I say, realizing I don't even see her in the room.

Mrs. Hansen picks up her attendance book. "No, you will not be partners anymore. But that's because Hayley is no longer enrolled in this class." Mrs. Hansen watches my face as she says it, giving her words time to settle. They sting, but I try to remain stoic even as a near crippling amount of shame closes in. Not only did I embarrass Hayley, but I also made her quit something she was really talented at. Great. But why would she stay? She hates me, and every memory of TV Production is probably tainted for her now. "You're going to be working solo this semester, Lewis."

"Solo?" I ask.

"Yes. I was recently talking to Mrs. Winslow. She serves as the faculty advisor to the prom committee, and they want an interesting senior video to show at prom."

"Don't they usually just put up a photo slideshow or something?"

"Usually, yes. But they want to do something different this year. Something more meaningful. And apparently a lot of the students on the committee have been impressed by your mini-documentaries."

Our documentaries, I almost say. "They want a documentary for prom?"

"Not necessarily. But something new. Something more sincere than just photos and music. I told Mrs. Winslow I thought you could pull it off, but this isn't something I want you slapping together in a week. Aside from your duties producing the announcements most mornings—by the way, I really had to go to bat for you in order for you to keep that position—this will be your only assignment this semester." What Mrs. Hansen's saying sinks in, and the weight of it is overwhelming. One assignment to determine my whole grade. This prom thing sounds like just the type of challenge Hayley thrives on. I know if she were here, she'd have at least half a dozen good ideas by the end of class today, and, if history is any indication, somehow they would all lead to us risking our lives in one way or another. Mrs. Hansen must sense my reluctance because she adds, "I know this is big, Lewis. I'm giving you a lot of freedom with this, but I think you're up for it. Take some time. Find what you want to say. Find your voice."

FORTY-ONE

HAYLEY

It's surprisingly easy to slip back into my old life. I start spending all my time in the AT wing at school, eating lunch with the smart kids and talking about postgraduation plans. I catch up with everyone I haven't really been spending much time with this year, and I ignore the announcements each morning by playing cards instead. No one talks about the documentary Lewis aired. Everyone is too consumed with being Ivy League–bound to care. I guess Dr. Kim was right. Some people are too focused on their own life to be concerned about mine.

But as the weeks drag on, I become increasingly annoyed at the realization that, even though I can spend all of my free time with my fellow AT students, none of them is truly my friend. I can sit through the whole lunch period and no one nudges my knee like Lucy used to when I would get lost in my own thoughts, and no one is so committed to seeing me smile that they make joke after joke until I finally crack like Lewis would. It grates on me, and I start playing a little game to see how long I can go without saying a word before anyone notices. At first, I don't last very long. Maybe half an hour before someone prods me with a question and I speak. But then it stretches on. A whole lunch period and then an entire day where I'm completely silent, just occasionally nodding as I listen to the same conversations we seem to have every day. Prom, graduation, college. Prom, graduation, college. The same topics again and again, constantly circling back with nauseating frequency. I get it, those are the next big things on the horizon, but there's only so much to be said about boutonnieres and tassels, limos and dorm decor.

Tonight, Parker is coming over for dinner. My parents insisted on having him over to celebrate since we both got accepted to Northwestern, our dual full-size envelopes with welcome packets arriving on the same day. When I got the package, I sat at the kitchen island and read over the congratulatory letter three times, waiting for the excitement to arrive. Waiting for the buzzing that usually forms in my gut when I'm eager or exhilarated. But it didn't come. It didn't come when my parents wrapped me in a big hug and told me how proud they are, and it didn't come the next day at lunch when Parker shared the news with all the other AT kids. I just sat there with a dumb smile on my face and chewed my peanut butter sandwich, the thickness coating my throat.

My parents are pulling the roast chicken from the oven when Parker shows up at the front door in an ironed white button-up. As we all take our seats at the table, I'm dreading sitting through another meal talking about college, and I'm actively trying to think up ways to change the subject. Maybe I can get Tanner talking about basketball or something. But before I even have a chance to open my mouth, Dad already has his glass raised for a toast. "To Hayley and Parker. You've both worked so hard, and you deserve all your success."

"Hear! Hear!" my mom says.

"Hear! Hear!" Tanner echoes, a little too enthusiastically.

"I can't believe you're already graduating," Mom says, giving me a dreamy look from across the table. "Seems like just yesterday we were bringing you home from the hospital."

"Okay, pull it back, Mom," I say. "There're still three months of school left. You're going to exhaust yourself if you get weepy at every mention of graduation this soon—"

"Two graduations this year," Tanner interrupts. "Both equally important, I think."

Dad rubs the top of his head. "That's right, bud. Graduating from middle school is an accomplishment too."

Tanner nods approvingly and stuffs a forkful of chicken into his mouth. Under the table, Parker finds my hand and gives it a little squeeze. We've been spending more and more time together lately. Especially since he's pretty much the one real friend I have among a sea of acquaintances. When we were dating, we used to dream about going to college together, imagining how glorious our lives would be, living on the same campus without our parents to answer to. But whatever it was about that plan that used to excite me doesn't seem to have the same power anymore. Now it feels more like trying to fit into an old sweater that shrunk in the wash.

"Well, we're going to have to buy you a better winter coat, that's for sure," my mom says.

"That's right," Dad adds. "Chicago is no joke."

"It'll definitely be an adjustment," Parker says. "But I'm excited. There's just so much to see and do." Parker starts talking about museums he wants to visit and restaurants he's already looked up, and the words glide over me like water across a stone. I try to imagine us walking around the city together, the hoods of our parkas pulled up over our heads as the snow swirls around. I try to envision us studying in the library or going to see a play, and it just doesn't feel right. I'm reminded of my old childhood felt board again, where I would swap the girl's head with different bodies.

Can I really spend four years playing dress-up in Chicago, forcing a smile through selfies at the Bean and the observation deck at Willis Tower?

I manage to grin my way through dinner, offering very little input, happy to just nod and smile as Parker and my parents run away with the conversation. After dessert, I hug Parker goodbye at the door, and he sneaks a quick kiss on my cheek. On the way upstairs, I hear my mom say, "It's so good to see them spending time together again," as she and Dad load the dishwasher.

Everyone seems so happy. So why can't I be?

In my room, I check my phone and find I have a missed text from Lewis. One sentence. *Hey, can we talk?* Part of me wants to call him up, but I'm still so hurt. This is the type of thing I would usually consult with Lucy about, but we're not on speaking terms either. I open up my text chain with her, hoping against hope there's a missed text, but there's nothing new. Instead I'm staring at a screen of photos, the series of shots she sent me from the night we all TP'ed Harold's car. Selfies where she and Cal and Lewis and I are all squeezed into frame, beaming and holding up our shaved ice cups. Looking at them now, I'm filled with an ache, a longing for something missing. Is that feeling gone forever?

I lock my phone, turn off my light, and crawl into bed.

FORTY-TWO

LEWIS

Trying to come up with a clip for prom is turning out to be a nightmare. I spend most of my time in TV Production trying to think of some theme or interesting idea, but everything I come up with just seems too corny or trite, so a lot of days I just end up flicking paper footballs across the desk while Cal holds his fingers as makeshift goalposts.

I thought meeting with the prom committee might give me some insight into what they're envisioning, but that turned out to be a very bad idea. Everyone had a different vision. One person suggested that the video should be quiet and sentimental, while someone else interrupted and said it should be loud and celebratory. Someone said it should feel big and immersive, while someone else kept reiterating that it should be under four minutes long. When someone suggested the clip culminate in a wide, sweeping shot of our entire graduating class, the conversation shifted into a debate about the logistics of getting everyone on the football field at the same time and trying to find out if anyone owns a drone we could use to get a cool elevated shot. If that's how all their meetings go, I'm pretty sure prom is going to end up being three DJs all playing different music and half a bowl of Doritos (if they can decide between Nacho Cheese or Cool Ranch, that is).

I've been running more than ever, tossing on some sweatpants nearly every night to go out and pound the pavement. I'm getting better at it, I think. My breathing techniques have improved, and my distances are growing longer. It's turning around that's always the hardest part. When I'm running, I can forget about TV Production and Groveland and college decisions. I imagine what would happen if I just kept going. Could I be in the next state by sunrise?

I start carrying a video camera with me everywhere, hoping some sort of inspiration will strike unexpectedly. That's how I end up filming Cal at the sporting goods store as he tests out golf clubs. His parents have promised him a new set as a graduation present, so now he's trying to decide which one he wants. We're standing on the plastic practice green when he says, "I think you're stressing out about this prom clip too much," bringing his putter against the golf ball and sending it into the hole a few feet away.

"Well, it's been a month, and I've still got nothing," I say, setting down the camera and picking a putter from the railing that lines the fake green. It's silver and purple and all sharp angles, like a prop from a sci-fi movie about golfing on the moon.

"I'm sure it'll be fine," Cal says. "You really think Mrs. Hansen's going to flunk you over this? We're three months from graduation. You're basically already in college."

A lot of seniors are talking about college nonstop these days, but it's not a topic I'm particularly interested in. Over winter break, I finally buckled down and applied to some places, but there's nothing I'm particularly excited about. I just can't find anything motivational about four more years of sitting in a classroom. Even if it does mean getting to move away from my parents and drink beer. I don't want to wade into all of this with Cal, so I stay focused on the TV assignment. "I don't know. This clip is worth my whole grade."

"Maybe this is one of those things where you need to stop thinking about it and an idea will just come to you. Isn't that a thing?" Cal asks, lining up his next putt.

"So I should just think about something else?"

"Yeah, like what's going on with you and Rebecca?" Great, another subject I'm not particularly interested in discussing.

I look up at Cal across the green. "What do you mean?"

He collapses out of his putting stance and gives me a look of annoyance. "Well, she's, like, the girl of your dreams, isn't she? You guys made out on New Year's, and now what? It's been over two months!"

"I think the girl of my dreams wears shorter skirts," I joke.

"Yeah right. You're into that sexy librarian shit," Cal says, pointing his club at me like a sword. "Your dream girl isn't wearing a short skirt. She's wearing a chunky sweater and drinking chamomile tea or something."

"Okay. That was weirdly specific," I say, taking my putt. The ball misses the hole by a couple inches and bounces off the wooden guard with a dull thump.

"You're just easy to read," Cal says, sending another ball across the green and into the hole I just missed. "But seriously, why aren't you pursuing this? I thought this year was going to be different for you two."

I think back to the kiss Rebecca and I shared in my car. "Yeah, me too." For a while, I thought the way Rebecca and I didn't really talk about the kiss meant we were both taking our time to sort our thoughts, figuring out the right words for the right moment. But the longer time has stretched on, and the farther we've moved away from that moment, the more I feel like a canyon is forming between us. A gap neither of us can clear. I've tried to drop a few hints to figure out where we stand. Last month, I slid a small box of chocolates across the counter at Graze Daze on Valentine's Day. I had printed a picture of John Cusack from *Say Anything* in his classic boom-box-over-the-head pose and glued it to some cardboard, then attached it to the top of the box so that he stood up on his own. Not a grand gesture, but something small and intentional that I thought might help bridge the gap and remind her of where we used to be. But that didn't happen. She was appreciative and thanked me and even gave me a free milkshake in return, but any spark of reconnection I was hoping for just wasn't there.

"I know you got distracted with Hayley for a bit, but she's out of the picture now," Cal says. Is that what Hayley was? A distraction? If so, I think I'm still distracted. As much as I try to push the thoughts out of my mind, it still bothers me that I've never really had a chance to talk to her since the day of our big fight. I haven't even seen her in the halls at school, and she hasn't responded to any of my texts. It's like she's completely reoriented her life around avoiding me. And as the weeks go by, I find I'm missing her more and more, wishing she was there when I think of a joke and wondering if she's going on after-school coffee runs with someone else now. "It just feels like things haven't been as weird lately," Cal says.

"Weird?" I ask, picking Cal's ball out of the hole and rolling it back to him.

"Yeah, with you and Rebecca. You guys had private jokes, and you were always smiling at each other. Sometimes, I felt like a third wheel, honestly. It hasn't felt that way as much lately."

"So you want us to be more sexual around you?"

"God, no. I'm just saying you guys might be going separate ways soon. Rebecca's probably leaving the state for college. You need to figure out what you want or you're going to regret it. Especially when she starts posting pictures of her hunky college boyfriend and you're left all alone at night." Cal lifts his eyebrows as he wraps his thumb and forefinger around the shaft of his putter and starts moving them up and down suggestively. He stops only when he catches an employee giving him a stern look.

"You're so gross," I say. But Cal does have a point—I need to figure out what I want. I pull my phone from my pocket and check my text log with Hayley. Nothing there but a handful of texts from me that she never responded to. What do I do if what I want is not the thing I thought I wanted for so long?

"Talk to Rebecca," Cal says, taking another putt. "I know all of my relationships up to this point have crashed and burned, but even I know communication is the foundation of a good relationship."

"I'm pretty sure one time when you were drunk, you told me a nice ass was the foundation of a good relationship."

"Okay. So a nice ass is the foundation, and communication is the bricks you use to build the house."

God, I need new friends.

FORTY-THREE

HAYLEY

oward the end of March, I finally go with Dr. Kim to check out the support group down at the local university. I tried to avoid it, but one day, Parker invited me to a trivia night with several other AT students in front of my parents, and I told him I was busy. Tanner couldn't keep his big mouth shut and asked what I was doing, and the support group was the only valid excuse I could come up with off the top of my head. Then Mom got super excited when she heard I was going, so I couldn't back out.

Dr. Kim opens the door of one of the gray stone buildings on campus and leads me down a hall of shiny green tile. We enter the last door on the left, where there are chairs set up in front of a wooden podium, and a bunch of college kids are huddled around a table of free coffee and doughnuts. I'm relieved that at least the chairs aren't in a circle, which is what I was envisioning. Dr. Kim squeezes my shoulder and says, "Come on. It'll be all right." Then she leads us to a couple of seats in the back row.

After a few minutes, once more people have filtered in and filled over half the chairs, a girl with bright red lipstick and a yellow hijab steps up to the podium. "Hello, everyone. Thanks for coming tonight. If you're new here, welcome. Feel free to grab some coffee and a doughnut. If you want chocolate glazed, you better hurry before Glenn goes back for seconds."

"Why you gotta call me out like that, Naj?" a muscular guy in the second row yells, his mouth half full. Several people laugh.

"Anyway," the girl at the podium continues, "like always, this is an open space. If you want to come up and share, great. If you want to just sit and listen, that's cool too. We just ask that everyone be respectful and open. Now, who has something they want to say?"

I press my hands firmly into my knees to keep my legs from bouncing. Dr. Kim better not expect me to get up there. Talking to her is one thing, but I'm certainly not about to get up in front of these strangers and share the details of my life. *Hey, everyone, nice to meet you. I'm about to go off to college with my ex-boyfriend, and I haven't talked to my best friend in several months. Also, have you seen the YouTube video of my mental breakdown?* Yeah, no thanks.

Luckily, there's no real opportunity for me to speak because other people keep going up. There are all sorts of stories, some funny and some heartbreaking and most somewhere in between. A guy with a black Mohawk talks about how his mom died last year, and this past Christmas was their first real holiday without her. A larger woman tells a hilarious story about how her friends recently convinced her to try skiing for the first time. Another girl with full tattoo sleeves talks about coming home from work one day to find that her girlfriend had moved out.

No one really asks any questions or offers any advice. They just let people tell their stories. If this is a support group, it's a weird one.

Eventually, a girl with spiked brown hair sitting toward the front raises her hand.

"All right, Cody, come on up," Naj says.

Cody pulls the mic from the stand and leans against the side of the podium. "So, who here has cried in a Target recently?" There's some light laughter, and a guy near me and Dr. Kim lets out a small "Woo!"

"Great, so just me and Marco," Cody continues. "Awesome. Well, I'm going to tell you all this story. Last month, my grandmother passed away." A handful of people offer sympathetic *awws*. "Thank you," Cody says. "It was very sad. My grandmother was very considerate and so nice. Nice to the point where you couldn't really correct her. You know anyone like that? Like, here's an example: I was eight when the first *Despicable Me* movie came out, and let me tell you, I was very into that movie." A few people in the crowd chuckle. "Seriously, I had shirts and posters and bedsheets. You name it. And that was the one piece of information about me that my grandmother really clung to. So every birthday and every Christmas, you can bet there was something *Despicable Me*–related under the tree for me from dear, sweet Granny. And for a while, it was great, but then my interests shifted, and Grandma didn't recognize that. She just kept the *Despicable Me* stuff coming. For my high school graduation, part of my gift from her was a stuffed minion in a graduation cap! I think she had to special order it!" People are laughing in earnest now, even me.

"So, anyway, I'm at Target the other day, and I see this little girl in a shopping cart holding a minion toy. Guys, I just lost it. I don't know what happened to me. All of a sudden, I was bawling in the cereal aisle. Eventually, I just grabbed a box of Cheerios and ran away. I was sprinting through the aisles of Target crying and clinging to some cereal. If it was filmed in black and white and played at slow motion and set to some violin music, it would have made a great art house film about the perils of suburbia or something. I don't know. So what did I do? I went home, ate some cereal, and you bet your ass I watched *Despicable Me*." Cody looks up toward the ceiling. "Miss you, Grandma." She grabs the stand and slides the microphone back into place as people cheer. Some even stand and clap. Several people pat her on the back as she makes her way back to her seat.

I'm stunned. This girl who's only a couple of years older than me just took this tragic and embarrassing thing and made it . . . funny. It was a private story that she could've kept hidden, but she chose to get up and share it with all of us, telling it in a way that was powerful. No one here is making fun of her or laughing at her. We're all laughing *with* her. And I kind of want to be her friend.

After an hour or so, Naj concludes the meeting. People get up and start talking to one another, and I'm surprised when Dr. Kim waves at Cody, who smiles and comes to give her a hug.

"Dr. Kim! What brings you here?"

Dr. Kim gestures to me. "I'm actually here with Hayley."

"Hayley, hi, nice to meet you," Cody says, extending her hand. "How did you like our little group?"

"I really enjoyed it," I say, surprising myself. Out of the corner of my eye, I can see the smug grin on Dr. Kim's face, satisfied that I actually liked something I've been actively avoiding for months. "I guess I'm just a little confused. Is this just a storytelling group, or . . . ?"

"Sort of," Cody says. "Half storytelling, half support group, I guess. We started as a group for people who were struggling with the transition from high school to college, but we've grown over the last several semesters. Still, I think the heart has remained. At our core, we're a group of people who feel like everyone deserves to be part of a community. We want to make sure no one's being pushed to the fringes here on campus, so anyone can get up and talk about anything going on in their life, and we promise to listen."

"That's pretty cool," I say.

"Yeah, it basically saved my life," Cody says. "I love college now, but my first semester was pretty rough. I probably would've dropped out if it wasn't for this group. And Dr. Kim, of course."

"Hayley's headed to college next semester," Dr. Kim offers.

"Oh, nice," Cody says. "You just gotta find your people, you know? Sometimes you walk around campus and you see people smiling and having a good time, and you convince yourself everyone has it all together except you. Listening to people talk about their lives reminds me that everyone's dealing with their own shit."

I completely understand what Cody's talking about because it's what I've been trying to do all year—project an image of having it all together.

"I got to go," Cody says. "Nice to meet you, Hayley. Come back any time. Dr. Kim, see you for our appointment on Thursday, right?"

"See you then," Dr. Kim says.

As we walk back across campus, Dr. Kim and I are silent for a bit, and then I say, "Okay, you can say 'Told you so' now."

"I don't know what you're talking about," Dr. Kim says, but then she smiles and winks at me. "I'm just glad you finally decided to come. I wanted to bring you here to show you that lots of people are dealing with the same kinds of things you're going through, Hayley. Trying to figure out who they are and working out who they want to be. People you see every day are dealing with difficult struggles. What's important is that we find people who care about us, people we can be honest with, people who won't judge us."

During my drive home, I keep thinking about it, and I know Dr. Kim is right. I've spent so much of this year trying to cover up my insecurities or trying to force people to change their perception of me. Even this semester, I've been working so hard just to blend in with the AT crowd, while someone like Cody has chosen to stand out. She's chosen to make herself the center of attention by grabbing a microphone and stepping into the spotlight, not shying away from her issues. Even though she was telling an embarrassing story tonight, no one thought she was frail or damaged. They saw her as strong.

As I cruise past the shaved ice stand, I notice yellow light spilling from the inside, so I pull into the parking lot. The door is cracked open, and when I tap it with my foot, I find Lucy sitting there, stabbing at a cup of clear ice with a plastic spoon.

"Mrs. Cambridge called me and said she needed me to return her keys this weekend so she can give them to the new girls she found to work here this summer," she says without looking up. "Seemed like I should come one more time." After a moment, she extends the cup my way, and when she shifts, I see she's wearing a red USC sweatshirt, vibrant and new.

"Piña colada?" I ask.

"Piña colada."

I lean against the counter and take a bite of the shaved ice, letting the cold sweetness rest on my tongue for a moment before swallowing it down. Lucy and I have had fights and disagreements in the past, but never anything like this. We've never gone months without speaking. I'm not really sure how to start this conversation. I take another bite to just give myself something to do, and then I start talking, hoping I'll find the right words along the way. "I finally let Dr. Kim take me to that support group thing down at the university." Lucy raises her eyebrows at me but doesn't say anything. "I got to hear a bunch of people share their stories. It made me realize I've been so scared this year. I kept thinking there was some sort of fault line in my brain, and I was just waiting for the moment when everything would shift, and it would mess up my whole life."

"Hay, that's not going to happen," Lucy says.

"I know. It took me a while to get there, but I really do believe you." I hand the shaved ice back to her. "I remember when I was a freshman at Groveland, I would see these seniors in the hall, and they all looked so mature and carefree. I wanted that for my senior year. I wanted to win awards and have a perfect GPA and be relentlessly happy and look tan in every photo."

Lucy snorts. "When have you ever looked tan?"

I smile. "Shut up. It was a dream, all right? Maybe that's corny or stupid, but it's what I wanted. And then everything went sideways. I haven't won any awards, and I'm certainly not relentlessly happy. After my meeting with Wexler and Mr. Keith at the start of the year, I knew things were going to be different, and I thought different meant worse. I thought it meant I'm worse."

"You're not worse, Hayley."

"I think in some ways I am, just not in the ways I was consumed with. I was worried about my reputation and my status, and that made me a worse friend. I see that now. I was obsessed with myself. I'm so sorry, Lucy. I'm sorry for the ways I ignored you this year. I'm sorry for the ways I kept putting my needs ahead of yours. I'm sorry for the way I've been unsupportive and uncaring. You're my best friend. I've missed you a lot."

Lucy smiles at me. "I've missed you, too."

"I want to get better," I tell her. "I'm trying to get better." Lucy extends her hand to me, and I take hold of it. For a moment, we just sit there in silence, the only sound an occasional car passing on the street. Then I slide up onto the counter and lean against Bertha's cold metal body. "So, do you want to tell me about USC?" I ask, gesturing to her sweatshirt. Lucy's smile grows wider as she starts talking about the application process and how she mulled over each admission essay for days, and for the first time in weeks, I'm genuinely happy to hear somebody talk about college.

FORTY-FOUR

LEWIS

S pring break isn't real.

I mean, it's real in the sense that we all get a week off school, sure, but there's a folklore surrounding it that's little more than some MTV fantasy propped up by social media influencers and frat-bro movies. Not everyone is going to go on a seven-day liquor-fueled sex romp through Fort Lauderdale, you know? You're not going to lock eyes with some hot blonde over a beer pong table and then find out that you must be soul mates because you both lost your virginity to the same Drake song. It's just not realistic.

Maybe the nonstop-party version of spring break is real for some people. As I walk across the Groveland parking lot, I spot several cheer-leaders rocking new tans and airbrushed Panama City T-shirts. Still, I'm willing to bet their week was less about meeting their soul mate and more about experimenting with hand stuff on some Florida townie under a pier.

Normally, I wouldn't be in such a bad mood after a week off school, but my time away wasn't particularly fun. Rebecca was spending the week with her dad, and Cal's parents took him to visit some relatives in Tennessee, so I mainly slept, watched a lot of daytime game shows, and tried unsuccessfully to think of what I should do for this stupid prom clip.

I also ran a lot. Since I didn't have to be up early for school, I would often go out late at night, jogging past lit-up gas stations and glowing fast-food joints at ten or eleven. Late-night exercising definitely has a different vibe. People who have their life together go running at dawn, greeting the day at sunrise and listening to some upbeat carpe-diem-I-am-the-master-of-my-fate podcast. If you're out jogging by yourself when other people are crawling into bed or watching Jimmy Fallon, something is wrong. You do not have your shit together. I don't even have the strength to muster up any fantasies during my runs these days; it's just putting one foot in front of the other. There were multiple times when I jogged past Hayley's house, wondering if I might spot her up in her window or catch her sitting on her porch. But it never happened. Will we ever speak again?

In TV Production, Mrs. Hansen stops me at the door. "Lewis! How's your assignment coming along?"

"Uh, yeah, the assignment. I'm making progress. Piecing it together." Good answer, Lew. Vaguely positive. Technically not a lie.

"Okay. Well, don't take too long. Prom's only a few short weeks away."

"Yes, it is." Just receive information and affirm it.

"As I'm sure you'll understand, I will need to approve the clip before handing it over to the prom committee."

I nod. "Indeed. Yes." Such good receiving. Such good affirming.

"Are you okay?"

"Mm-hmm. Just so pumped for . . . the stuff . . . you know." I duck past her, an awkward move that basically requires me to bend over sideways since she's a head shorter than me. I stumble into class and have to grab hold of a desk to right myself, but I don't look back.

During class, I hang out in the studio, lazily scrolling through old footage from this year, letting the clips silently move by, hoping something might inspire me, even though I've done this at least a dozen other times. I'm only half paying attention when the cursor lands on some footage I'd forgotten about. It's a clip from my GoPro on the day Hayley and I filmed Rohan playing laser tag. Onscreen, we're standing outside Lazer Labyrinth, and Hayley's face fills the frame as she smiles up at the camera mounted on my forehead.

"How do I look?" I hear myself ask.

"Oh, real good," she says.

"You're not being sarcastic, are you?"

"What's sarcasm?"

"You know, you can't really make fun of me for this since you have to wear one of these things too."

"Yeah, but I look good in all sorts of head accessories." Hayley smirks and then starts counting off on her fingers. "Bonnets, sweatbands, cowboy hats, berets."

"Berets?"

"Oh, I look great in a beret."

I'm smiling at the footage when my phone buzzes with a group text from Rebecca. *Meet me at Graze Daze tonight at 10:30. We're celebrating, boys!*

Celebrating what? Cal replies.

You'll find out tonight!

When Cal and I arrive at the restaurant, all of the lights are already off because the place closes at ten, and when we get out of the car, Rebecca beckons to us from the roof. "Up here, boys!" She motions for us to go around to the back, and soon, for the second time this year, I'm climbing a ladder and hauling a video camera to the roof of a local business. At least this time, I didn't have to mount a dumpster first.

When we get to the top, Rebecca helps us over the ledge and ushers us to three camping chairs she has set up near the front of the building. She makes Cal and me take a seat before handing both of us a milkshake. There's a chill in the air, so she's wearing a sweatshirt, the curls of her hair tucked away into the pulled-up hood.

"Okay, what's all this about?" Cal asks.

"Are you ready?" Rebecca says.

"Yes," we answer.

She does a little shifting dance in front of us. "Are you sure?"

"Why do I feel like you're probably building this up too much?" Cal asks.

"I'm not," Rebecca insists as she pulls a crinkled envelope from her hoodie pocket. "Your girl has officially . . . been awarded a scholarship . . . to the journalism program . . . at the University of Texas! I'm going to Austin!"

The words hang there for a moment as the crickets chirp and my stomach clenches. I stare at Rebecca, trying to process exactly what this means, as she holds the letter over her head with her mouth frozen in a huge anticipatory grin. The realizations come rushing in.

Rebecca's leaving.

She's going to another state.

She's leaving me behind.

Cal glances over at me. This is the thing I've been worried about all year, that Rebecca would leave town before I ever got a chance to really talk to her about my feelings. I wait for a beat, expecting the sting of regret to hit sharp and fresh.

But it doesn't come.

The construction crew in my mind quickly reminds me that stunned silence is not the proper response when your best friend gives you good news.

"Seriously?" I ask, lurching forward a little.

"Yes!" Rebecca proclaims, shaking the letter.

Then Cal and I are both out of our seats, and we're all hugging and jumping up and down a little.

"Like, a full ride?" Cal asks.

"Well, not a full ride," Rebecca says, "but enough. I'll still have to take out some loans and probably pick up a part-time job when I get there."

"So should we get you some cowboy boots or something?" I ask.

"Oh, I'm one hundred percent getting into bolo ties now, so get ready."

After a few minutes, we all settle back down into the camping chairs. Rebecca pulls out a blanket and tosses it over all our laps as we drink our milkshakes and stare up at the night sky.

"I can't believe you're going to Texas," Cal says.

"I can't believe I'm going to Texas," Rebecca echoes, her voice above a whisper but only just. "I will miss this place, though," she says. "There have been plenty of times I've wanted to quit this job. Times I've been frustrated with rude customers or had to clean unconscionable messes in the bathroom. But I have great memories here too. This was my first job." Her hand finds my knee under the blanket, and I look over at her, surprised to see her eyes glossy with tears. "I love so many things about this place, but that doesn't mean it's meant to last forever. This place was my first, and I'll always carry that with me, but I have to move on. This place will go on without me, too."

And suddenly I realize she's not just talking about Graze Daze anymore. She's talking about us.

Rebecca and I will probably never be together, and I can't really figure out where things shifted for us. I'm probably to blame. Maybe Cal's always been right that I waited way too long to ever make a move. Maybe the fact that Rebecca and I never really talked about our kiss shows that neither of us were passionate enough about the idea of being together to make it happen. At this point it's not worth dissecting because the only sadness I feel is a dull ache. Nostalgia for a moment that isn't even gone yet. I'll miss Rebecca because she's one of my dearest friends, but the romantic longing I once felt burning so strongly faded to glowing embers when I wasn't fanning the flames. I put my hand on top of hers, and she smiles at me before resting her head on my shoulder. "The world is big," she says. "There's so much for us to see and do. But who knows? Maybe one day we'll end up back here."

Maybe, but for now, I'm ready to let Rebecca go. Part of seventeen-year-old Lewis Holbrook will always love Rebecca Woodruff. Part of me will always belong to her. And her to me. Maybe one day when she's old, she'll find some photos of us buried in a closet or think of me when she hears an '80s song. Maybe that's enough.

"Will you still be able to get us free milkshakes?" Cal asks, tossing his straw at Rebecca.

"Yeah, think about how this affects us, Rebecca! Stop being so self-ish," I add.

Cal leans down and pulls something from his backpack, a long, skinny tube with colored paper running over the entire thing.

"Is that a Roman candle?" I ask.

"It is. Left over from last Fourth of July. Rebecca said we were celebrating, so I thought I'd bring it. Seems like it might be a good time."

"I don't know," Rebecca says. "What if we get caught?"

"What are they going to do, fire you?" Cal asks, standing up and tossing off his blanket. He pulls a lighter from his pocket and flicks it on, letting it hover near the tip of the Roman candle and looking to Rebecca for approval.

"What the hell. Let's do it," she says, letting go of my hand and rising from her seat. The end of the firework catches fire, and a small stream of smoke drifts up before a glowing blue flame bursts from the tip. It arches out over the Graze Daze picnic tables and bounces in the parking lot before extinguishing into nothingness.

Rebecca releases a shriek of laughter, and Cal pushes the candle into her hands. "Come on, it's your night," Cal says. She takes it and lifts it overhead as a green flame bursts forth.

I turn on my camera and pull it to my eye to record the scene. Rebecca's face is lit up by orange and yellow and purple as different colors shoot from the firework, her smile large and luminescent. It's a beautiful scene, and I'm filled with pride watching her. In this moment, she's the leading man. Leading woman. She earned this moment. And even though I know I'll miss her terribly, even though I know this will hurt, I'm still so happy. I'm happy, even though this has nothing to do with me.

The realization comes slowly.

I finally know what my prom clip should be.

FORTY-FIVE

HAYLEY

Lucy takes three french fries, dips them into her vanilla milkshake, and then shoves them into her mouth.

"This is one thing I didn't miss during our time apart," I say, frowning at her.

"You just have an unrefined palate," she says, tucking a fist under her chin and smiling broadly, as if posing for a portrait. There's a small trail of ice cream sliding down her chin. I lift my phone and snap a picture.

We're sitting in McDonald's next to the large front windows, the sun beaming down on our table and the college catalogs spread out between us. I take a sip of my own shake and savor the sweetness. Even though there are still two weeks of school left, it feels like a summer day. The cloudless blue sky stretches on forever, and people are walking around in shorts and sunglasses. While I add a filter to the photo of Lucy and work on uploading it, I consider how thankful I am that we made up before the end of the school year. I can't imagine going through this time without her.

Ever since our conversation at the shaved ice stand, we've been hanging out almost every day. It turns out when you don't talk to your best friend for several months, you have a lot of catching up to do. She told me about going to visit USC over spring break, while I mainly complained about the AT crowd and told her she was right, I shouldn't have quit TV Production.

She's also encouraged me to reply to Lewis. I haven't done it yet, but my list of reasons not to is dwindling. Despite how mad I once was at him, the burning rage seems to get smaller with each passing day. Even when I try to dwell on it and purposefully add kindling to the fire, I can't dredge up that same anger I once felt. The other day, I found myself outside the television studio, staring up at the ON AIR light, and I couldn't help wondering about what he might be doing on the other side of the big wooden doors. I imagined the producer's headset pushed into his hair as he coordinates camera changes. In two weeks, we'll graduate and go our separate ways. Is the last conversation I ever have with Lewis really going to be a fight?

"I have something for you," Lucy says, brushing my college catalogs aside and sliding a white paper ticket across the table.

I pick it up. "Prom?"

"Come on. Don't you want to celebrate?"

"Eh, I don't know. Won't it be weird? I don't exactly have a date." Parker's been distant since I broke the news that I'm not interested in going to Northwestern. It was an awkward conversation. Multiple awkward conversations actually, since I also had to tell my parents, but it had to be done.

"What are you going to do? Spend four years at a school you don't really like just to avoid a couple unpleasant conversations?" That's what Lucy told me, and she was right. I couldn't just let momentum carry me to somewhere I didn't really want to go.

"You can be my date," Lucy says. "I think you kind of owe me."

I slink down into the booth a little. "Ugh. Fine. I'll go."

"Yes. Good decision."

I twirl the ticket in between my fingers. "It's kind of weird that it's all almost over, huh?"

"Are you about to make a sappy, nostalgic speech?" Lucy asks. "If so, I think I might need more fries."

"Hardly. With so much crap that happened, it's hard to be nostalgic about this year."

"Eh, it wasn't all bad."

"We didn't talk to each other for three months, Lucy."

Lucy nods. "Yeah, there were some rough parts, I guess."

"It was a giant dumpster fire sitting on top of a garbage truck that was also on fire."

Lucy looks at me for a moment as if she's pondering a question in her head. Then she slides out of the booth and says, "Come on, we should go. I want to show you something."

"What about helping me pick a college?" I say, gesturing to the catalogs.

Lucy quickly shuffles through the pile, finds the catalog for State, and drops it in front of me. I look up at her, and she gives me a knowing smile. I've been going back to the support group on campus without Dr. Kim. Cody remembered me and introduced me to some other regulars. I still haven't gotten up to speak, but last week after the meeting, a bunch of us went out to a diner together. For so long, when I imagined college, it felt like I would never fit in anywhere, but I actually felt like myself when I was squeezed into that corner booth, eating greasy fried food with people I was just beginning to get to know. Maybe there's a place for me after all.

Twenty minutes later, Lucy and I pull into the parking lot of the downtown library branch.

She holds the front door open for me, and I step inside, staring up from the lobby at the floors of books overhead. Lucy directs me to a hall on the right with a sign that says SENIOR PHOTOGRAPHY GALLERY. I give her a questioning look, but she just smiles and waves me forward.

When we turn the corner, there are matted photos in black frames hanging on every wall. They're in clusters, with a portrait of the photographer hanging by each display. We move halfway down the hall before Lucy comes to stop in front of her own portrait. "This is my corner," she says, gesturing toward the photos. In front of me is a small collection of her work, some of it in stark black and white, and other photos in stunning color.

"Oh my God." My eyes sweep across the collection, too eager to see the next photo to stop on any one for too long. "You . . . What . . . H-how," I stutter, my mind unable to figure out which question to ask first.

"There was a contest," Lucy says. "Every photography student in the county was eligible to enter, and the top five were chosen to be displayed here at the library all summer."

"And you were in the top five," I say, taking hold of her shoulders and shaking them a little.

"Yeah. Apparently more than a hundred people entered."

"When did you enter the contest?"

"Back in March."

"And when did you find out you won?"

"A few weeks ago. They just put up the gallery last week."

What Lucy's saying confirms what she shouted at me in my bedroom so many months ago. I've been obsessed with myself this year, too lost in my own concerns to be a good friend. I knew Lucy enjoyed photography, but I had no idea she was basically a rising star. It makes me wonder what else she's been up to all year that I never noticed.

"You're like a local celebrity," I say.

Lucy scoffs. "Hardly. But it did come with a two-hundred-and-fifty-dollar prize."

"Wow. Getting paid for your work. That's legit."

I force myself to slow down and look at each print. My eyes land on a sharp black-and-white shot of Lewis and Cal, and it takes me a moment to realize they're sitting in the guidance office on the day they fought Harold. Cal is staring down at his shoes, looking like he might vomit at any moment. Lewis has his elbow propped on the arm of his chair, his battered face supported by his fist. I have no clue how Lucy managed to get this picture, but somehow this single image tells a whole story. There's something about their terrible condition juxtaposed with the common waiting room setting that strikes me as funny, and suddenly

I'm laughing. I never thought a moment from such a terrible day would create such a joyful reaction, but here we are. *I have to show this to Lewis,* I think, and almost say it out loud before I remember.

My focus drifts to another photo that seems vaguely familiar, and then I recognize that it's me and Lewis sitting on the bench outside the shaved ice stand. The picture is taken from behind, and Lucy must have used a longer exposure because even though Lewis and I are perfectly still, my head resting on his shoulder, in front of us are the streaking lights of a passing car, blazing lines of yellow cutting across the whole shot. It's beautiful, and an ache I've tried to bury stirs within me.

"You remember those days?" Lucy asks.

"Of course, but I don't remember you taking these pictures."

"I'm very sneaky."

"They're stunning."

"But if I remember correctly, some of these were the result of some pretty terrible days." She points to the one of Lewis and me on the bench. "This moment would've never happened if Harold hadn't posted that video of you drunk."

"I remember."

Lucy drapes an arm over my shoulder. "I just thought this could help you see that maybe this year wasn't as bad as you thought. Yeah, we had some bad moments, but they were kind of beautiful, too."

"Now who's making the sappy, nostalgic speeches?"

"How dare you mock a renowned photographer whose work is being displayed prominently next to a public bathroom."

I laugh and hook my arm around Lucy's, congratulating her. I get her to explain about each shot, asking her about angles and composition. It's fun listening to her talk about something she loves. Her face lights up, and she becomes so expressive. I make a mental note to make sure I ask her more about stuff like this in the future.

FORTY-SIX

LEWIS

So far, Cal has spent a full seven minutes adjusting his hair in the rearview mirror. He's literally using his thumb and forefinger to lift individual curls and drape them in just the way he likes. I know it's been seven minutes because 8:34 is printed on the ticket the parking attendant handed me when we pulled in, and now my phone says 8:42. I'll assume it took me a minute to actually park. "Are we ever going to go inside?" I ask, flipping my tie and smacking it against the steering wheel.

"Dude, don't be in a bad mood," Cal says, not taking his eyes off the mirror. "You got to at least try to have fun."

Several hours ago, I found Cal standing in my driveway when I got back from a run. He told me he thought I needed to go to prom tonight, and when I asked him why, he said stuff like "You only get one senior prom" and "You'll regret it if you don't come," but mainly I think he just wanted me to come with him because he doesn't have a date and I'm not even convinced he had a ride.

I had already decided I wasn't going to come to prom. After I finally figured out what I was doing, it took me more than a week of long afternoons in the studio to splice together the prom clip. When I finished, I saved it to a flash drive and left it on Mrs. Hansen's desk. I didn't even want to be there when she graded it, so I definitely don't have any desire to be in the crowd when they show it at the dance. If they actually use it. Then Cal told me if I came to prom, some hot girls would grind on my junk, and I'm only human. So I took a shower and put on some nice dress pants and the suit jacket Rebecca helped me pick out at the beginning of the school year, and now my senior prom is raging a couple hundred yards away while I watch Cal primp in my mirror.

Since Cal always planned on going to prom, he actually has a proper tux. It's slick and black, and once he's satisfied with his hair (even though, to me, it basically looks the same as it did seven minutes ago), I must admit I feel a little underdressed walking in next to him wearing my now-slightly-too-big suit coat.

Once we get into the ballroom, I realize that the prom committee must have gotten their shit together because the place actually looks pretty nice. There's a large disco ball hanging over the dance floor, spinning slowly and sending shards of light bouncing off the walls. Above it, wide white drapes extend upward and bounce along the ceiling before sliding down the windows. Strings of golden Christmas lights are twinkling everywhere.

We're barely five feet in the door when Cal starts waving the Ellis twins toward us. Riley and E. J. are stars of the track team, and they are incredibly gorgeous. They're brunette and tan and somehow look good even when they just wear sweatpants and a hoodie to school. If I wear sweatpants and a hoodie, I look like I've managed to escape from some institution where they don't trust me with even the dullest of scissors. Of course, they look particularly amazing tonight in their short, shiny dresses that show off their legs, toned from hours spent on the track. In fact, they're so dedicated to track they're perpetually single, too focused on being the best to waste time on something as frivolous as dating. All the work has paid off, though, because apparently they're going to Texas A&M on full scholarships. Cal knows them since he's also a student athlete.

"You guys know my friend Lewis, right?" he says, placing a hand on my shoulder.

"Hi," I say, trying to keep my voice from cracking.

"Yeah, hi, Lewis," Riley says, bending forward to give me a quick hug. "You look great."

"He's been running," Cal says.

"Oh really?" Riley asks.

"Yeah, you both inspired me to start running."

"Really?"

"Well, you two and the fact that the good people at McDonald's started to know me on a first-name basis, so I figured it was time to make a change." Riley and E. J. both laugh, but the feeling is bittersweet as I realize I've slipped back to being the same Lewis from last year who was content with getting shallow laughs from cheap self-deprecating jokes about my body.

"Well, whatever it is, it's working for you," E. J. says.

"Thank you," I say, using all of my effort to maintain eye contact.

"Would you guys like to dance?" Cal asks.

"Sure," they say, and E. J. takes my hand and pulls me to the dance floor.

When you've been overweight your entire teenage life, it's hard to have any sort of confidence when it comes to dancing. The dancing I did when I was bigger was mainly done to get a laugh. *Oh look, big guy's doing the Worm.* Trying to actually dance well is not a skill I've ever invested in, so I basically just smile and try to exude confidence. I've heard the key to success sometimes is just *looking* confident. If, like me, E. J. is just faking it and exuding confidence, she's doing a damn good job. I figure she's spent years training her body to do as she wills it, so she probably doesn't need to fake anything. She places her hand on my shoulder and glides against me. I take hold of her waist with one hand, feeling pretty weird about being so intimate with someone I barely know. I'm not saying I don't like it; I'm just saying it's kind of weird.

For several songs, the music pounds through the crowd, seeming to vibrate the floor. Every once in a while, E. J. and I will yell something to each other over the music, something like "I love this song" (her to me) or "You're a good dancer" (me to her) or "This is great" (my penis to me). Despite the signals my body is sending, the novelty of the whole thing starts to wane after a while. It's fun, but it's hard for me to shake the fact that it's not particularly meaningful. E. J. and Riley will dance with plenty of other, better-looking guys tonight. Guys with defined jawlines and acne-free skin. Then eventually, they'll go on to be Olympians and marry doctors or underwear models or at least someone who knows how the stock market works. I won't leave this dance with E. J. We won't go to Waffle House after this and laugh as we share a couple of mugs of hot chocolate.

When I look up, I catch sight of Hayley near the far wall.

This is main reason I didn't want to come to prom. I assumed Hayley would be here, and she's made it pretty clear that she has no interest in ever speaking to me again. As I watch her line up with Lucy and several other girls to take some photos, I'm blown away by how genuinely happy she looks. She deserves a fun evening with her friends. She shouldn't have to deal with knowing she's in the same room as the guy who betrayed her confidence and embarrassed her in front of the whole student body. I tell E. J. I'm going to get some fresh air, and I make my escape to the parking lot.

FORTY-SEVEN

HAYLEY

Senior prom is weird.

Maybe it's the fact that everyone's dressed up and there're twinkle lights everywhere, or maybe it's the fact that people are feeling nostalgic about high school ending, or maybe it's the fact that half of these people are already pretty buzzed. Whatever it is, the vibe at the dance is a significant departure from a normal day at Groveland. For starters, a lot of people are actually talking to me. And not just the casual "Hey. You look great. I'll catch you later" sort of talk either. No, this is grab me around the neck and yell, "Hey! Oh my gosh, I love your dress! Let's take a few selfies!" stuff.

Mallory Scott, who has barely said three words to me since getting me drunk at the football game, insists on getting a picture with "the old gang," which includes half the tennis team. While we all gather around, Camilla Rodriguez slips her arm around my waist and gives me a wink. I wonder how she feels about the fact that the documentary about TwilightTin never aired. She's probably relieved. Mainly I think she just enjoys the fact that she basically took us on a police chase. After the tennis team photo, Kasey Hillford, who I had one class with junior year, tells me she's going to miss seeing me all the time. Then Chad Epelstein says I have a nice rack. He might be more than just buzzed.

I keep giving Lucy wide eyes as if to say, *What is happening right now?* and she just smiles in return as if to say, *I don't know, but I'm just going with it because some of these white girls are weirdly strong.* Lucy looks absolutely stunning. She's wearing a sparkling silver backless dress that sweeps the floor when she walks, and it fits her perfectly.

Rohan Bakshi shoves his phone in my hand and insists I take several photos of him and Lucy together. Lucy indulges him and even kisses him on the cheek for a couple of the pictures. After he reviews them and gives his seal of approval, Lucy starts moving toward the dance floor. I'm about to follow her when I spot Mrs. Hansen near the entrance, standing with a plate of chips and swaying slightly to the music.

"I'll be over in a minute," I tell Lucy.

Mrs. Hansen gives me a wave when she spots me approaching.

"Having fun?" I yell over the music.

"Oh yeah," she says, doing a small twist with her body. "I'm gettin' my groove on."

"Oh no," I snort.

"It's good to see you, Hayley."

"Thanks. I actually came over to apologize. I'm sorry I dropped your class without really talking to you. When everything happened, I just needed some space. And I never really got a chance to tell you how much I appreciated it when you helped me that day you found me and Lucy in the bathroom."

"Well, I'm glad I could help. And I owe you an apology too. I'm sorry I never expressly cleared that clip with you before it aired. I just assumed . . ." I can see where this is going, and that video clip is honestly the last thing I want to talk about, so I wave it off.

"But I'm glad you're here tonight," Mrs. Hansen continues. "And I'm sure I'm not the only one. There's a funny kid from my TV Production class around here somewhere who will surely be happy to see you." She moves her head a little to search the crowd.

"You mean Lewis?" I think of how he stopped texting me a month ago when I never responded. "I'm not sure he's too interested in seeing me these days."

"I'd be very surprised if that were true considering the clip he turned in last week," Mrs. Hansen says, chomping down on a carrot stick.

"What clip?"

"You'll see. Now go have fun and stop being the loser in the corner hanging out with the teacher because, girl, you are wearing that dress!"

"I do what I can," I say, placing my hand on my hip and tilting my head slightly before turning to make my way onto the dance floor.

"Make smart choices!" Mrs. Hansen calls.

Out on the dance floor, Lucy has tossed aside her shoes. Several other girls are already barefoot too. Some of the guys have ditched their ties, and others have them wrapped across their forehead, swinging them around as they nod along to the beat. It's nice to see so many people smiling and enjoying themselves. I close my eyes and allow myself to get lost in the music, the bass rhythm acting as my heartbeat and sending blood pounding through my veins. I lift my arms and sway my hips, trying my best to ignore the self-conscious voice in the back of my mind. I've spent enough time feeling sorry for myself this year.

After several songs, the music fades, and there's a whirring sound as a projector screen descends behind the DJ booth. Everyone stops dancing and pivots toward the display. Lucy appears beside me, hooking her arm through mine. I wipe a strand of hair from my damp forehead and catch Parker's eye across the dance floor. It's been several weeks since I told him I wouldn't be joining him at Northwestern. It was a tense conversation, and we still haven't really cleared the air. I give him a closed-mouth smile, hoping it seems as sincere as I'm intending. He waves back. I guess I have another stop to make on Hayley's Apology Tour tonight. I owe him an explanation for so many things.

A teal haze alights on everyone's face, and I shift back toward the DJ booth. For a moment, the projector screen is a bright blue square, but then the video starts up. An empty wooden chair sits in the middle of Groveland's auditorium stage before Lewis walks in from the right side of the screen and sits down. He sighs, moves his hands along the length of his thighs until they're resting on his knees, and then looks up directly into the lens. "Earlier this year, I made some documentaries with a friend of mine," he says. "Documentaries about some of you. I had the pleasure of watching several of you pursue your greatest passions." Footage of Camilla spray-painting comes onscreen, the shot slowed so dramatically, you can make out individual beads of paint as they move through the air and explode against the brick wall. It's followed by a shot of Rohan pointing his laser tag gun at the camera, his sight line aimed right down the lens. "My friend and I worked really hard on these documentaries," Lewis says. "We really wanted to share some untold stories, show people a side of their peers we previously knew nothing about. And I think we did that. But I also know there are a lot more stories that we didn't tell."

New footage runs across the screen as a piano medley begins building in the background. The robotics club controlling a robot down the main hall at school. The senior girls' powder-puff team celebrating their championship win. The boys' baseball team dumping a cooler of Gatorade on their coach. Someone popping a wheelie in their wheelchair. Mr. Keith opening his suit jacket to reveal a T-shirt with a picture of Einstein sticking his tongue out.

Lewis's voice comes up over the music. "The truth is, all of us have a story. For each of us, this past year has been fun and tragic and meaningful for a bunch of different reasons. I know I was hoping to have a good story at the end of this year. I wanted this year to be like a movie where I was the leading man." The screen jumps to an image of the poster for the '80s movie *Say Anything* with John Cusack standing in front of his car and holding up a giant boom box. The poster shifts to the left side of the screen, and the right side fades up to a shot of Lewis re-creating the poster in front of his own car. There's a small wave of laughter in the crowd that builds as the poster fades away and the shot of Lewis pulls out to reveal he's standing in Groveland's parking lot, and there are a lot of confused students walking around as he stands awkwardly motionless. I wonder who was behind the camera filming. A pang of jealousy shoots through me at the thought that it wasn't me.

The video transitions back to Lewis sitting on Groveland's stage;

now it's a tight shot of his upper body. "Ironically enough, this is my first time getting in front of the camera ever," he says. "Trying to be a leading man didn't go very well for me. I thought being a leading man meant I needed to be strong and cool and good-looking, but that pursuit just turned me into someone selfish. Someone so inwardly focused that I ended up hurting someone very important to me." I keep my eyes on the screen, but I feel Lucy's grip tighten on my arm. "Now, after filming so many of you doing amazing things this year, I'm realizing that being a leading man really isn't about all the surface-level stuff I thought. It's about being brave . . . brave enough to be vulnerable. So that's what I'm going to do."

Groveland's main foyer appears onscreen. It's eerily empty as the camera glides down the hall and Lewis narrates. "All this year, I've been worried. Worried about what might happen when I leave this place. Worried I have no future." The image transitions to a darkened classroom, the camera panning over rows of empty desks. "This year hasn't been like a movie because even though graduation is an ending, it's not *the* ending. There won't be scrolling credits. We won't fade to black. We'll all keep going." The video jumps back to Lewis sitting onstage staring down the lens. "So I don't really want to be a leading man anymore. I'd rather be part of a great ensemble."

The lingering piano melody shifts to something more upbeat and pulsating as new footage plays out across the screen. Some theater kids laughing as they rehearse a sword fight. The color guard lifting their flags in unison. Cheerleaders tossing a girl into the air as football players rush by behind them. All the images bright and oversaturated as they play out one after another after another. Around the dance floor, people point and cheer when they spot themselves onscreen. After a couple of minutes, the video cuts back to Lewis. "I wish the same for all of you. I hope you find your ensemble. Looking at this footage, I know a lot of you already have. And if you haven't, there's still time. Your life isn't a movie. There's always another scene, a chance to be better, to make amends, to take a risk and take another if the first one doesn't go so well. Yes, graduation is a beginning. But it's also a beginning. And a middle. Keep going."

The screen fades to black, and there's scattered applause. It's slow at first, but soon the clapping sweeps through the crowd until everyone is cheering and the flashing lights start back up and the music builds and the dance party continues. I stand there, frozen as everyone jumps and bounces around me. I catch sight of Cal through the crowd, and he must already know what I'm thinking because he nods his head toward the wall of windows. I make my way over and cup my hands to the glass to block out the glare. Down in the parking lot, a lone figure sits on the hood of an old Mazda.

FORTY-EIGHT

LEWIS

P arty's inside, you know."

I turn and see Hayley making her way across the parking lot toward me. She's wearing a dark green dress with an intricate jewel pattern on the top, and her hair is pinned up in a way that makes her look older and more mature. I thought I felt underdressed next to Cal, but now that feeling climbs to another level. "The loud music and flashing lights kind of give it away," she adds.

"Just getting some fresh air," I say.

Hayley leans against the hood of my car, and I catch the scent of her perfume, light and sweet. "They just showed your film," she says. I nod, happy to have missed the big debut. It was enough for me to watch as I edited it. I didn't need to see it again. "I think they liked it," she says, motioning back toward the ballroom. Then, after a moment, she adds, "I liked it."

A small smile tugs at the corners of my mouth. "I'm glad. It only took me four months to create."

"Four months?"

I nod again. "That was my only real assignment in TV Production this semester."

"Mmm. I noticed there weren't any more senior documentaries. You decided not to keep doing them?"

"Mrs. Hansen didn't really give me a choice. But it wouldn't have felt right to continue without you. Not after what happened."

Hayley releases a long sigh as she slides up onto the hood beside me, a motion that takes some extra effort with the size of her dress. "Yeah. What happened."

"I obviously owe you a huge apology," I start, realizing now might be the only chance I'll get. After what happened with Rebecca, I'm done missing the opportunity to have important conversations.

"That's funny because I was about to apologize to you," Hayley says, shifting toward me so that her knees touch mine and I can make out the scattering of freckles across her nose.

"For what?"

"I've been apologizing a lot lately, actually. I'm sort of realizing I went about so many things the wrong way this year. All of my energy was focused on how everyone else saw me, and I couldn't see that that was really stupid." She lets out a quiet laugh and shakes her head. "So I made some not-so-great choices and nearly destroyed all of the good parts of my life. This past semester, I just retreated from every good thing. TV Production. Lucy. You." She looks me in the eyes. "I'm sorry I did that."

I shake my head. "You had every right to run away from me. You were trying to move past this traumatic event, and I just brought this toxic sludge back into your life without even asking you because I thought the documentary was good and in some completely mis-guided way thought it might help you. That was selfish and dumb. So clearly you're not the only one who didn't make the best decisions this year."

"Yeah, but I was obsessed with those documentaries too. It felt like everything else was taken away from me and those were the one thing I had left that I was really good at, and it got out of control. I just wanted to show people I was still the Hayley from before my breakdown. Smart and capable and steady."

"There's nothing wrong with wanting to show people that," I say. "I shouldn't have said those terrible things to you just because you have ambition."

"But my ambition consumed me. I let it poison everything, and I don't even know where this need to be number one comes from. It's like I'm scared that if I'm not the best, I'm not anything."

"I know that feeling, that feeling of not knowing who you are. I was never outstanding at anything until these documentaries came along. I liked that feeling, so I just kept pushing, and I took it too far."

"For what it's worth, I think there's a lot about you that's outstanding, Lewis. And I missed making those documentaries with you this semester."

"I missed it too." We're quiet for several moments, with only the distant sounds of throbbing bass moving through the stillness. I glance toward Hayley, but she's staring up at the sky, so it's hard to make out her expression. I move my hand until it finds the top of hers, and I wrap my fingers around her palm. "Sorry things turned out so shitty."

"Well, it wasn't all shitty," she says, tilting her head toward me. "Lucy showed me that recently. There were certainly parts I wouldn't want to experience again, but there were some great moments too."

"Like when we got busted with that flask?"

"Oh my gosh, that stupid flask," Hayley says, her smile cracking wide open. "You know I could never look Mr. Rosco in the face after that. There were times I saw him coming down the hall and I would purposely go out of my way to avoid him."

"Ah, so that's the real reason you've been hiding in the AT wing this semester. You were too intimidated by Mr. Rosco."

"Definitely." We're quiet again, but this time it's a comfortable silence. After a moment, Hayley hops off the hood and extends her hand toward me. "Come on," she says.

"What?"

"We just talked about how our senior year was pretty terrible, and

I know it's not going to get any better sitting around being pensive and moody."

"But I'm so good at it," I protest.

"Come on," she says again, taking my hand and pulling me off the hood. She wraps her hands around my neck and begins to sway to the music drifting softly from the ballroom. I place my hands on her waist, feeling her body move beneath the silky fabric.

"I like your dress," I say.

"Thanks."

"It's a shame it's probably going to get oil stains on it because, you know, we're dancing in the parking lot."

Hayley tilts her head up at me. "Lewis, just be quiet and enjoy the moment." I have a sudden flashback to summer, where I was standing in a dressing room with Rebecca. A moment that was so intimate that it scared me, and I had to cut it with a joke. I remember resolving to not be that guy anymore, so I take Hayley's advice and shut up.

FORTY-NINE

HAYLEY

When Lucy and I arrive at Parker's after-party, he's standing on the front porch like a bouncer, collecting car keys from people who intend to drink. "You don't turn over your keys, you don't get in," he shouts over the small crowd of gathered students. This is why Parker's our class president. Even though he could be cutting loose for senior prom or living it up at his own party, he's not. He's taking care of others.

"Any chance I could relieve you for a few minutes?" Lucy asks when we get to the porch.

Parker glances over her shoulder at me and says, "I don't know. You sure you can handle the responsibility?"

"You mean can I be rude and demanding until people drop their keys? Yeah, I think I can handle it."

Parker smiles and hands over the bowl. As he and I make our way upstairs, I hear Lucy say, "Come on, Kowalski. We both know you're gonna get hammered. Just hand over your keys."

Once we're in Parker's room, he shuts the door to deaden the sound of the music drifting up from downstairs. I sit on his bed and straighten my dress over my lap. It's a little weird to be here considering Parker and I used to make out on this bed. He must feel the awkwardness too, because instead of coming to sit beside me, he just leans against the door and stares down at his shoes. He's ditched his coat and tie, but his navy vest remains buttoned, and his shirtsleeves are rolled to his elbows.

"Did you have fun at prom?" I ask.

"I did. I did," he says, nodding a lot. After a moment, he adds, "Good DJ."

"Great DJ."

"Mm-hmm."

"I liked the decorations, too."

"Really nice decorations."

"Very . . . nice." God, this is excruciating. Clearly, it's time to do away with small talk. "I owe you an apology," I say.

"Oh yeah?" Parker says, looking at me for the first time since we stepped into his room.

"Yeah. For a lot of things, actually. This year, you've been nice to me and you've reached out to me, and I've been kind of all over the place. Last semester, I kept my distance because I was jealous. You're class president, and you're supersmart, and basically everyone loves you, and I was . . . struggling. So instead of being your friend, I was closed off."

"I didn't realize that was the issue. I just assumed things are always kind of weird after a breakup. I didn't really know if you were interested in being friends."

"I do want to be friends. I think I'm remembering how to do that. But I know there's some stuff I still need to work out. I've spent this past year trying to run away from things, and that's obviously not working, so I'm going to try staying still for a while. Something that doesn't come easy for me."

"Yeah, I remember," Parker says, smiling. "I'm sorry this year was so hard for you. I wish I could've done more."

I stand and go over to him, placing my hand on the side of his face. "You've done enough. Honestly. Now please go off to college and let loose a little. Be reckless for once. And send me a postcard."

"All right," he says, standing up straight like he's making a pledge. "I promise to fully embrace the wild college lifestyle."

"Good. I look forward to the day I can watch an embarrassing video of you on YouTube." I give him a light kiss on the cheek, and then I slip back downstairs.

"We're really doing this?" Lucy asks, squeezing my hand.

"We're really doing this," I say, looking down at the calm blue water of Parker's pool. We're standing on the balcony railing, still in our prom gowns but barefoot, our toes curled over the edge of the railing. It's a warm night, but a shiver runs through my body. Parker's party has been raging for more than an hour now, but I've only been drinking Coke. I wanted to be absolutely sober for this moment. Cal is sitting on the diving board with his pant legs rolled up so his feet can dangle in the water. Lewis is standing at the edge of the pool looking concerned.

"You're sure this is a good idea?" He cringes.

"No, not really," I reply.

Parker steps out of his house. He looks at Cal and Lewis and then follows their sight up to Lucy and me. "Oh no. This should not be happening!" he says. I give him a look, and he shrugs. "But hey, what the heck? I'm chill. Let's get nuts. Do you . . . all the way to the hospital."

I'm already bending my knees and pushing off the wood. I know if I stand on this rail for too long, I will eventually talk myself out of it, so I force myself forward. For a moment, it's as if I'm suspended in the air. Parker looks horrified, and Cal's wearing a huge grin. Lewis has his hands up to his face, and he's peeking through his fingers. Lucy's hand is still in mine. When I look over, she's staring down at the water, her mouth opened so wide I can see nearly all of her teeth.

Then everything snaps back to speed.

My dress bunches around my knees, and air rushes over my legs as gravity pulls us down. The impact is cold and brilliant. The water moves up over my waist, my arms, my head, and then cradles me beneath the surface, spinning me and turning me onto my back. Looking up, I see distorted faces peering over the edge of the pool. I stay there for a moment, feeling the coolness on my skin and in my hair, watching the way my dress moves in slow motion underwater and listening to the gargled voices overhead. I feel amazing.

Then I break the surface. Lucy is already there, laughing and shaking the water from her ears.

"Oh my God, you could have died!" Parker shouts. "That was insane."

"I've always been a little crazy." I smile, brushing my wet hair away from my face. "That's why they call me Messed-Up Mills."

Cal starts clapping. "I'm impressed," he says.

"Me too," Lewis adds, already pulling at the knot of his tie. He tosses his suit jacket aside, slips out of his shoes, and jumps into the pool. Before he surfaces, both Cal and Parker follow his lead.

FIFTY

LEWIS

The morning of Groveland's graduation is brilliantly sunny. The football stadium is crowded with grandparents fanning themselves and dads who clearly regret their decision to wear a tie. Even at eleven a.m., I already have sweat building on my back, and I'm itching to get out of this green robe. We all march out onto the field and take our places in the rows of white chairs, the sun glistening off the shiny band instruments as they play "Pomp and Circumstance." Once we've all settled in, Parker steps up to the podium and starts welcoming family and friends, his face projected on the large screens that flank both sides of the small makeshift stage. My phone buzzes, and I hike up my robe to get to my pants pocket. It's a text from Cal.

Just look at the size of those screens. Your big head's gonna look ginormous on those things. They're gonna have to zoom out to make it fit.

I turn and catch sight of Cal several rows behind me. He has his cap resting on the back of his head so that a tuft of blond hair curls out the front. He smiles broadly and waves at me enthusiastically. I nod and turn back toward the front just as my phone buzzes again. This time, it's my dad telling me to look to the right. When I do, I see him waving from the bleachers while my mom's face is half obscured by her phone, taking several dozen pictures, no doubt.

A few days ago, she woke me before my alarm, nudging me and saying, "Get up. We got to get going."

"School doesn't start for another hour and a half," I said, pulling my pillow on top of my face.

"You're not going to school. Get up. Put on a nice shirt. Do something with your hair."

I stumbled out of bed and threw on some khaki pants and a button-up shirt. When I got downstairs, Dad was making pancakes at the stove and proclaimed, "There he is!" as I took a seat at the kitchen counter. Mom looked up from her coffee, gave my outfit a once-over, and then nodded her approval.

"There's a very weird vibe in this kitchen," I said.

Dad pushed two pancakes onto my plate and said, "Eat up. Important meeting today."

"Important meeting where?"

"At my work," Mom said, not taking her eyes off her phone.

When it became clear she wasn't going to elaborate, I looked to Dad for help, but he just frowned a little and said, "Sorry. I've been sworn to secrecy."

The drive to Mom's station was weird. She kept humming along to her old Beach Boys CD while I tried to figure out if what was about to happen was good or bad. When we got inside, Mom led me down a narrow hall and knocked on an open door. I stood beside her as a large man with cropped gray hair eased out from behind a cluttered desk.

"Lewis, this is Bill Wilson," my mom said. "He's the lead producer for our morning news program, and he's been working at this station for nearly twenty years. Bill, this is my son, Lewis."

"Nice to meet you, Mr. Wilson," I said, extending my hand.

He wrapped both of his large hands around mine. "Lewis! I hear you're very involved with your school's TV Production program."

"Yes, sir. I was the senior producer this year."

"Well, your mom sent me the link to some of the segments you worked on this year, and I have to say, I was quite impressed. But she tells me you have no immediate plans for college. Is that true?"

I looked toward Mom, and she gave me a small smile. We hadn't exactly had an extended discussion about my academic future. "Yes, sir. That's true."

"Well, we could use an intern for our morning crew. It's paid. Not much, but it's something. It'll be a lot of early mornings and, if I'm being honest, a lot of grunt work, but I'll make sure you get paired with some people who can really teach you a thing or two if you're considering a career in TV."

I was stunned. "You want me to work here?"

"If you're interested. It is an internship, so that means you do have to be enrolled in college even if it's just part-time. I suggest you sign up for some classes at the community college if you really want this." I do want it. All year, I've listened to people talk about how stoked they are for college, but it's never really resonated with me. How do you work up excitement about more years of books and lectures? But this is different. A door opened at the end of the hall, and I caught sight of the studio. A real television studio with modern equipment and specialized lighting. This is an opportunity to step closer to something I really like. Even if it is a lot of grunt work.

"Yes, sir," I said. "That sounds great."

Everyone starts clapping, and I realize Parker has wrapped up his speech. As they start announcing names and handing out diplomas, Lucy is the first of us to walk across the stage. When she shakes Wexler's hand, a loud whistle erupts from the crowd to my left. Her father is up on his feet, both pinkies tucked into the corners of his mouth. It makes me smile. When I collect my diploma and see my face projected on the giant screens, it's easy to imagine my life as a movie. In this moment, it's undeniable that I'm the leading man. But as I look out at my fellow graduates, I know I'm not the only one. Hayley catches my eye and gives me a thumbs-up. Cal puffs out his cheeks and holds his hands up beside his head, letting me know just how big my face looks on the screen. This is my ensemble. These are my people.

After the ceremony ends, I find Mrs. Hansen among the teachers. She gives me a hug and congratulates me, and now I don't know if I call her by her first name or just continue to refer to her as Mrs. Hansen for the rest of my life. "I guess my one assignment was good enough to earn me a passing grade this semester," I say, holding up my diploma.

Mrs. Hansen smiles. "Well, you didn't think I'd want you back again next year, did you?"

"Wow. And here I was about to thank you."

"Oh?"

"Yeah, I really enjoyed TV Production. It might be the only thing about this place I truly enjoyed, and I know a big part of that is because of you. And now, you might be interested to learn, I actually have a new studio to work in. My mom helped me land an internship at the TV station where she works."

"That's great. Congratulations, Lewis."

"Thank you. I'm sure it will mainly be hours of hauling equipment and wrapping cables, but who knows? Maybe if I stick with it long enough, one day I'll have the opportunity to air rogue segments on the five-o'clock news."

"Oh God," she says, bringing her hand to her face, but she's smiling. She gives me one last hug and tells me not to be a stranger and then points over my shoulder. "I think you might have people waiting for you." I turn, expecting to see my parents, but it's actually Rebecca and Cal standing there.

This is my first time seeing Rebecca since she told Cal and me about going off to Texas. When I walk over, she extends a wrapped gift in my direction. I take it and realize Cal is holding an identical present. "What's this?"

"Just open it," she says.

Cal shrugs at me, and we both tear into the paper. Once I get it unwrapped, I immediately start laughing. It's a framed poster from the 1989 movie *Bill & Ted's Excellent Adventure*, except Rebecca has cut out photos of Cal and me and taped our faces over those of the actors. She has also scratched out Bill and Ted and written in our names. "It's incredible," I say.

"It really is," Cal agrees, looking down at his own poster.

Rebecca shrugs. "I'm a pretty great gift giver."

She hesitates for just a moment before extending her arms and wrapping us up in a big hug. I don't know what will happen with Cal and Rebecca and me once Rebecca heads off to college in the fall and Cal starts his classes at State, but I know I don't want to waste what could be our final summer together. As we separate, I say, "Hey, Cal, you should hang yours by the foosball table."

"Yeah, so you have something to cheer you up after we crush you this summer," Rebecca says.

"Excuse me?" Cal asks.

"I have a feeling this might be the summer of upsets," Rebecca says, smiling at me.

"We're kind of due," I say.

"All right. Tomorrow night. My basement. Seven o'clock."

Rebecca shrugs again. "Okay?" It's such a simple and beautiful invitation.

"Okay," I say.

"All right, I'll see you tomorrow, boys. Come by and see me at Graze Daze sometime. I have a couple of milkshakes with your names on them."

Cal and I watch as Rebecca heads off toward the parking lot. "Is it going to be weird with you two all summer?" he asks.

"Probably for a little while. Yeah."

He sighs and looks out at our graduating class, green robes speckled among siblings and parents and grandparents. "I can't believe I went to this school for four years and you're, like, my only real friend."

FIFTY-ONE

HAYLEY

'm trying something new for the summer," Dr. Kim says, motioning to the glass pitcher of iced coffee on her credenza. I pour myself a cup and then add some cream, watching the white swirl in the brown liquid. Today, Dr. Kim is wearing brown sandals and a sleeveless blue-and-white dress patterned with large palm branches. Her hair is pulled back in a loose ponytail, and she looks like she could easily step out of this office, hop in a Corvette, and cruise to the nearest coast. I'm wearing some faded gray shorts and a loose short-sleeved button-up that's more wrinkled than I would like. Maybe someday I'll look as put together as Dr. Kim, but not today. "So . . . you graduated," she says, smiling at me as I take a seat across from her.

"I did. One diploma down, several more to go if I'm going to catch up with you."

"Well, I had a head start," she says, glancing at her framed degrees. "How do you feel?"

"Good. Weird. Lucy and I aren't working at the shaved ice stand anymore, so I've had a lot of free time. My brother has already beaten me in multiple games of H.O.R.S.E. I've still been going to the support group on campus on Wednesday nights. I didn't know they kept meeting during the summer."

"They do. Though I hear there's a drop in attendance."

"There is. But that just means I have a better chance at getting the good doughnuts."

Dr. Kim smiles. "I'm glad you've been going. And now you'll already know people when classes start up in the fall."

"Yeah, it should be good. And even though it's here in town, I convinced my parents to let me live in the dorm. Dad's not thrilled about the boarding fees he could be saving if I lived at home, but I think I need the community of dorm life. Is that weird?"

"Not at all," Dr. Kim says. "Plus, it's college, Hayley. You're going to have lots of weird experiences." I laugh, and so does she, and that's how the rest of our session goes. I tell her about the courses I've signed up for and the part-time jobs I'm thinking about applying to, and I don't feel self-conscious or like I need to censor myself.

I used to think my brain was damaged and Dr. Kim was supposed to help me fix it, but I don't think that anymore. Now I think I'm just someone who went through something hard like so many other people have, and working through difficult things takes time and other people. Dr. Kim is helping me, but she's not fixing me. Because I'm not broken. Lucy is helping me too. And Lewis. And my family. And hopefully I'm helping them find their way too because my life shouldn't be all about me.

When I get home, Tanner is playing basketball in the driveway. I sit in my car for a moment, watching him shoot around, and it strikes me how much he's grown this year. The rest of his body is starting to catch up with his long arms and legs. He's already getting excited about playing on the JV team at Groveland, and I'm hoping his high school experience will be a positive one. Years where he's not tormented or tormenting others. Maybe he'll get lucky and it will just be four more years of basketball and seeing which one of his friends can pee the farthest.

Up in my room, I strip down to a tank top, and as I fold my shirt back into its drawer, I spot the corner of my corkboard sticking out from behind the dresser. It's been there ever since I tore it down on the day I fought with Lucy. I pull the board free and lay it on my bed, looking at the collection of ribbons and certificates. I trace my fingers over the fabric, remembering when I won each one. Then, slowly, I start removing them, placing each one neatly in a box on my desk.

It takes a while, and when I'm done, I'm left with a blank corkboard, a wide expanse of brown nothingness. On my desk, I spot the State pennant my parents gave me after graduation, and I tack it to the top left corner of the board. Next, I add my Groveland diploma.

There's still a lot of space.

After a moment, I remember the small envelope of photos Lucy gave me last week. Some of them are copies of her award-winning prints. Some of them are pictures from prom where everyone is shiny with sweat. Others are pictures from graduation, all of us crammed in close and smiling big. When I tack them on, they fill up the rest of the board, some even overhanging the edges. I take the whole thing and place it back on the hooks over my dresser.

Tanner's laugh drifts in through my open window, and when I look outside, I spot Lewis in the driveway. He's telling some story that involves him sticking the basketball under his shirt and waddling around like a pregnant woman, one hand clutched to his lower back like he's having problems balancing. His hair is cut shorter than the last time I saw him, and there's a redness baked into his cheeks, probably from not wearing any sunscreen during his runs. After a minute, he spots me in the window and yells at me to come down. I grab my tennis racquet and a fresh can of balls before taking the stairs two at a time. When I step out onto the back porch, the warmth of the sun feels nice on my bare shoulders. "Ready?"

"Are you ready . . . ?" Lewis says, pulling a collection of red, white, and blue striped sweatbands from his pocket. He places one on each wrist and a larger one over his forehead. Then he pulls a pair of orange-tinted sports glasses from his back pocket and slides them onto his face. ". . . For this?"

"Wow," I say.

"Next John McEnroe right here," he says, bouncing on the balls of his feet.

"Wow, are all of your pop culture references from the eighties?"

"Pretty much."

"I'm assuming that's the only professional tennis player you can name?"

He stops bouncing. "Well, I also know Venus and Serena, but that didn't seem like a good comparison."

"Good call," I say, tossing him the can of balls.

In the car, Lewis puts on his latest mix, which consists of his favorite '80s cover songs. It opens with a band singing an upbeat version of Cyndi Lauper's "Time After Time," layers of electric guitar and snare drums pushing the tempo. As we drive, I roll the windows down and let the warm air sweep over my arms and through my hair. When we pass Groveland, the light's green, so I lean into the gas and shoot through the intersection as Lewis laughs, all of his teeth visible as he leans his head back. I hope I get the chance to make Lewis smile more this summer.

When we get to the tennis court, Lewis walks around to my side of the car and grimaces at something on the collar of my tank top. "What is that?" he asks.

"What? Is it a bug?" I say, pulling at my shirt to get a better look.

"No, I can't even tell . . . ," he says, moving in closer.

"I can't see what you're talking about. If it's a bug, I'm—" Then Lewis is lifting my chin up and pressing his lips against mine. It catches me so off guard that I nearly drop my racquet. Just as I start to ease into his embrace, he pulls away.

He glances down at my shirt and frowns. "Hmm. It's not there anymore. Weird." Then he turns and starts walking toward the courts.

"Okay. That was cheesy," I say, chasing after him.

"I don't know what you're talking about."

Two days after graduation, Lewis showed up at my house at dusk wearing flip-flops and a pair of swim trunks.

"You know I don't have a pool, right?" I asked.

He rolled his eyes. "Duh, just get some clothes on you don't mind getting wet. It's time to go."

After I tossed on an old T-shirt and a pair of denim cutoffs, Lewis drove us downtown. Once we had parked, he pulled out a map of the area dotted with several Xs.

"So where do you want to start?" he asked. "This fountain's a little bigger, but this one has a better waterfall feature, I think."

That's how we ended up spending the night fountain diving, splashing through shallow aquamarine water and shuffling over coins tossed in as wishes. We only got chased off by a security guard once, which is apparently becoming a habit of mine and Lewis's. We ran down the block laughing, holding our sandals in our hands and dripping water on annoyed twentysomethings lingering outside the bars. The night concluded with us sitting on the edge of one of the fountains, sharing some pizza from a late-night food joint. Lewis's hair was slicked to the side, and I took hold of his damp shirt and pulled him to me, kissing him for the first time.

I don't know exactly what will happen in the fall or where things might lead with Lewis and me, but for once I'm not trying to plan it all out. I'm not thinking three steps ahead.

Lewis readies himself on his half of the court, breathing onto his ridiculous glasses and wiping them with his shirt. Once I crack open the balls, I step to the service line and spin my racquet in my hand, refamiliarizing myself with the weight. I run my thumb over the grooves of the grip, letting it fall into the most worn spot. When I bounce the ball, it snaps back with a surprising amount of spring. I toss it into the air, hoping muscle memory will recall the motion, as I let it land back in my open palm.

"Ready for this?" I yell across the court.

"Ready for anything," Lewis says.

I toss the ball again, this time bringing my racquet down and making contact. The ball sails over the net and lands in the service box. Lewis is already moving forward with determination, so I take my stance, waiting for his return.

ACKNOWLEDGMENTS

Since this is my first novel, I feel like I should thank everyone who has ever helped me with writing, all the way down to the people who used to sit beside me in creative writing class in high school (Hi, Joey and Rachael!). But I'll try to keep this brief rather than writing multiple pages about how my love of literature was shaped at an early age by episodes of *Wishbone*.

First off, thank you to my incredible agent, Claire Friedman, for believing in this book when it was a meandering plot that was roughly thirty thousand words too long. I'd be lost without your vision, support, and reassuring replies to my panicked emails. Thank you!

Thank you to my amazing editor, Alex Borbolla, for fighting for this book and convincing me that every chapter doesn't need two additional pages of dialogue just because I thought of some funny things for the characters to say. I haven't forgotten I still owe you an Edible Arrangement! This book wouldn't exist without the hard work of so many great people behind the scenes, such as Becca Syracuse and Bex Glendining (who created a fun, beautiful cover), Jeannie Ng, Elizabeth Blake-Linn, and Chantal Gersch.

Thanks to all of my former mentors who encouraged me to keep writing over the years (even when what I was writing was moody teenage poetry), including (but not limited to!): Gary Egan, Tara Wilkinson, Moe Conn, Kim Miller, Gina Herring, and (my own high school TV Production teacher) Tonya Merritt.

Thanks to the incredible folks (both members past and current) in my Chicago writing group, Write Club! I would have given up on this book on the first draft without your continual encouragement and feedback.

Thanks to my parents for letting me get an English degree and always encouraging me in all my artistic endeavors (even when it meant listening to me stumbling through scales on my alto sax at eleven o'clock at night).

Thanks to my old community house roommates—Jon, Sarah, David, and Jamie—for letting me skip out on every game of Dominion ever so I could be introverted and write this book. I owe you all a heaping helping of Meatball Nirvana!

Finally, my eternal love and gratitude to my wife, Cary Anne, for letting me read her early passages of this book late at night when all she wanted to do was go to sleep, for listening to me vent about writing frustrations, and for letting me spend a bunch of our money at various coffee shops in our neighborhood because I don't like writing in our apartment. I love you!